Praise for Lorelie Brown's
An Indiscreet Debutante

"...difficult to tell who the seducer is and who's being seduced in this sexy story..."

~ *RT Book Reviews*

"...brings a contemporary erotic flair to the Victorian bedroom..."

~ *Publishers Weekly*

Look for these titles by
Lorelie Brown

Now Available:

Jazz Baby
Wayward One

Dear Sarah

An Indiscreet Debutante

Lorelie Brown

Enjoy!

Love
Lorelie Brown

SAMHAIN
PUBLISHING

Samhain Publishing, Ltd.
11821 Mason Montgomery Road, 4B
Cincinnati, OH 45249
www.samhainpublishing.com

An Indiscreet Debutante
Copyright © 2014 by Lorelie Brown
Print ISBN: 978-1-61921-899-4
Digital ISBN: 978-1-61921-478-1

Editing by Sasha Knight
Cover by Kim Killion

First Samhain Publishing, Ltd. electronic publication: May 2013
First Samhain Publishing, Ltd. print publication: May 2014

Acknowledgments

The past few months have been a difficult time in my life, and I've discovered who my true friends and family are. To everyone who's supported me, I thank you from the bottom of my heart. Special thanks go to my mother, who made returning home something that felt good, and to Carrie Lofty and her husband, Keven. Love to Sarah Frantz, Zoe Archer, Dayna Hart, as dear friends. Last but not least, to TLTSNBN and to The Sekrit Illuminati Ninjas. I hope one day you'll make peace again.

Chapter One

Miss Charlotte Vale had a problem. More than one, including her father's recently renewed intentions for her future, but at the moment only one stood in the doorway of her small office. The man was tall, slender and elegant—with a scowl that threatened to do war. A maid hovered at his side, making apologetic eyes and wringing her hands.

"Sorry, miss. He barged right by," Mary said.

"Quite all right. You may go." Lottie's nod dismissed the girl, though she'd lurk nearby. Lottie's school had an efficient system set up for self-protection. She stood from her leather chair with calm borne of years' experience dealing with strange men. Nerves still rushed through her after her father's most recent letter, sent from their country estate. Unfortunately she didn't have time to dwell on his glowing review of neighboring Lord Cameron. "Sir, we aren't open to general inquiries. This is a by-invitation society."

Men occasionally attempted to visit at unapproved hours. Along with education and etiquette lessons, the school survived by courting subscriptions from men of fair education and newly burgeoning wealth who sought wives. Their quarterly soirees were quite popular.

She wouldn't have guessed this man had need of a marriage service. He was sharp. A keen-edged smile tipped finely shaped lips, and lines scored his cheeks. Most of all, he arrowed in on her with an intensity that made her toes curl.

"I'm not here for membership." His gaze finally flicked off hers, taking in the rest of the office with one go. Papers piled everywhere, overflowing bookshelves and the small clutter of slates. A chair needing repair listed in the corner. Judged, condemned and dismissed in one tiny glimpse of pale blue eyes. That must be a handy skill. "If I had my way this moment, I'd shut this whole foolish enterprise down."

She sat. If she were to be lectured, she'd much rather be comfortable. Her skirts shifted and swooshed as she fidgeted one foot up and down. "How lucky I am that you've no authority over me or mine. Is this for any particular offence, or do you simply have a virulent dislike for untidiness?"

"Harboring thieves."

The laugh that loosed from her chest was part hysteria and part real amusement. "I think not. I can personally speak to the character of almost every one of our girls."

He still hadn't moved from his position inside her doorway. He wore a dark, voluminous coat, obscuring most of his clothing beneath. His top hat was made of quite fine beaver, and he carried a gold-capped ebony walking stick. "You think none of them are capable of indelicate or licentious impulses?"

"I wouldn't dream of making such sweeping pronouncements, much less agreeing with a man whose name I don't know." She paused then, letting her gaze unfocus and looking beyond him. Her teeth bit into her bottom lip, and even in her looking-past-him state she saw his gaze drop to her mouth. She felt it, the weight, the attention. "Though I'm not sure what name would actually have any influence on me. Perhaps I could be swayed if you were the second coming of Christ."

He hissed in a breath. His chin jerked back into the crisp points of his collar, as if he were a startled turtle. She pinched her lips together to hold back her grin.

Under her palms were stacks of paper. Bills needed to be paid before she could go home to visit her mother for their daily tea appointment. An invitation to the Duchess of Marvell's ball in two months nestled along with the note from her father. More tasks than she had hours in the day. She would prefer this man hustle himself out, but that didn't seem likely.

"I'm Sir Ian Heald."

She waited. Let the draught from the window swirl through the air between them. She kept a pleasant curve to her mouth, which her mother would approve of. *Always turn a sunny disposition to the world.* Though it had never worked for Mother, she'd insisted Lottie smile, as if that would make unpalatable events easier to swallow. Lottie placed one hand atop the rough paper she'd been making tallies on. The clock on the mantle made quiet ticks as the seconds dragged by.

Men were so accustomed to having women fall all over themselves to acquiesce, they didn't realize how much they took for granted.

One small advantage of her mother's madness meant Lottie could dispense with some of those expectations. She so adored playing with men and never filled silences with idle chatter unless it served her purposes.

He took her small game better than she might have thought, never faltering and his expression placid. "You're Miss Charlotte Vale."

"I am. You haven't run astray on that score."

"I'm looking for Patricia Wertherby."

She kept her smile, but her palms turned damp. Her fingertips wanted to curl into the papers. "I don't know her."

"You're lying."

"Maybe." Her biggest, brightest grin didn't make him blink. "But you've no proof of it."

He came closer. She hesitated to add the word finally, but it hovered in the shrinking space between them. Like he were the sort to linger and watch and only move forward when he'd taken stock of the entire situation.

Rather than an actual frown, his bottom lip pinched into displeasure. Twin divots dove between his brows. "You don't understand. I have to find her. She stole from my household."

"Did she steal an item of yours?"

"Not exactly." The displeasure carved on his expression flittered away momentarily, turning into exasperation. "Suffice it to say, the item in question is important to me."

"Of course it is," she drawled. She waved a hand at the seat opposite her desk. "Please. Sit."

"Funny that you'd invite me to sit now. Have I hovered long enough for your tastes?"

"More like I'm tired of feeling like my neck is about to break." He was rather tall, after all.

"I should hate to inconvenience you." His teeth gritted around the words, and a muscle popped and shifted in his lean jaw. He sat nonetheless. His long legs folded, knees rising and poking at fine wool trousers. She'd bet that at some point in his childhood he'd shot up a half dozen inches in a few short months. He had that sort of narrow build.

Lottie laced her fingers, considering how to continue. Asking him to sit had been a diversion. She needed time to go forth without endangering the girls of her school. "Let's suppose that you had a dear friend."

"I have a few, as the case may be," he said with dry humor.

"How lucky for you."

His head tilted toward her a fraction, and dark brown hair slid across his forehead. The tumbled, messy locks were his one error in dressing. He looked every inch the rising gentleman, except his coiffure was in ruins.

She wanted to delve her fingertips through the mass, see if it were nearly as silky as she thought it must be.

She jerked her hands to her lap. Fingers curled into her palms. How very curious. She knew lust, of course, and had indulged in tastes now and then. This was new, the sharpness with which it lodged under her ribs and turned her heart heavy and foreign in her chest.

"But I wonder," he went on, absolutely oblivious to the fact that the air in her small office had suddenly become ten degrees warmer. "Do you often call serving girls your dear friends?"

"Why do you assume I'm talking about a servant?"

One of his eyebrows quirked, giving him a rakish aspect she wouldn't have guessed at moments ago. "Because Patricia Wertherby's most recent position was as an upstairs maid. Before she ran away to the city."

She waggled her fingertips at him. "Details. Nothing says I'm talking about Patricia. If I knew who this girl was."

"I see."

She managed to keep her smile. He was certainly droll when he meant to be, infusing his words with both doubt and humor. "Now, let's return to this dear friend. She's come to you for help and assistance, wishing to make herself into a better person. She relies on you."

He stacked his hands over a fine waistcoat of wool and silk and embroidery that covered a flat torso. "More fool her."

"Someone *else* comes along. Asking where this friend of yours is. They're bigger and more powerful than your dear friend. More than that, they seem entirely displeased with her. I might go so far as to say they seem positively furious, though they're hiding it admirably well." She infused her smile with sweetness. "Would you give this person your friend's direction?"

He managed to surprise her. She knew men and liked them for the most part, even when the men of her class spoke first and thought later. She'd not have thought Sir Ian much different.

Except his mouth stayed closed. His eyelashes flickered, and he rubbed his bottom lip with one thumb. When he spoke, the words oozed like treacle. "No. I'd likely not."

"Well done," she couldn't help but say, like he were a five-year-old who'd added his numbers, and she thought for a second that now, *now* he would take offence. Now he would run his mouth off and say something rude or crude or demanding, in the way of men.

He didn't. His mouth tweaked into a bare curve. He lowered his chin as he watched her. "So I think you should take me to her."

Ian liked surprising people. Making their eyes widen and their expectations tumble sideways was particularly satisfying.

Miss Charlotte Vale gave a lovely, distinct reaction too.

Her skin was pale enough that the slightest blush showed in the flush of her round cheeks. Her eyes were the true source of his satisfaction. She had amazing eyes. Large, almond-shaped and fringed with lashes that turned her exotic and remarkable. Those smoky eyes shifted darker as they went wide with surprise. The black center grew.

Straight white teeth worried at her bottom lip. "Certainly not."

"Why not?"

Her gaze darted about the room, as if looking for some way of escape. She gripped the carved wooden arms of her chair and settled her shoulders across the back. Staking her territory. He rather admired a woman who established her place in the world.

That he was in this position was entirely his sister Henrietta's fault. Their father had carried the family through the initial boom of tin mines, and it had given him hope for a new elevation for their lower gentry family. Etta and Ian would both marry well and have solid, steady lives of comfort.

Etta had refused to marry any of the men their father suggested, all of whom had been well-titled men in need of cash infusions. She'd run away to marry a millwright. The family had managed to cover that up well enough, including her husband's unfortunate early death.

The problems had come only six months ago, when the blackmail notes started.

He pushed away the cold churn in his stomach. His father had wanted so very much for them both.

Ian gave the most reasonable smile he knew, though from the way Lottie's cheeks flinched perhaps he'd failed. "I understand your reluctance to simply hand over directions. You don't know me from Prince Albert."

"Actually, I know Prince Albert reasonably well." Her brows tipped up in the center, and her chin rose. "You'd best keep talking or I'm likely to think you're entirely too dangerous. Perhaps I should have you seen out."

"That's unnecessary. I'm harmless. My point is that you don't know that, and that makes me understanding." He spread his hands wide. "So go with me. Take me there. You can see for yourself that I mean her no bodily harm."

"No bodily harm?" she echoed. "Seems to me that leaves you plenty of room for other sorts of harm."

"Nothing she won't have earned. I will wish to inspect her lodgings to look for the item I seek."

"This might be easier if you told me what that was."

Not a chance in hell. His spine went rigid, though he never let his intentionally casual posture straighten. No need to encourage her doubts. The tiny muscles and pings along his back told him how much tension he carried, as if he didn't already know from the pressure across his chest.

It never went away. Not fully. He'd too many things to do and too many responsibilities, along with an entire family to lift up. They'd barely hung on to the bottom rungs of gentry for years. His father had been well respected in their small village, but he'd dreamed of something better for his children. He'd wanted respect for his daughter and son, only to die before he'd seen it happen.

Perhaps that was for the best, considering the muck-up Henrietta had made of her life.

"It is a document."

"The Magna Carta is a document."

"I'm not looking for the Magna Carta."

"Seems a shame. That would be worth helping you with."

He let an exasperated breath through his teeth, which clenched so hard pain spiked toward his ear. "You're quite clever, aren't you?"

She had a bold mouth, in color and in shape. Full lips had a deft dip at the topmost point. He had an urge to rest his thumb there. Perhaps she'd dart out that active tongue and taste his skin.

More likely she'd clock him. "You say that as if there's something wrong with being clever. Being smart. Wouldn't you like to be smart? Perhaps someday when you've grown up into a big, real man?"

He held up a single finger and wagged it once, twice. "Miss Vale," he said on a heavy sigh. "You've gone straight to the base insults. I'm so disappointed."

She smiled, but that wasn't apparently enough to grab him by the balls and twist. Because then she *laughed.* Low and husky, with enough mirth that made him think she really, truly meant it. Her head went back and her face turned up toward the ceiling, and she only laughed harder and harder, until her chest rose and the white, white skin of her throat practically begged for a man's attention.

He smiled, watching her and waiting, and the remarkable thing was that she didn't stop. Didn't feel herself alone in her laughter enough to dry it out artificially. Instead she let the peals trail away as the humor demanded.

"You're right," she said once she'd gotten her breath back. "I went too far. I'm almost tempted to apologize."

He shouldn't be smiling at her. Not considering the situation he was in, not with potential disaster overhanging him. "I should hate to think you'd give up your convictions so easily."

She shifted in her chair, leaning her chin on one small fist. It drew her into a slender shaft of sunlight. The reddish tone to her hair gleamed. Like a halo, but entirely more indulgent. Earthy.

She was temptation and promise all wrapped up together.

If he were the least bit sane, he'd stay as far, far away as possible.

He needed a wife, truth be told. If this disaster with Henrietta were to come to light, he needed to have already found himself a respectable wife with societal connections that could elevate him a degree or two. Not a hoyden who taunted men she'd newly met.

That didn't mean he was capable of wiping away all thought of dalliance. Miss Charlotte Vale wasn't wife material, but she was a fancy lady of the very best sort. He wished she'd stand again so he could look at that slender figure. Her curves had been slight, though plenty sufficient for his tastes. He wanted to unwrap her layers, find out what sorts of treats he could find.

He'd keep his hands to his damned self.

"Take an entire army of footmen with us, if you like," he offered in as conciliatory a tone as possible. He kept his expression pleasant. Happy. As if he hadn't been imagining stripping her with rough hands and applying his teeth to every inch of her pale skin. "Whatever would keep you comfortable."

Her smile turned from amused to inquisitive. "You're well versed in keeping women comfortable, are you?"

He shrugged. "Safety is a concern of yours."

"How can you tell?"

"The emergency bellpull set up behind your chair."

She jerked upright. Her chin twitched. A tasseled pull dangled among the curtains behind her, at the windows. Not the usual placement, but subtly within reach of her seat. "Observant cuss, aren't you?"

"What kind of establishment are you running that strange men barging in with barely time enough to be announced don't warrant a pull of that bell?"

"This is a charity that depends upon the kindness of strangers."

There was something about the way she said that which made him doubtful. At the very least, she was defensive and prepared for verbal assaults on her words. Her neck locked tight, losing much of its soft elegance.

So he intentionally decided to let it go. This place mattered little to him, only in how he could use it. Only in its relation to Patricia Wertherby—who would be entirely easier to find if Miss Vale willingly took him. He spread his hands wide, smiling. "And a worthy one as well, I'm certain. Which is why I should hate to muck around and cause difficulty. It'll be best if you simply escort me. Wouldn't you like me out of your hair as hastily as possible?"

"That I would. You'll see that we harbor no thieves here, not of the kind you're insisting. We'll get this sorted out in no time. However, as much as I'd like such to happen quickly, I'll have to insist you come back tomorrow."

He managed to hold back his immediate response in favor of a more politically chosen one. He'd been chasing Patricia across hill and dale for almost six months. To be so close and yet so far drove him up the wall. "Why not today?"

"I'm terribly sorry, but I have commitments. It's tomorrow or nothing." She stood, making for the door. "And now, if you'll excuse me, I must insist on escorting you out."

"If you insist." He stepped back, gesturing for her to precede him out the door with one arm and a little hint of a bow. But really, truly, he wanted no such proper thing. No honorable thing. He wanted to watch her skirts sway with the sensuous shift of her hips. Somehow he knew she'd walk like a lioness. Purpose and intent in every step, but with tension that made men think of inappropriate things.

She knew it too. The way she looked back at him, cutting her eyes so their exotic shape caught him.

The faster he got his hands on the maid, the better. Otherwise he had a disturbing feeling he'd be trying to get his hands on Miss Vale, which would be completely unacceptable.

He hoped.

Chapter Two

Lottie found herself unaccountably nervous as the carriage twisted and rolled farther into Whitechapel. She'd been unsurprised when Sir Ian had showed up precisely on time for their trip into the bowels of the city. A man on a mission was easy to predict.

Sir Ian had taken the rear-facing seat, but his feet bracketed the half-circle of her pale violet skirts. Inside their safety, she drew her feet backwards until her heels tapped the front of her seat. As withdrawn as she possibly could be without letting the smile slip off her face. A phalanx of footmen and groomsmen clung to the exterior of the carriage and windows opened from each side. She and Sir Ian were very much not alone.

There was no reason to be nervous.

Which was why it made no sense that beneath her white gloves sweat dampened her palms or that the skin over her forearms prickled every time he looked at her.

Maybe it was the strange cant of her thoughts. She hardly knew what to do with the swirl in her mind.

Taking a lover had become a distinct concern to her as of late, but in an arbitrary and theoretical way. She wished to live her own life and stay in her mother's sphere, which directly contrasted with her father's hopes for Lord Cameron. Somehow she had to convince her father of her unsuitability toward marriage. Though she'd be damned if she could figure out why her father thought her right for marriage considering what he'd had to put up with from Mama.

The easiest way to do that in their world would be to remove her value on the marriage mart. As she wasn't foolhardy enough to throw away her inherited fortune, she would have to prove she wasn't likely to provide babies of the proper lineage and breeding. The most simple solution was to rid herself of her virginity.

Though Sir Ian was handsome enough, she was lucky she knew plenty of other, more amenable men. She needed a man who could smile rather than indulge in tiny quirks of his lips. Even if those lips were perfectly shaped enough that she wanted to touch.

"Tell me about your charity." He snapped the words out. Two divots appeared at the inside of his brow like mirrored commas.

Surprise pulled her chin up. "It's a school, not a charity. Not that it's any concern of yours."

"I expect not." He tugged the sleeve of his coat down a fraction. "But I should like one good reason why I shouldn't tell the world at large that my path toward a blackmailer and a thief ended at your doorstep."

She couldn't afford that. Funds supplied to meet the needs of the women they helped always ran short. The school survived on men's patronage. None of them would wish to marry a blackmailer or thief. The school would be destroyed. The recent infusion of cash that had come with Sera's marriage only went so far. Lottie's best friend provided a budgeted amount.

She crossed her hands over her waist and flashed a false smile. "To do so would necessitate admitting you'd been blackmailed. Which would *then* lead to questions as to *why* you'd been blackmailed." She made a show of shaking her head. "How desperately sad for you. Though I do find myself wondering as well. What have you to be blackmailed over, Sir Ian?"

He didn't act furtive or guilty despite the soft aspect of his chin. A weakness she made herself focus on. He seemed less handsome when she wasn't looking at those pale, incisive eyes.

"No one has ever blackmailed me," he said with enough haughty aplomb that she almost believed him. If he had his way, ice wouldn't melt on his tongue.

All of which ignored that he'd been the one to bring the word up.

"I wonder what you did. I can't believe you're innocent." Her head tilted to the side, and she let herself look at his mouth, his eyes. She lingered on the lean frame of his body in its fine suit. He wore the clothes well but seemed different than most of the men she knew. More...at ease, perhaps? Like he belonged in his skin.

"I never said I was innocent," he protested. And then he did a cruel, unthinking thing. He grinned, mouth lifting on the left side first. White and bright, the expression took over his entire face. The tiniest flush of red swept over his cheeks. "I've been lucky enough not to have left proof behind."

"It's generally the women who're left with the proof." She managed her usual air of calm and amusement, but it felt strained and a little harsh at the corners. She was tired—so very tired of holding on.

"Is that why you run that charity?"

"School," she snapped. Her fingertips rose to her brow, where she found warmth and a tiny throb in her temple.

She seldom lost her temper. There was no point to it, after all. Nothing resulted from such outbursts except to add to the general air of difficulties. Plus she so hated losing control of herself. She didn't have the same sort of lax emotionality that other women could get away with.

Sometimes she wished she were still at school with Seraphina Thomas and Victoria Wickerby, her two closest friends. The world had been easier then. She'd gotten by, and on troubling occasions when she felt low, she'd been able to turn to them. Sera was a born mother and loved her friends with calm, unchanging affection. Victoria was logic and sense, able to work through the worst possible problems. Unfortunately her family had recently insisted she toddle off to the ducal estate and allow her titled fiancé to lavish attention on her at his leisure.

The carriage drew to a halt, thankfully distracting Lottie from the strange angle of her thoughts. She wasn't the type to travel lost roads and indulge in nostalgia. That way lay trouble and malingering.

The door opened, and the redheaded footman bowed. "I'm sorry, Miss Vale, but this is as far as we can go. The rest will have to be on foot."

"I'm well aware of that." Though she didn't make a habit of it, this wasn't her first visit to the part of town where streets became too skinny and closely set for carriages to venture down.

They stepped from the carriage, and Lottie found herself watching Ian. His nostrils flared, and he whipped a linen cloth from an inside pocket when he noticed the open gutter running through the center of the cracked pavement with its rancid offal and putrid water.

"Is that excrement?"

She shrugged, scooping up her skirts as she led the way. "It is. Would you like to turn back? The girl is certain to attend our next quarterly soiree. You can come back and see her there."

"I think not." He followed with resolve in his spine. Most gentlemen walked with a lazy insouciance and a rolling predator's gait, since they saw the entire world as their prey. He was intent. Focused. His shoulders arrowed toward his destination. "Where is it from?"

She waved toward the dark windows above them. Those that had glass were sooty and filthy. Paper covered some. Still others were open, with laundry hanging out on poles across the narrow alleyway. "There's no telling."

"What fresh hell the cities create."

"Spoken like a true country dweller." The knot of footmen behind them had been chosen for their size and intimidation factor, yet when she looked over her shoulder, Sir Ian was a good two inches taller than any of them. For all his size, he had a certain reediness, mostly in the long line of his neck. As if a stiff breeze could puff him away like a dandelion. Lucky his features were so handsome, that constantly active, mobile mouth first and foremost. "Let me guess. You've lived in the country all your life in the same village. Your grandest excursions have been to school. Did you get to come to town for the Season?"

"Once." He all but drawled the word, turning it into agreement and doubt at the same time. "Though to say 'get to' implies a certain level of excitement that was entirely lacking."

"I love the city."

"How can you not?" He craned his head up, up, up toward the gray-tinged strip of sky barely visible at the tops of the buildings. "So healthy for one's constitution."

She shook her head as she came to a crossroads of alleys. To the right was a brighter, cleaner-looking row of smashed-together tenements that led to a larger road. She consulted the small scrap of paper in her hand upon which she'd scribbled the only address that the school had on file for Patricia. "Blast," she muttered.

"I do so hope you're not about to say we're lost. I'll be left a gibbering pile to collapse right into the gutter."

"Don't do that," she said. Though she flicked only the shortest glance at him, she'd have guessed that gibbering was far from his list of intentions. His posture was supremely casual, and he continued to take in their surrounds. "We're not lost."

"Good."

"I just don't know which way to go next."

"Blast."

Her grin was completely unplanned. She did so hate to be taken by surprise by pure emotions. "I do believe that's what I said."

"Much more appropriate coming from me than a lady."

She made a little hum in the back of her throat. "You're quite the wit, aren't you?"

"I try." His changeable mouth moved again.

What would those tweaks and shifts feel like against her skin? "It would be more helpful if you knew where we were going."

"If I knew where we were going, I wouldn't need you at all."

She had the childish impulse to stick her tongue out at him and stomp her foot. Preferably on his, smashing his toes. He was rather frustrating at times.

Four footmen stood side by side behind him. "Any of you? Are you from around here?"

They shook their heads as one, and the redhead stepped forward. "I'm from Bethnal Green, and Tim's from Southwark. The other two mates are from the north."

She turned away to focus on the knot of choices laid out before her. Sir Ian's gaze upon the nape of her neck made her less inclined to mutter the curses she wished. Instead she nibbled on her lip until a flash of pain made her let go.

Then she saw it. A door opened two buildings down and disgorged three women into the street. They laughed and giggled in a way that made Lottie miss her friends.

"Ah-hah," she said with no small measure of satisfaction. "We'll have our direction in no time."

Sir Ian's hand flashed out, wrapping around her elbow. His grip was firm but not painfully so, and yet her first inclination was to yank away. Her heart fluttered. She didn't like things that affected her strongly. They made her nervous. She couldn't risk feeling something so intense.

"You can't go speak with them. Send a footman."

"Can I not?" She jerked her arm away and smiled as widely as she could manage. Curling her fingers under his lapel was beyond rude considering they'd recently met, but she did it anyway and was gratified that the dark centers of his eyes flared. From such a close distance, his crisp scent undercut the sticky rot of the open gutter. She patted his chest, which was solid, despite its narrowness. "I recommend you never, ever tell me what I can and cannot do. You won't like the results."

Ian hadn't thought before speaking. There had been a moment, as the words slipped out from between his lips, when he'd known he'd spoken wrong. Miss Vale wasn't the sort to take bold-faced direction. She bristled. Her green eyes went wider, her lips parting on an affronted sharp intake of air.

He'd never admit it, but she looked more handsome for the emotion. Mostly because he thought it might be one of the few true reactions he'd seen from her in their short acquaintance.

She gathered two handfuls of her fine, silk skirts and hopped over the trickling line of liquid that wandered down the center of the road. As bold as anyone he'd ever met, she walked right up to the trio of women. The three watched her warily and clutched wool wraps about their shoulders.

Henrietta would never, ever have been capable of such boldness. Of course, had they approached her, Etta would have been talked into giving up every scrap of clothing on her back, but that wasn't at all the same thing. Etta was sweet, though inclined to be too sweet. Her involvement with Archie and Patricia had proved that. Gullible and inclined to accept people at their word. Who in the name of God gave her marriage certificate to her sister-in-law to keep safe?

But that was different. Ian and his family were lower gentry at best. Association with the middle rungs was necessary if one wanted to have any socializing at all in their little village.

Miss Vale was obviously of a different sort, fine and high flying. She was the kind of girl who was lovely to look at and enjoyable to watch, but not exactly the sort who'd make a good wife. Not for Ian. He wanted the kind of woman who'd settle down in a true love match with him. Eventually. It wasn't as if he were looking to shove his head in the parson's noose the next day.

It had taken him six months to track the unsigned, threatening notes from Devon to London, and that was even with their money demands. Patricia had taken a while to work up her courage to full larceny. Ian had no hope this would be figured out in a matter of days.

He hustled as quickly as he could without running to catch up with the girl before she made a hash of things. These women wouldn't take kindly to arrogance, as Miss Vale seemed likely to issue.

But Miss Vale surprised him. She walked right up to the cluster of women and smiled brightly. "Hello, ladies."

Obvious suspicion wrinkled across their careworn faces. Their mouths were all turned up in smiles that wavered under Miss Vale's attention. The one in the back of the knot nodded and stepped forward. Her hair was a dingy, dark blonde and dropping around her cheeks, but under papery skin it was apparent she'd once been a beauty. Her eyes were wide and innocent, though wary. "Hullo, missus."

In contrast, Miss Vale shone like a bright star dropped to earth. Her pale lilac skirts all but glowed with color compared to the dark, work-ready colors of the other women. "It's Miss. Miss Charlotte Vale."

The flash of recognition that turned two of the women's smiles real was surprising. The one who'd spoken remained cautious, however. "We haven't many visitors of your cant around here."

Miss Vale shrugged. "I know. Terrible, isn't it? Those fancy pieces like me who stay in our faraway castles and can't be bothered to spread some blunt around."

Ian grabbed her by the arm again. This time she didn't pull away. He'd have gambled ready money that the working women would have been offended by such impudence, but instead the last one melted under Miss Vale's charm and honesty.

"We around here could always do with a little of the extra."

The one with dark hair on the right smiled. Her eyetooth was black at the gums, but the way her eyes lit up made up for it. She was still a pretty woman. "It makes a girl almost tempted to give in to some of them lads about here, for an extra coin."

Ian sealed his lips and kept his expression calm. He couldn't believe either the crudeness of the group, nor that Miss Vale seemed so inclined to chat along, smiling and nodding along with the rest of them.

"You can't let them have it, though. That coin will be fast spent and you'll be left up against the wall with your skirts a mess and your pride tinier." She pulled a tiny sheaf of calling cards from the reticule hanging by braided cord from her wrist. "Are you already married?"

"Pshaw," said the one in front. "Not the three of us. Same boys keep asking the same questions and they're not apt to get us anywhere good."

"If you'd like a step up, you'd best come to see me. My friends and I will teach you a few tricks. No cost involved for you in any way. After, we'll introduce you to choice men looking for wives." She handed over three of the small, cream-colored cards.

"Miss Vale," Ian interjected. He hadn't time for her to recruit victims for whatever scam she ran. He wanted to wrap his hands around Patricia's scrawny neck and destroy her for having threatened his sister. He wouldn't, of course. He'd have to settle for her rotting in prison while he carried away the key.

Didn't mean he liked standing around.

Miss Vale waved a hand at him. But then she shot him a glance out the corner of her eyes that said she entirely knew what she did to him. "Did we have a deadline, Sir Ian? Somewhere we have to be?"

"Sir Ian?" echoed the girl who'd been silent up until now. She added a tipsy-sounding giggle at the end. "I've not met a sir before. Not out walking on the street in this part of town."

"And speaking of such, we're almost lost," Ian said.

Her head tilted to the side and confusion darkened her eyes, but Miss Vale only laughed.

"Almost lost?" she echoed. In the dim light of the alleyway, her verdant eyes shouldn't have been so lovely. Didn't matter. "I had no idea you were quite so whimsical."

He curled his fingers against his palms to hold back the urge to touch. "There's a lot of things you don't know about me. Such a short acquaintance and all."

"There are certain things one knows at once."

"It's not whimsical," he insisted. "We're not precisely lost, as we could easily return to the carriage. But we don't know how to get where we're going."

"Too true." She aimed that keen-edged smile back at the women. "Which is where we were hoping you three could come in."

The one in front laughed. "Have at it, though we've little resources any better than the protection at your back."

Miss Vale waved her hand again in an airy, open gesture. "Oh, they're mostly for show. If anyone should try to molest me, they'd have to answer to Fletcher Thomas."

"Is that right?" the woman said with a fair measure of surprise. "I wouldn't have figured your sort to get mixed up with him."

Ian watched the byplay with no small measure of curiosity. His brows knotted together as he tried to work through the puzzle that was Miss Vale. She didn't talk down to the women, and she had acquaintances that struck awe and no small measure of fear in the area's denizens. But she didn't once lose her brightness or shine.

"It's a long story, anyhow. What we really need is simple. Directions. To this address." She held forth the slip of paper with Patricia's information writ upon it.

"Can't read, lovey," said the other woman, as plain as can be.

"I thought not." Miss Vale gave a decisive nod. "Now you must promise to come visit my school. We'll teach you to read."

It was obvious such an enticement intrigued the woman, though not so much her friends behind her. "Maybe I will at that."

From there, it was only a matter of moments to get directions. Miss Vale wasn't above touching the women, patting their shoulders and backs as they eventually moved on by. She waited and gave a little wave as the black-haired woman who'd been most tempted by the idea of the school looked back.

Ian and Miss Vale started toward the turn they needed, which was apparently two streets down and past the wig maker. The footmen ranged behind them, keeping close.

Ian found himself at a loss for words. As his mother and sister would tell the world, that wasn't a particularly common problem for him. He didn't quite know what to make of Miss Vale. She was a flippant society girl, that much was assured. Yet he couldn't help feeling she must have depths beneath that.

He rubbed his thumb over the etch work atop his walking stick. "You'll marry those three off, will you?"

"Likely as not." She studied the dark buildings that passed, gaze flicking over the soot-and-mold-covered brickwork. A baby cried in an upper window, and she craned her neck backwards to look. "It's easiest to get them into the school with the possibility of matrimony. The idea is accessible. Something they can understand."

"And what sorts of fantastical things would you say if you thought they'd believe it?"

Chapter Three

Lottie was fast coming to dislike this man. Or maybe she was coming to like him too much considering their short acquaintance. Her mouth pinched into a frown. Indecision crawled along her skin. She couldn't afford it, not when the specters overhanging her life wanted their way. "I would tell them that they could train for inside service or to be a shopgirl. Or to perhaps remain in their current jobs but agitate for unions to gain better pay and benefits."

"You would encourage them to noble heights indeed." He said it so dryly that she had no hope of discerning his true meaning. The way his mouth bent up on that left side again made her inclined to think the best of him.

"You approve of unions?"

"I couldn't care one way or the other about unions. They're a waste of time."

She laughed as they made the turn the women had described. "Spoken like a man who's never worked for a penny in his life."

Lottie's pin money was less controlled than most women, but its use was split between keeping up appearances and funding the various needs of the school, which had plenty of work in itself. Any least little problem could tip the balance between a solid school and a crumbling edifice of no use to women.

Trepidation fluttered down her back as the street got narrower. The tall buildings leaned in overhead, obscuring more of the dim London sunlight. Night fell sooner in the depths of the city than it did in idyllic neighborhoods. They'd be well served to be on their way back to more familiar environs in less than two hours.

Not to mention she had her daily appointment with her mother.

"You'd be wrong." His shoulder brushed hers with heat. They pressed too close together when she tried to push away from the wetness in the center of the road. "I've increased my family's fortunes tenfold since taking over."

She inclined her chin, giving him a measure of respect earned by those words. "Well done of you."

He had to bend his neck to peer at her, since he was a full head taller. Yet he managed to look in her eyes, even as they kept walking. "Is that sarcasm?"

"As a matter of fact, it's not." She drew to a halt, looking up at the building on her left. No numbers designated the address, but it was between a tinker's shop and a pawnbroker as the women had said to expect. "I've known plenty of men who do their level best to squander every pence that falls into their hands. It's a sickness."

His mouth curved into an appealing smile. "I'm pleased you can see my position."

"Your position is still entirely invalid." She grinned up at him. His height appealed to her. Most likely it was the illusion of being sheltered. Though Lottie knew how false harbor could hurt. "Unions are not simply recommended, they're a necessity."

His eyes widened, but he didn't respond with the vigor she might have assumed. Instead he pursed his bottom lip as he concentrated. "I'm not sure whether to be more shocked that your charity is a front for union agitation or that you should so boldly admit it to a near stranger."

She bit her lip around a smile. "Neither. My *charity*, as you insist on calling it, is a place for women to advance themselves. Nothing so bold as union agitation. But nothing so lost as to pretend it doesn't exist."

"Lords and masters do what is best for their employees as it leads to what is best for the business as well." He puffed up another inch, his collar white and blindingly clean against the dismal grayness of the surrounds.

"You're almost adorable in your stubbornness." She patted his cheek. Though she'd have liked the gesture to be about putting him in his place, she couldn't quite lie to herself that much. She wanted to feel his skin. Smooth and yet rough with his beard's evening growth. "Now let's find Patricia so we can get you away from my *charity* and on your way."

The stairs inside were decrepit. Lottie hardly knew whether to trust her life to the rickety balustrade, so she settled for holding her skirts up and keeping her chin lifted so that she wouldn't see the stickiness in which she stepped. She allowed herself to be much comforted that Sir Ian followed behind her as they went up two stories.

If she fell, she'd take him with her on the way down.

The amusement that would arise made the idea worth considering. If it weren't for the footmen trailing behind, as alert as soldiers, she would play at it. See his true colors if he were to think she was falling.

Instead they arrived on the proper floor, and she knocked on the door of Patricia's small flat. Sweat and chills sprang up on her hands, though she had no idea why she was so unaccountably nervous.

She wanted to think well of the girls who attended her school. Their very appearance signified willingness to better themselves and take advantage of opportunity. That didn't mean they all had the best *reasons* for wanting to better themselves. They'd already had a few instances of petty theft, but that was different from blackmail. It was also different from theft serious enough to have the gentry on her tail.

Only Patricia didn't open the door. Instead a tiny woman with bird-thin bones and a wan smile appeared. "Miss Vale. I didn't expect you to call."

"Finna, I didn't realize you roomed with Patricia."

Finna bobbed a small curtsy. "We met in Lady Victoria's elocution lessons, and Patricia needed somewhere to stay. Since my previous roommate moved on, it seemed like a good combination." Her voice lilted with the softest touch of Ireland. She was a long way from home.

"I'm glad you found each other, then." Lottie had drawn Finna's story out one evening when she had lingered late at the school. There had been a man involved, of course, as well as the lure of better paying jobs than Finna could have found in the north of Ireland. But she'd quickly found herself on her own. She was lucky to have steady work in a porcelain factory, but she was working herself to the bone and wanted a better life.

Like all Lottie's girls. Which was why she had to keep them safe.

Finna's glance jumped over Lottie's shoulder, toward Sir Ian, who was likely glowering in that way of his. When Finna looked past him, down the stairs to the footmen, her eyes got wider.

Lottie angled her shoulders and stepped a half pace to the side. Not that she could obscure the alarming set of men with her, but so it would be more clear they waited on her orders. "Don't worry your head about them. We brought them along so Sir Ian here wouldn't be frightened of Whitechapel."

"I beg your pardon?" Sir Ian began, but she cut him off as soon as she could.

She kept her voice calm and light. The same voice she used for placating her mother when the megrims came upon her. "You see, Sir Ian's a bit of a worrier. He knew Patricia in Devon."

"She grew up there," Finna provided.

Lottie smiled. "Of course she did. Sir Ian is under the misapprehension that Patricia is in possession of something of his. Is she in?"

Finna shook her head. "I haven't seen her a couple days now. I'm worried, truth be told. It's not like her. But then, she's gotten stranger and odder over the past little bit."

Sir Ian stepped to the side, making himself seen. Finna shrunk further, her shoulders curling about her ears. "How long have you roomed together?"

"Five months," she provided, and Sir Ian nodded along as if he'd expected no different.

Lottie shot him a look, but he willfully ignored her. Simmering tension made the space between them palpable in a way he couldn't possibly ignore. Attraction was a matter of bodies, and she'd felt it before. Lord Cameron was a handsome man, also tall with dark hair. Too bad her father had been pressing him on her so directly. Made a girl want to run fast into the next available man's arms.

She must have a certain affinity for dark-haired men. That would be good to know in finding someone to be with.

She pushed away those silly thoughts and smiled at Finna. "May we come in?"

Her gaze flicked from Sir Ian to the footmen and back again. "All of you?" Her accent slipped under the strain. "It's a small room…"

"Of course not. Only Sir Ian and me. He'd like to peek around. He won't make a mess or treat your belongings with anything less than the utmost respect." She turned her biggest, brightest smile on Sir Ian. "Isn't that right?"

The amusement his mouth quirked into was wry and to Lottie's eyes, doubtful. But he made a rumbling, purring sound of agreement anyway. "Quite right." The girl melted a little under Sir Ian's approbation, her spine curling and her hand loosening around the edge of the door. "My mother and sister raised me better than that."

If Lottie didn't know any better, she'd think a measure of truth filled his words about his sister. But she had him agreeable, and she'd best press her advantage for the benefit of her girls. "And he promises to behave himself as well. Doesn't he?"

Ian wasn't used to women telling him so bold-facedly what to do. He wouldn't have guessed that he'd easily accept. A surprising sense of amusement kept him willing and happy. He nodded his agreement. "As Miss Vale says. My very best behavior." He swept two fingers over his lapel in a King's Cross. "I swear it."

"As you like, sir." The girl with frail shoulders stepped back and held open the door.

He could understand her reluctance to have their entire troop inside. He wasn't assured there'd be enough space on the battered, worn floorboards for all their feet. Two tiny cots lined each side of the room. At the far end was one bare windowpane. A shelf underneath was stacked with belongings—a doll made of a few twists of cloth and a round head, a chipped vase that Ian couldn't imagine anyone paying money for. The crack that ran through the center alone would have made it useless. Yet either this girl Finna or Patricia kept it as their special treasure, in a place of pride under the window.

Ian could almost understand why Patricia would be moved to blackmail.

That didn't mean he was inclined to pay it.

Tucked behind the swing of the door was a sink and a small stove. A single cabinet there had a couple pots and a loaf of bread wrapped in cloth.

Four steps landed Ian in the middle of the room. He schooled his expression into something genial and kind as he turned back toward Finna and Miss Vale, but it was difficult. He'd come so far to lose Patricia from his grasp.

"Which side normally belongs to Patricia?"

"The left," answered the girl. Her voice was subdued. She darted a look toward Miss Vale. "I hope she comes back soon. The rent is due day after next and I've my half, but that's it."

Lorelie Brown

Ian knelt by the left-most bed, but his attention was split between checking beneath the woefully thin mattress stuffed with cornshucks and watching Miss Vale's response. Most women would have fished a bob out of their purse and handed it over to gushing thanks from the girl. Hell, Ian would have likely done so himself. This poor, draughty room wasn't much. If Finna were kicked out, Ian couldn't imagine what the next step down would be. Sleeping in a cold alley? A tenement packed ten to a room?

But Miss Vale's bright expression never wavered. She patted Finna on the shoulder. "If she hasn't returned by tomorrow evening, come let me know at the school. We'll find you someone new to room with. There are always girls looking for safe situations."

"I do know that feeling," Finna agreed. Her spine eased from its rigidity, and the tendons stretching her thin neck softened. "Not as I'd want to get rid of Patricia, but if she can't be bothered to be around, well..." She trailed off with a shake of her head.

"Was she a good companion until now?" Miss Vale asked.

He tried to make his poking and digging subtle, but when he was looking for a sheet of paper, it became difficult. He leaned down to peek in the space between the baseboards and the yellow-tinged walls, to make sure no folded papers were secreted.

"Well enough," Finna said, but her gaze shifted and her jaw worked over what seemed to be a lie. "That is, she was always sweet. Kind. Except for when her man came calling. I didn't like him as much."

"Her man?" Miss Vale prompted. "Who was that?"

"I don't know as such. She never talked at length. But she liked him a great deal."

Ian hoisted a loose floorboard and found nothing but dust and thick cobwebs. He dropped it in flat-out annoyance, but

Miss Vale's eyebrows lifted and her mouth pinched into a displeased shape.

He shifted the floorboard neatly into its place, then used the heel of his shoe to push down an errant nail. The smile he aimed her way said, *There. Sufficient to your high standards?* Silent communication was the only option considering their audience.

Except he wouldn't have guessed that she'd understand him. Or that she'd curve her mouth and lower her lashes into an expression that said so very clearly, *Yes. For now.*

He didn't enjoy the idea that he might have some deeper level of communion with this woman. She was flighty and giggly and entirely too *much*. He hardly knew what to do with her kind, except she'd never lower herself to his level. Best to admire her sort from afar.

He dusted his hands off, flecks of dirt falling to the floor. "Sweet and kind sound like wonderful attributes in a friend."

Her throat worked on a nervous-looking swallow. The woman came to Miss Vale's chin and Miss Vale, in turn, was petite when compared to Ian. How obvious the poor effects of childhood malnutrition could be sometimes.

Finna was still capable of lying, however. "She was the very best sort of roomer. I do hope she comes back," she said, ignoring the strain in her words.

That didn't sound at all like the Patricia once known by Ian. Her brother Archie had been a bluff, kind man, that much was for certain. He'd been the second son born to a large farming family, but he'd been apprenticed out to the local millwright at twelve. No one had been thrilled when Etta ran away and married Archie, not by half. Screaming battles between Etta and Ian and their parents left everyone going round and round in awful circles. That she should lower herself so fully to a man who wouldn't ever leave the village. Mostly that she would so disappoint their father's hope with such sound dismissal.

That didn't mean the family was incapable of understanding Archie's appeal. He'd treated Etta like a queen among women and loved her every step. There was no doubting his love for her, nor his goodness. He fed stray cats, nursed ill hedgehogs and would give a beggar the boots off his feet if he thought it would help—the same sort of person as Etta.

Patricia had been nice enough, but not in Archie's league. Plus she'd always had her eye on moving on. Nothing in their small village or even their county was good enough for Patricia. When she'd disappeared after Archie's death, no one had been astounded. Nor, honestly, had Ian been particularly shocked to realize she was the only one with Etta's marriage certificate and therefore the likely choice for blackmailer.

The difficulty had come when she'd proved adept at hiding.

Etta, as sweet and gentle as she always was, gave Patricia credit for allowing the mourning period to pass unmolested.

Ian shoved his hands in his trouser pockets. No marriage certificate. No paper at all among Patricia's meager belongings. The anger trying to knot his fists would leave Finna scared and confused. There was no reason to take his fury out on any but the intended target.

Which he would gladly do. "Nothing here."

"I see that," said Miss Vale. Her amusement poked fun at him and how he'd dispensed with the fiction he was looking for Patricia for dutiful reasons. "If you would tell me what you're looking for, I might be more help."

"Find me Patricia."

She let silence weave between them, let his words go unchallenged for a long moment. "I'm doing my part."

He blew out a rough, gusting breath. "I know."

She turned to Finna, who'd watched their interaction with rapt fascination. "As you might guess, Sir Ian here isn't only on a charitable call for his mother."

"Lady Victoria said in class that lies were occasionally acceptable for the benefit of society as a whole."

"What *is* that school of yours teaching?" Ian spat.

"We teach women what they need to know in order to better their lives." Miss Vale's smile turned harsh and a little bitter. "Whatever the cost."

"Lovely. Just lovely." Ian ground his teeth together. "I find myself less and less surprised that a harridan like Patricia found your school. It might be best if the world at large knew."

"You wouldn't dare." Her eyes flashed.

"Try me."

Her next words were aimed at Finna, but she kept her gaze trained on him. "Finna, dear. Tell Patricia that I am looking for her. Me. Not this man."

"You hide her from me, you'll be harboring a fugitive."

"Words you have yet to prove." She finally looked at Finna, her expression softening. "I'm very sorry if we've put any sort of an imposition on you. And don't forget to come to the school if Patricia doesn't come back and you need a new girl."

"I will, miss," Finna said on a hint of a curtsy.

Miss Vale swept from the room and down the stairs in high dudgeon. The footmen split to allow her past, pressing up against the wall and the decrepit balustrade. Her color was up, red splashes across her high cheekbones turning her into some sort of fiery sprite. The angle of her chin lifted her neck to an imposing arc. She was absolutely and completely furious with him.

Ian had no intention of telling her that she was rather adorable when in a temper. He hadn't much association with women who lived wildly or were so free with their emotions. His mother and sister and other women he knew were calm and prepossessed.

It seemed more and more that Lottie was a force unto herself.

Chapter Four

The walk back through the alleys was much shorter than the route they'd taken inward. This time they stopped to chat with no one, nor did Lottie talk to Ian, the smug bastard. She would have stomped if it weren't for the uneven pavement and the conviction that falling over face first would negate her righteous position.

She couldn't indulge in her temper. Couldn't let it take her over. She'd seen enough of that from her mama to know how foolish and troubling it could be.

She intentionally calmed her breaths. Made her cheeks pull her mouth into a smile, even if they didn't want to head that way, because sometimes a smile *caused* happiness, damn it.

She refused to hand her life over.

That also meant she wouldn't let some stranger malign her girls and accuse her school of harboring bad women.

By the time she arrived at the carriage, she'd smoothed herself into an approximation of calm. Her blood eased in her veins, and she simply ignored the tight bands around her ribs. She'd not lose control, not in that way. Her happiness was her armor, and she liked it.

She smiled at Sir Ian. "Where can I drop you off?"

"You don't stay angry long, do you?" He put out a hand for her to balance fingertips on as she mounted the stairs of the small black carriage.

She put her fingers in his, ignoring the tingling rush that swept over her skin and lodged in the damp, hot points behind her ears. When her temper and emotions flared, the rest of her body followed. Anger and lust wrapped up together. More proof it was a good idea to find someone halfway appropriate to slake this want with, before she did something she'd regret all because of raging emotions.

"I couldn't," she said, forcing a laugh. "When one gets as royally furious as me, one can't afford to cling to the emotion."

"Royally furious, eh?" Dark brown hair fell over his brow as he followed her into the cab. "Every woman I've met claims they're incapable of such emotions."

"Every woman gets angry," she scoffed.

He folded himself into the opposite seat. His knees were skinny, his legs long. She had the impression he was rather like a colt or a puppy. Someone who hadn't grown into his limbs despite appearing nearly thirty years old. "I never said otherwise," he continued. "But I've found that most of them *claim* they have the temper of misplaced angels. Even Lady Cotrose."

She lifted a single eyebrow. "I don't know Lady Cotrose."

"No, I don't imagine you would. She's a country bumpkin like me. Her husband tired of her screeching and screaming and throwing vases at his head."

"Are we certain it's not his fault?" She smoothed her lap so the silken, knotted flower decorations aligned down the outside edge of her thigh. "Certain behaviors could all but demand such a response."

"He is known for chewing with his mouth open. A dire, horrid habit, I'm sure. But there was doubt that such habits required him being roomed with the hunting dogs."

"Lady Cotrose demanded such?"

"Hard to tell. She was tied to a tree in the back gardens, so one must assume he decided to sleep with the hounds all on his own."

She saw it then, through the dawdling remains of her temper. She'd forced herself to fake good humor, but that wasn't exactly the same thing as being truly relaxed or happy. So he was *teasing* her. His eyes were sparking, and the tiniest quirk of a smile lingered on his lips. The way he watched from under canted brow, his chin tucked toward his chest...

He was having her on.

She tongued the inside of her teeth, trying to appear as if she was considering the situation. "Did he have a bed installed in the kennels? Or did he sleep on the paving stones?"

"Does it matter?"

She made a humming noise and rubbed her thumb over her bottom lip, trying to hide her smile. "It does. Considerably. As much as it matters if Lady Cotrose were tied to the tree with a silken cord. One must observe standards."

He wasn't half so circumspect with his grin. She liked that, liked the way it shone through the carriage. She knew entirely too many people who were afraid to demonstrate emotions, even the pleasant ones. Sometimes she was among them. Rather often, truth be told. "Is that all it takes? Observe the standards and one can get away with anything?"

"Not even that, most of the time. Take me, for example."

"I'm sure most men gladly would." His eyelids drooped, and if she hadn't known better, she'd have thought he'd suddenly decided he was interested. She could almost think it involuntary. If he had any idea what that husky tone of voice did, he'd have used it straightaway.

As it was, she flicked a wry glance from under her lashes and went on with what she'd been saying. "I ignore all the rules. I'm positively wicked. I tell bad jokes, I drink port with the men whenever I can, and I wear the wrong colors. My mother is so mad, she would have given George III a run for his money. And yet curiously, no one has kicked me out of their presence."

His cheeks hollowed on a shot of amusement. "I can't imagine why not," he said with dry aplomb.

"It's a mystery, is it not?" She gave him her cheekiest grin.

Truly, she knew why people put up with her. Money and charm and beauty went a long way, which said ill things of the society she kept. She shouldn't have started this line of conversation. But it was strange how easy he was to talk to and how their senses of humor meshed. Normally she would only suggest a silk rope to Victoria. Sera would have been shocked.

"Where are you taking us?" he asked, as if hearing her silent pleading to change the subject.

"You may take the carriage anywhere you like. I'd drop you myself, but I'm going to be late."

"Late for what?"

She didn't let the hard jolt of panic that clenched her chest show on her face. "I'm going to have tea with my mother."

"The mad one?"

"The very same." Her heart leapt into her throat. She wasn't normally reckless when it came to her mother.

He let silence spin through the air between them, though the wheels kept churning over rough roads. They came to a halt in traffic, and costermongers and rag-and-bone sellers called out their goods. Outside the window, a boardman had hanging from his shoulders a two-sided ad for the smallest chimneysweeps in London.

"I'd like to go with you."

"No."

The carriage turned down Cheyne Walk. She didn't have much longer before she could wave him away. Time with her mother could be fraught for many reasons, but at least she could always be herself. What parts of herself she wanted to be, that was.

He leaned forward to look out the window. His collar pulled at the back, revealing skin barely warmed by the sun and the ends of his dark hair. "I wouldn't have expected you'd live in Chelsea."

"My mother insists." She said the words with a smile and a light air, but that was usually enough. She never had to lie—no one ever bothered to ask further. They took her surface explanations and everything was fine.

But Ian transferred that intense gaze to her. His mouth stilled for a moment, as his exacting gaze scanned her from head to toe. "And your father? He goes along with her?"

She swallowed. Once, twice. A strange knot lurked at the back of her throat. The street turned relatively quiet as they drew to a halt before gray stone and the green-painted front door. "What Mother wants, Mother gets."

"But you called her mad." When the door opened, he put one hand out. The footman hardly blinked, but Lottie flinched. He turned his hand, held it palm out. She liked his long, graceful fingers. This was a man who should play the piano. Or a woman.

"I called her mad because she is."

"Insane, you mean?" He leaned forward. "Not angry?"

She pushed past him and stepped down. The sun was low in the sky. Across the street was the Thames, but before her was the building she both loved and dreaded. She smoothed her skirts. "I meant exactly what I said."

"Yet you and your father let her determine where your household resides." Then he did something she'd never expected—stepped down from the carriage. His top hat tilted at a rakish angle, he looked up at the tall building. "I think I'd like to meet her."

"Not a chance in hell." Her heart flipped in her throat. She couldn't breathe.

"Such rudeness." He smiled a slow-burn grin. "Will you kiss your mother with that mouth?"

She shook her head, almost frantic. The footman behind Sir Ian had the grace to avert his gaze, as if he didn't want to witness her explosion. It was no surprise he'd expect her to blow. Everyone treated her like she'd snap at any point, but she knew better. Her mother's madness hadn't come until the stress of childbearing, like her grandmother's. Hence Lottie's determination to avoid marriage. "No. This isn't happening. Take yourself away. Right now."

Ian wasn't being kind. That much he knew. But he set one hand at Miss Vale's spine and gently guided her up the white-painted stairs. She didn't want to go with him, that was obvious in the way she all but dug her heels in and leaned back. It served only to increase his touch by flattening his fingers against her spine. The curve of her waist was sleek temptation.

"Would you like me to be honest?"

Her nose wrinkled with all the abandon of a young girl. "I do generally appreciate it."

"My desires have little to do with wanting to meet your mother or be any sort of a bother to you." He smiled at the butler when the door opened. "I simply don't trust you."

She came to an abrupt halt then, her steps clattering at the threshold. She held a hand up and out as if she'd stop the air. "Perhaps I'm wrong and you're the one who's lost all sense of your wits."

"How do I know you won't immediately run out the back of your house and find Patricia? Your loyalty to those who attend your charity—"

"School," she insisted. Her cheeks pinched, and her mouth set into a mulish line.

"So who's to say you haven't a plan to warn her at your first opportunity? I'm afraid I can't let you out of my sight yet. Not until you've calmed."

Her gaze jerked to the butler who waited inside the foyer. He kept his face pointed straight forward, as if looking through them toward the Thames. The gray-brown rush of water was nearly obscured by trees, but the salt-and-pepper-haired man seemed to find it fascinating.

Or he was an expert in ignoring awkward situations.

"Martin." Miss Vale greeted him with a brief nod. "Is my mother well today?"

"I believe so, miss."

47

"Fine." Miss Vale swept forward, away from Ian's touch. His fingertips tingled with the need to get her back, but that wasn't likely. Not with the haughty lift of her chin and the way she all but spit when she addressed him again. "You're in luck. I've decided it's simply easier to have you to tea than to deal with your incessant whining when my men throw you out bodily."

He followed along behind her, stacking both his hands flat across his own back. No touching. Not her. Not that long, graceful sweep of her spine into neck and the delicate knots there. Her reddish hair had been swept and pinned up haphazardly enough that a wisp fell out to touch her collarbone.

"Just curious, but if you have me thrown out of the house, how would you be able to hear my whining?"

"I notice you don't deny that there would be such." That impish good humor was back in her expression. Her smile curved, her body canted toward him.

How much of it was real and how much was falsified? A fake designed to ease everyone around her and deflect. The curious part was what she hid. If she could so boldly admit insanity in her family, what could possibly be left as an enigma?

He wanted to peel her apart, see what mysteries she kept for someone with such a bold mouth. Truths could hide the deepest secrets.

But he didn't have time for such nonsense. Etta still waited at their family home in Devon, along with his mother. If he knew them both, they'd be working each other into frenzied balls of worry. They were good women and didn't deserve to have to fret the way they were. No one deserved to be blackmailed by a piece of trash like Patricia, much less his sweet, kindhearted baby sister.

Ian intended to do whatever was necessary to ease her heart. Best-case scenario would involve seeing Patricia in wrist and leg irons, marching into the bowels of a dank prison.

"Whether I whine or not is beside the issue." He felt his mouth quirk, thought of her skin and the way she'd taste under his lips. "What matters is that we're going to take a lovely tea *en famille.*"

She shook her head as she pushed open a pocket door. "This certainly isn't a public sort of occasion."

That much was apparent when she stepped in and revealed the room. At some point, the position and airy windows on the front street said it had likely been a parlor. The sofa toward the far end lent credence to the idea, as well as the marble-surrounded fireplace.

But that's where the similarities to normal decorating ended.

The whole room was soft. A giant jumble of cloth and fabric and large pillows that had been stripped from the beds of giants. The entire south wall was covered in fabric, starting at the plaster medallion in the center of the ceiling and falling in gathers of pale, pale yellow. A line of half-done paintings leaned along the edge of the wall. They'd been stacked while still wet, as many had drag marks through the oil paint. Whoever had painted them lacked focus, as seven different subjects ranged widely from landscapes to nudes.

It took him a moment to spot Miss Vale's mother, mostly because she was curled up in the corner of the room. If it weren't for the fact that she were on a cushion only four inches off the ground, she might have been any woman of leisure in the afternoon. She had a pile of books at her elbow and another open in her hands as she flipped through speedily.

"Mama," Miss Vale said, with a French-like accent on the second syllable. "I've brought company. Lady Vale, allow me to present Sir Ian Heald."

Lady Vale looked up, her eyes slightly unfocused as she flipped onward two more pages, as if she weren't able to switch activities. Then she grinned. She stood with a surprising amount of grace, tucking her pale yellow dressing gown around her waist and retying a lace sash.

"Oh, Lottie. You really shouldn't have. I'm not dressed." The protest seemed unauthentic from the avid way she inspected Ian from head to toe. "Though if one must be seen half dressed, how fortunate it should be by an attractive man. Perhaps you should leave me with him, Lottie. Better that than endure such strangely mixed company."

Ian bowed. It was either that or gape at the woman.

Lottie's response was curiously absent. Her lips still bent upwards in a smile, but there was something about it that looked un-right. She was only half there. It was her eyes, he was fairly sure. The bright spark that drove her normally had fled. The tiniest dots of red color flushed the tops of her cheeks, below thick lashes. "Mama, have you ordered tea yet?"

"They'll bring it on the hour, I think. Always do. They think I can't take care of myself," she said with a charming smile directed at Ian. "A team of little rats, taking after their queen. That's me, the servants' queen. They do love me so." She talked at a rapid cadence with endearing verve. She shrugged, which made the neckline of her gown gape. Her skin had a strange, bright red tinge across her neck and upper shoulder. Lady Vale looked more like a laborer who'd been too long in the fields than a lady who spent her time sheltered.

Lottie noticed too. She touched two fingers to the back of her mother's neck, concern drawing her brows down. "Were you out today?"

"Nicolette went with me," she replied with a guileless innocence that Ian suspected was wholly manufactured. "I wished to paint a bird's nest in my tree. You should have seen the light over the river. The park is lovely this time of year."

"You say that all year," Lottie said with a gentle smile.

"It's particularly true in the spring." Lady Vale strode toward the windows then and yanked back the curtains. "Look! Look at all that light. It's amazing. I was using it to paint my vision of the goddess Aphrodite. I want her streaming through the scene as if she's been transported."

"Mother," Lottie said. "Please. I'm sure Sir Ian doesn't want to hear all about that."

In all honesty, he had no idea what the woman was talking about. Her avenues of conversation were easily transported to raptures about the fairly ordinary street views outside the window. He gave a small bow, as the polite thing to do. "Certainly don't worry on my account."

"See? Sir Ian is a man of taste, I'm certain of it." She spun and leaned back against the windows, which made her gown part inelegantly. Her lower leg and knee were on display.

Ian coughed into his fist and averted his gaze. At some point, she'd drawn directly on a six-foot-square section of the wallpaper. Charcoal lines took a moment to coalesce into a roughly hewn face.

Lottie's face.

Once the lines fell into place, Ian couldn't see anything else. Her wide smile and the almond eyes slanted to the side, secretive.

Beside him, Lottie spoke in a calm, sure voice to her mother. "Why don't you run upstairs and have Nicolette dress you in your new silk moiré? You haven't had a chance to wear it yet, and I'm sure Sir Ian would find it beautiful."

"Oh, that's a lovely idea. I'll be back in a moment."

She disappeared out of the room in a tide of yellow dressing gown. The blue lace sash trailed out behind her, and long red hair fell down her back.

He shouldn't say it. Shouldn't say anything. He knew it, knew it as well as he knew that he'd find Patricia and serve her up to Etta on a silver platter for having tainted his sister's memories of her short but happy marriage. The words burned like coals behind his teeth. "What's it like?"

"I beg your pardon?"

"Acting as parent to the woman who ought to be your mother?"

Chapter Five

Lottie's chest became a tangled ball of tension. Rolling her bottom lip between her teeth gained her no relief. "I've no idea what you're talking about."

He watched her for a long, steady moment, making her blood turn to prickling wires inside her veins. She pressed her palms together for calmness.

When he turned away, her entire body unclenched.

She let out a slow, shaky breath.

No one ever asked. No one ever wanted to know.

With his hands stacked at the small of his back, he wandered the room. His head was bare, his dark hair soft and touchable. His steps picked carefully between pillows and low tables. At one, he stopped and bent to inspect a tumbling pile of her mama's collection.

He had elegant bones in his wrists, peeking from beneath his starched cuffs. When he picked up a small skull, bleached white with age, he cradled it as if it was an expensive artifact rather than her mother's eccentricity left upon a table.

He held it up toward a shaft of light that had managed to peek through the excessive curtains. "Is she an anatomist?"

"At times." Her hobbies were endless, her interests varied. Few lasted long, especially when it came to motherhood and being a wife. "I believe that one was from an attempt at taxidermy."

His mouth quirked. "Taxidermy?"

Lottie shrugged. "Which in turn was more about the painting. She was displeased with how she represented animals."

He carried the skull over to the stacks of paintings below the windows. He bent slightly, and it was enough to draw his coat taut over his backside. "I see no animals in here."

"She burned them."

He straightened. In his eyes, she saw every word she left unspoken, the rest of that story. How terrifying it had been, how her mother had started in the fireplace and then dragged a burning, charred painting to the back terrace when it wouldn't fit. Mother had wept the entire time. She'd damned her work as pointless, as horrible, as the worst expense of a destructive, self-aggrandizing indulgence.

Sir Ian said nothing. And Lottie was playing make-believe. Filling in the silences with things that she wanted to hear.

Except he'd asked. He'd seen the extent to which she'd been forced into the position of mothering her own parent.

Sir Ian was the only man—or person, for that matter—who'd ever dared to cross that unspoken boundary. When she called her mother mad or crazy or insane, everyone dismissed her. Told her she was exaggerating. Or those who knew and believed...consoled her.

"Arson is a rather unusual hobby for our class."

"We encourage her painting, for the most part." She flipped through a couple stacks, until she found her favorite of the recent batch. "She has a large measure of talent. Certain periods are better than others in terms of production."

"Is that why you live in Chelsea rather than Mayfair?"

The painting wasn't particularly large, only a foot across. Lottie propped it up on an easel. "Some of it, yes."

"The rest of the reason?"

She smiled hugely. "So if Mother goes traipsing about the neighborhood in her shift and garters, it's only a passel of other artists who see her."

He held the tiny skull balanced in his palm as he neared her. "You're teasing."

"Oh, but I wish that I were." She shook her head and stepped back to examine the painting. "But see? She's not like most."

"Beautiful."

Lottie crossed her arms over her stomach and cupped her elbows. She took a deep breath, letting the comfort of the painting ease through her. Oil strokes showed two girls in white dresses. They faced away from the perspective of the viewer, toward an open window. Their voluminous skirts covered the bench they sat on, but a sad-eyed beagle peeked out from the one on the right.

"And yet Mama is not happy with it." She reached out to trace the air above the window depicted. "This portion here. She doesn't like it. Says the colors are off."

"I don't see it." He stepped closer to the painting, which brought him nearer to her. "I know I'm no art expert. I went to Winchester, after all. But it's perfect to me."

"To me as well." She rather liked a man who had no problem admitting his shortcomings. If he did so while praising her family, all the better. "I've tried to have her submit it to the Royal Academy, but she'll have none of it."

"It's a moment of great friendship. The way their shoulders lean in together."

Lottie and Victoria had had a lovely month, chattering and gossiping while they posed. Lottie's mother had been in one of her good periods. "It is."

"That's you too. I can see it in the line of your back."

"Oh, gee," she said with dry humor. "And here I thought it was my red hair that gave me away."

He cut his eyes toward her, mouth quirking. "How easily you wound me."

He didn't mean it. They'd had one of the most hectic afternoons she'd participated in for a long time, and yet he didn't seem the least bit bothered, not truly. Worried and concerned, yes, especially when talking about Patricia or his intent to find her, no matter the cost. He had intrinsic good humor that Lottie could appreciate. After all, she'd been seeking a little bit of that for herself for such a very long time.

The delicate chimes that wound through the room made her jolt. The gold-wrought fingers of the clock on the mantelpiece had ticked over a surprising amount. "What is taking Mama so long?"

Sir Ian blinked, his gaze shifting from her to the clock. "Has it been long? I thought women were forbidden by the rest of the fairer sex to dress in anything less than thirty minutes."

"Aren't you so very amusing," she grumbled, but most of her mind was already preoccupied. "Not my mother, and not when she has a handsome man waiting."

"You think me handsome, do you?" He liked that.

Worse was that she liked him liking it, and around they went in a terrible, wonderful, mesmerizing circle. She had no time for such nonsense, and if anything, this moment was proof of why. She was split. Divided between the tempting flirtation she could begin and a steadily growing sense of worry for her mother.

She broke the spell Sir Ian wove and stalked to the door. A passing maid stopped. "Milly, run upstairs and see what's taking Lady Vale so long."

"Is that necessary?" Sir Ian asked. "She's a grown woman in her own house. She can't have gotten far."

"How little you know."

Indeed, it didn't take long before Milly all but tripped over her own feet as she tumbled into the room. "Your pardon, miss."

"It's all right." Really, her fingernails dug into the soft meat of her palms, sending pain swirling up her wrists, though it was nothing compared to the prickling worry stealing her breath away.

The maid gasped for breath as if she'd hustled upstairs and down. "Lady Vale has gone out, miss."

"Blast. Does anyone know where?"

The girl nodded. She didn't want to say it, that much was in the way her eyes flicked and her mouth worked. "Mrs. Lafevre says, that is... She went to the park across the way."

"Alone?" Lottie clarified.

Milly nodded. Lottie could feel the weight of Sir Ian's presence. She was trying to keep herself grounded, keep her mien calm. But she was rapidly losing control. She should have shoved him back in that damned carriage.

Without a word, she swept through the foyer. The butler scrambled toward the door in time to open it for her. Carts and carriages rolled past the house. Lottie bounced on her toes, looking for an opportunity to skip through.

Sir Ian arrived at her side, throwing around manly arrogance. He held a hand toward traffic. A black brougham stopped quickly enough that horses neighed and whinnied in their traces. Lottie darted forward. Across the street. Over the Albert Bridge.

"Where do we start?" asked Ian.

Her breath spiked. She panted fast. The oxygen wasn't enough to keep away the dizzy, spinning feeling threatening to overtake her. Worry converged and split and spun into fear. "This way."

The park was lush. Large. If Lottie didn't already know where she was going, there would be entirely too much ground to cover. Mama's favorite spot had a large oak that overlooked the boating lake. She moved fast, hiking her skirts up to her knees and cursing her corset for disallowing running.

Because it was as bad as she feared.

Mama had actually climbed the goddamned tree, like she was a monkey or a child. Exactly so. At least she'd changed out of the yellow dressing gown. Instead the pale pink skirts of a gown best worn by a woman ten years younger draped from her perch on the gnarled branch.

Lottie's hand fluttered toward her throat. "Mama, come down."

"There's a bird's nest up here, Lottie love. You should see it. The fragments are so pretty and intricate. How do you think they know to put all those pieces together?"

Her back was a spike, her arms rigid. Her every muscle colluded to contain her. If she tried hard. enough, she could ignore the fact that Sir Ian was witnessing this embarrassment. "Mama, I thought we were going to have tea?"

"Then I decided you should keep your gentleman all to yourself." Lady Vale, the very same one who was up a damned blasted tree, smiled with the pure conviction of a mother leading her child to bliss.

Lottie smiled. Because she was helpless and there seemed nothing else she could do.

Until the branch cracked.

Then she and her mother both screamed.

Ian had learned to swim so young that he had no memory of actually learning. His parents had been quite an unusual sort compared to most of the other gentlemen and ladies of the area. They'd taken Ian and Etta for picnics on a regular basis to the lake at the far end of the property, and Ian's father personally took on the task of familiarizing Ian with water.

It had led to happy, sunny afternoons in the high months of July and August. Now it led to instinctual action.

Lady Vale became a tumbling flip of ribbons and cloth and streaming red hair. The branch went with her, a dark slash. The pond cleaved in a splash, but the worst part was when half the screaming stopped.

Miss Vale clapped both hands over her mouth. Her wide eyes went wider as she ran across the rest of the grassy clearing. Ian ran beside her, pushing his pace faster. Harder. To get there first.

His coat came off and dropped to the ground. He yanked his braces and jerked his white shirt over his head, but then he was at the water's edge. His shoes were kicked off in the air.

Arms above his head, he dove in and aimed for the last place he'd seen Lady Vale. The water was cold, bracingly so. He blew air threw his nose against the hard shock. He kicked, pushed along under the dark, brackish water.

She wasn't there. Somehow, he'd missed.

Strands of watercress and lilies brushed over his face. Tangled in his fingers. With his eyes open, he couldn't see a damn thing. The pond was surprisingly deep. He flipped and pushed off the bottom.

His head broke the surface of the water. Until he had to gasp he didn't realize how badly his lungs burned. Water coursed over his face, and he shoved it back. Looked at the bank.

Miss Vale had caught up. She stood at the edge, one hand holding her skirts. Her toes were likely wet, she was so damn close. "That way." She pointed to Ian's right.

"How far?"

Despite the panic drawing her features and turning her into a living doll, she spoke calmly though fast. "Five feet? Maybe six. She came up."

"Get back from the bloody bank. If you fall in, I'll have to pick between the both of you."

She did it, stepping back, but her expression promised retribution. "Save her."

He kicked out the way she'd pointed. It took only a few strokes, then he was diving again. Down and farther and his hands stretching out until he felt it. Silk. Cloth.

A ribbon that snapped.

He swam again. On one deep stroke, his arm hooked widely.

He got her by the neck. Didn't matter. Better him to suffocate her than her to drag in a wheezing lungful of water.

She fought him. Goddamned fought him. Nails flew out with slow drag under the water and scratched the length of his arm. He had to readjust his grip. Eventually he had her in one arm, across the shoulders, and somehow they'd sunk to the blasted bottom again.

His toes squished through muck before he found purchase enough to propel them both toward air. He kicked and stroked with his one free arm. Their heads broke the surface at the same time.

Gasping, clinging weight made the swim to shore take entirely too long. His kicks tangled in her skirts. She weighed as much as three grown men. Once he'd gotten far enough in, he walked them the rest of the way.

He collapsed to the grassy bank, all but dropping Lady Vale beside him. He was fairly sure she was weeping. Through his own whooping breath, he could barely tell.

Now that the immediate danger was over, he was lost. Looking up at the gray-blue sky through the canopy of the very tree which had abandoned its post so badly.

Miss Vale dropped to her knees beside them. Her attention went to her mother first, clutching at her shoulders. "Are you well?"

Lady Vale cracked a sob, her tears rising with her volume. She leaned up on one elbow. A series of coughs wracked her. "I...I think so."

Miss Vale's fingers dug into her mother's shoulders hard enough to leave dents. She shook. Her mother's head bounced in the air. "How could you?" she cried. "Reckless and awful and—"

Ian scrambled to his knees. The arm he wrapped around her shoulders protested abuse against the already vicious scrapes over his forearms. He yanked her back anyhow. "Miss Vale! Stop this."

Nothing got through to her. "Horrible woman, how could you? How could you scare me like that?"

Lady Vale started crying again. Her eyes were pale spring versions of her daughter's verdant green.

"Miss Vale," Ian repeated, but she was still trying to grab her mother. "Lottie!" he said sharply.

She jerked, her entire body flinching. Her gaze flew to his. "She shouldn't have!"

She hardly made any sense herself, but he wasn't about to point that out. He framed her jaw in one hand. If anything, he was making her look at him. Making her focus. "It's over. She's safe. It's all well."

"It's not well. *She* isn't well." When she shook her head, tendrils of reddish hair curled around her neck, dipping down into the shallow opening of her bodice.

Ian realized suddenly, terribly, how close they were. They pressed together from knee to shoulder. He curled over her, his strength absorbing her. Her shoulders were slender, but she wasn't insubstantial. Beneath her lean curves there was potency. The bottom he had his arm wrapped around was firm. Pliable.

He folded his fingers over her shoulders and carefully set her back enough so that he could breathe.

His lungs would never recover from this day.

Lady Vale collapsed into a wet, sopping pile. Though she buried her face in her arms, broken sobs could be heard. Her weeping was the likes of which he'd never known before. He wanted to scramble away, find the nearest way out because he thought his own heart might break. Lottie seemed versed in what to do.

Her arms curled around her mother's back, and she pulled the older woman up enough to tuck into her lap. "Come, Mama. I'm sorry."

Lady Vale shook her head, face pressed against the poof and pile of Lottie's skirts. "You were right."

"I can be both right and sorry." Over her mother's head, her eyes met Ian's. She dug up a wan, lost smile, but it wasn't like her normal ones. This one he wanted to frame with his own lips and make it go away.

He didn't have time for this. Such dramatics were beyond his experience. Hell, he shouldn't be calling her Lottie, not when considering matters of propriety, and here he was, forever with Lottie in his mind. Her name and those pleading, lying, smiling eyes would forever be bound together.

He rubbed a hand over his temple. Etta. His sister was his bigger concern. There wasn't a stone he was unwilling to turn in the entire city of London if it meant easing her heart and mind.

That didn't leave much time for rescuing kittens or puppies or ladies who were more than a little bit insane.

He pushed to his feet, unwilling to admit how unsteady he felt. His head swam and his vision blurred. Taking a moment to breathe, one hand on the rough bark of the oak that had caused all this trouble, he looked out over the small clearing. "Is this area often frequented?"

"No." Lottie petted and patted her mother's hair. "It's quiet. Most people stick to the paths and the boat launches."

"I was afraid you were going to say that."

She cast an apologetic smile at him. "I'm afraid you'll have to venture out to find someone."

Indeed he did once he managed to corral his rubbery legs. At the path, he caught the first waif he saw by the shoulder. "Aye, guv," it squawked. "I was just on the way to me lushery, mind yer own."

From the child's dirty face and bedraggled hair, Ian couldn't tell if he'd caught a boy or a girl. The trousers meant probably male. "I need an errand run."

The urchin's entire demeanor changed. He gave a quick nod, tugging on his filthy shirtfront. "Two pence and I'm your boy."

"Here's one," Ian said, digging in his pocket. But he'd apparently lost every bit of change at the bottom of that damned pond. "That is, you'll get both once you run across the way to number nineteen Cheyne. Tell them there's been an accident and we need a cart."

"Promise you'll pay?" the boy questioned.

Ian couldn't help his laugh, though he probably seemed more than a little crazy himself. He was soaking wet in the middle of a public park. His mind was twenty feet behind him on a redheaded girl who seemed so unbearably lost in her own laughter. "I'll pay. Oh God, I'll pay. One way or the other."

Chapter Six

By the time a handful of servants came from the house and got Mama bundled in a blanket, then tucked into a cart, Lottie almost felt like she had a hold of herself. Almost.

Mostly she was a hysterical mess trying to keep her bits and pieces from flying away at the edges.

She walked behind the cart, a shawl folded around her shoulders and elbows. Though she kept her head down, she wasn't sure if it was to avoid the censure she might see from neighbors—or to avoid Ian's gaze.

Sir Ian, she reminded herself. She had no claim to call him by his Christian name. Yet she couldn't rid herself of the chant in her head. *Ian saved my mama. Ian saved my mama.*

Ian had done what she'd failed to do so many times.

Her discipline failed, and she couldn't help but look at him out of the corner of her eyes. She glimpsed enough to see the carved lines down his cheeks and the solemn downturn of his lips. That active mouth of his was completely stilled.

At the house, Mama was bustled upstairs by a handful of servants who acted with an extra measure of solicitousness. As well they should. Lottie stood at the base of the stairs and glared.

This never should have been allowed to happen. They had protocols in place, all of which had apparently been ignored. Nicolette was supposed to attend Mama when she left the house, and if Mama insisted, Lottie should've been notified. Immediately.

"If it's no inconvenience, I'd borrow your carriage to return home." The calm, wry words jerked Lottie's attention around.

"Oh!" she said as she spun toward him. "No. Certainly not."

His eyebrows lifted as one, in an expression that said he quite clearly held back a stream of words. He needed to go home. Bedraggled wasn't the word. He carried his suit coat over one arm, and his shirt's thin linen clung to his skin.

Clung. To his skin.

Beneath was the slightly darker outline of a sleeveless undershirt. But sweet heaven and the virgin's baby, where had all that muscle come from? His shoulders weren't wide, but they were assuredly deep—layered with stacked weight that spoke of strong muscles and arms that were built for cradling women and banging steel around. A sword.

With that build, he ought to be carrying a sword.

He had the temerity to make it worse. "Lottie?" he asked. Her name, but it was enough. A deep, purring curl that worst of all, she knew he didn't intend her to take in a tempting manner.

She pressed her hands flat over her stomach to keep in the tumbling feelings that threatened to shake away her calm. "That is, we cannot possibly send you home in such a state." She snapped her fingers, and a footman popped in. "Andrew will take you to a spare bedroom. We'll either get your clothes cleaned up and dried, or we'll find you something else to wear home."

"It's quite all right." His hair was plastered to his forehead, the dark brown strands almost black. She wanted to smooth them back. His skin might be cool to the touch. She could warm him.

"I insist. It's the least we can do." Her voice broke. Cracked and whistled away like a lesser person without control of her emotions. She stopped. Pressed her palms flat together and ignored the sticky sheen of sweat between them. "I would appreciate the chance to bestow our hospitality."

He saw too bloody much. The way he looked at her. Looked into her. Sympathy turned his eyes warm, and she wanted to fold her forehead to his surprisingly strong chest. Let the worries melt away.

If only it were ever that easy.

He nodded. "All right."

She had him seen to a guest bedroom, and then she ran to her own on the floor above. Only once she was in the privacy of her own rooms did she dare turn her attention downward. She flinched at the muddy, bedraggled hem of her dress.

She'd loved the pale purple silk when she'd seen it, and she'd selected the silver cording to go with it, but that mattered little now. Six inches of dirt ringed the bottom, and Mother's clutching hands had streaked smudges all over the lap.

This was why they lived in Chelsea. This was why she kept Mama away from everyone else. Things exploded, and her humiliation turned into everyone's purview. She couldn't think of that now.

The best way to push it away was always to find something else to concentrate on. She'd spent years pouring effort into the school and her friends. She had enough outside interests to absorb her time, keeping the school from tipping into destruction. Fallout from any scandal with regards to Patricia would be one scandal too much.

This was part of why she'd never marry. She never wanted to bring a new person into her crazy world. That wasn't considering her fear of *becoming* her mother. Mama's madness reached its peak with having Lottie—as her grandmother's had with bearing a child as well, though they'd managed to hide that from the world at large. Everyone thought her lake drowning had been accidental.

Calling her maid to assist, Lottie changed as quickly as she could with shaking hands and weak knees. She found herself in the corridor downstairs at the polished mahogany door. How very innocuous.

She shouldn't knock. It was one thing to offer him a chance to dry or that she'd sent in the tea promised two hours ago. She couldn't put herself in that room with him alone when she didn't know what kind of clothing had been found for him.

Her hand leapt up almost of its own will, rapping the dark wood.

"Come in," he answered in a rough, deep voice.

She darted in. Her back pressed against the cool door, but only for a moment. Her breathing tumbled and shivered, but it wasn't as if she were shaking. Not really. Not much.

She put on her best, brightest smile and tucked her hands behind her back. "Have you found everything to your satisfaction?"

He couldn't have been more shocked to see her. His lips parted on silence. Someone had found him a banyan. The dark blue silk wrapped around his torso, and he wore dark trousers beneath, but under *that* his feet were bare. He had pale and slender feet and toes with a tiny sprinkle of dark hairs across the top.

Her fingers curled into her palms.

They'd brought the tea, and he sat at a table next to the window. A tree's leafy green canopy obstructed most of the view through the window, but she knew that was no hardship. Next door was a brick townhouse.

She barely managed to restrain her hands from plastering along her temples. Apparently she needed some assistance keeping her brain inside her skull because she was losing it. The throbbing, heavy weight in her blood was expanding through her whole body, the way she'd always feared.

"You shouldn't be here," he said after a long moment.

Likely he'd tired of waiting on her to be less insane. "It's my house. I'm allowed to be anywhere I like."

"I doubt that." He leaned one elbow on the arm of the chair. The embroidered lapels of the robe parted enough to display three inches of his chest. There was a division between two thick muscles. He was a man who hadn't ignored his body.

He made her want to not ignore her own body.

Losing her virginity had been an idle thought, one born of convictions and supposition. Not need. Not any amount of want. She ranged closer to the table, closer to him. Her fingers trailed over the cold metal edge of the tea tray.

"I'm all but mistress of this domain." She nudged a plate of iced biscuits to the side in order to get at a tiny dish of cubed sugar. The piece she picked up was rough between her thumb and finger. She rubbed it over her bottom lip, then licked away the grains left behind. Sweetness burst over her tongue.

He never moved. His hands didn't shift, nor did his feet, nor any other variety of limbs. The tilted-down angle of his chin stayed still, and he watched her from under thick, dark lashes.

Despite not moving, he was...alive. Aware of her and of the heat that flowed back and forth between them. Far, far away in the recesses of the house a timepiece chimed. Between them was the thick molasses of promise and potential. His eyes all but burned her skin, turning the stretch between her shoulder blades into a tickling, sensitive place that begged for his touch.

Except instead of following through with those silent promises, he shook his head, so very slowly. "You don't want to head down this route."

She edged closer. Near enough that her skirts folded over and around his calves. His knees. She managed to smile, but no one would ever know what it cost her. The way her lips felt nearly numb. She wanted to run her tongue over them, just to feel.

Maybe she could feel his mouth instead.

She still held the sugar cube. When she lifted it to his lips, it almost seemed that the room would implode from what built and wove between them. He speared her with that wicked gaze, and despite the reluctance she could feel rolling off him, the tiniest quirk of his lips said she hadn't gone too far astray.

His lips parted for the cube. His tongue darted out enough to wet the tip of her index finger. A full-body shiver rolled over her skin and dove into her veins, turning her into both more and less.

"Maybe I don't want to wander down the route. Maybe I want to run."

Ian knew better.

Sugar melted on his tongue. Granules rubbed across the top of his mouth with sweet abrasion. Comparatively, her finger had little flavor, with the slightest hint of warmth and life.

She made him feel like he were Genghis Khan. A conqueror who didn't need to be bent on taking because the slave girl was already offering him everything she had. Everything she was.

Her lush bottom lip trembled, but her eyes were wickedly hot. Her gaze scalded him, made his brain fuzzy at the edges. She wanted to be taken, or so she implied.

Unlikely.

His fingers locked around the arms of his chair, but he wasn't sure what he braced against. The rising need, maybe. He didn't have time for her. Hell, he shouldn't have agreed to resting in her house long enough for his clothes to dry. The likelihood of him catching sick in a short carriage ride was negligible. But he'd wanted to help her. Those wide eyes, the obvious distress on her face. It all combined into a compelling desire to give her what she wanted.

Not taking what *he* wanted. "No," he growled.

She twitched, her elbows tucking in closer to her ribs. "No?"

His hips shifted in his seat, tipping forward toward her. He slid his knees out a fraction and made room for her voluminous skirts. Apparently his own body didn't believe his words. "It's a common word. Do I need to explain its meaning? I'm sure you don't hear it often."

She smelled so sultry and edged with temptation that his mouth watered. The sugar slid and spun and washed through him. No substitution.

She laughed. "I hear it often enough." She leaned down closer. Her hands rested on the chair's arms. Her dress was modest. Tight. All the way up to her collarbones, with more white lace edging toward her slender, graceful neck. He hated the damn thing. "I don't like the word."

He couldn't reach up and trace her pale neck the way he wanted. Otherwise all his control would snap. He shifted the first two fingers of each hand enough to rest them on her knuckles. Supple and hard in one, she was bone covered with silk. Barely concealed, barely hidden.

Though she didn't realize it, her every emotion rode right beneath the surface. He was shocked she triumphed in society. Sharks should have scented her blood and taken her down.

"You might be improved by a little extra experience with denial."

She shook her head. When she'd changed her clothes, someone had tried to repin her hair from the tumbled mess created during the park's drama. They'd succeeded for the most part, but feathery red tendrils curled around her cheeks and temples. "I'm perfect the way I am. You should kiss me and find out."

He hadn't ever laughed while kissing a woman before, but both responses rose together. His lips took hers. His hands lifted to cup her jaw and trace over delicate ears.

All the while, laughter wove between them, trading between their lips and teeth and tongues. She kissed exactly how he'd expected. Complete abandon and rapidly growing joy.

He leaned up even as she leaned down. Her hands came to rest on his shoulders, thumbs tucking beneath the open collar. Those two touches of skin were more than enough. Their lips clung, and Ian and Lottie laughed at the same time. There wasn't enough air between them. He'd lost control of the situation.

His body woke. Wanted. Needed.

He didn't dare lower his hands from her face, but he tilted them. Let his thumbs coast over that tender flesh under her jaw. He felt it move and work as she so eagerly kissed him, and he loved that sense of delicacy, with that extra hint of tenderness.

She was gilt. A shiny and beautiful layer over harder, more base emotions underneath. He wanted to see underneath that artificial brightness.

That wasn't his right. He didn't get to peel her apart the way he needed, because he'd be damned if he stayed long enough to put her back together. He'd return to his regular existence soon enough, in order to reassure Etta their world was safe. Maybe he'd revisit London to find a wife next Season, but he'd find someone more of his own sort. Ordinary.

He didn't get to keep Lottie, which meant that he didn't have the right to take everything he wanted.

His laughter faded.

With his hands as gentle as he could manage, he pushed her away, but he couldn't resist one last nip of her bottom lip. Flesh gave under his teeth.

She didn't straighten fully. With her cloud of red hair, she hovered over him like a depraved angel. He liked it. He liked her a hell of a lot, for that matter. Especially the way she grinned. "See? Perfect."

He chuckled again, until he realized that he'd been unable to let go. His fingertips smoothed over her soft skin, from her nape to her shoulders. "I concede the point."

Her hands were on his shoulders, and she dug in, like a kitten finding her nesting spot. She had blunt and square-tipped nails that scratched over his skin with an extra measure of temptation. Her gaze returned to his mouth. He could see beneath the gilt now. Darkness and worry altered her eyes to mossy green. "You were very brave today."

An uncomfortable knot settled in his stomach. He hadn't done anything unusual. "Speak nothing of it."

She shook her head, and then sank to her knees. His chest clenched on a spiral of restriction and control. Between his outstretched legs, she was a froth of silk and lace and all that pale, pale skin. "I can't say *nothing*. I owe you my thanks. My appreciation. My gratitude." Her mouth pinched into what was likely supposed to be a smile. "There's not enough ways in the world to say it. Or to...offer it."

Had it really only been six hours ago that he thought her a complete jade? She was more lost than found. Offering herself as repayment for him doing what any man should...

He wanted her. There was no denying that. He wasn't the sort to run around taking advantage of women either. Not to say there hadn't been temptation nor times that he'd dallied in delectable activities. He always chose partners who were on an equal footing, both in terms of expectations and potentials. He couldn't imagine any man who'd grown up with a loving mother and sweet sister doing anything else.

If a man took advantage of his sister in a similar situation, he'd gut the bastard from stem to stern.

That didn't mean he was perfect. His hands framed her face, his thumbs rubbing over and over that tender skin. Delicate insanity.

He took her mouth one more time. Sugar and velvet. Her lips pressed against his. He traced the inside tenderness of her bottom lip, then the hard edge of her teeth. His body curved over hers, offering shelter from the storm that no one would be able to keep away on her behalf.

She made a quiet noise that spilled into his mouth. Her fingers dug into his muscles, making the tendons across his neck shiver and pull tight. He had to put her back again. Move her away from his reach. She wasn't the only one traipsing down routes best left forgotten.

He turned his hand and rubbed her jawline with his knuckles. She tilted her chin into the touch. "You shouldn't be here."

"I think it's a little late for that sort of protest. Neither of us are spinster maidens."

"Let me put it this way, then. I thank you for what you're offering. But I have to decline."

She sat back on her heels, her mouth bending into a displeased frown. "You'll regret that. I'm sure of it."

Bugger yes, he was going to regret that. He already was. His cock all but reared up in protest. But he only shook his head. "Then that will be my regret to live with. Not yours."

Chapter Seven

By four days later, Lottie knew that Ian had been wrong. The regret was all hers. In the second best parlor of her school, she stood with her hands folded at her waist as she blindly watched three rows of girls practice curtsying. Mrs. Sera Thomas stood at the front of the room leading the class and occasionally shooting Lottie questioning looks.

It wasn't often that Lottie felt it necessary to watch a class. But she'd needed to reassure herself that she was on the right path. She hadn't lost her mind.

The whole last week had been a tumble of too many emotions at once. She didn't like feeling so...at sea. Flipped around. She wanted to be happy, wanted to be pleased. More than that, she wanted to be calm inside her own skin. The calmer she was, the happier an aspect she could present to the world, the less likely her mother's difficulties were to take hold of Lottie.

Kissing Ian had been the very opposite of that. In memory, her lips tingled and her heartbeat rushed to fill her head and senses. She pressed her hands together hard enough that knuckles bit into bone. The pain grounded her. Drew her back into herself and the moment.

She wanted more of that. That kiss had been a different kind of confusion, one she almost thought she could handle. If she'd been able to direct how things had gone.

Instead, he'd turned her down.

Denied her.

Lottie chewed on the inside of her lip until she tasted copper. Her tongue probed the tiny sting as she watched Sera dismiss the class. She gave a single clap and gracefully beckoned. "Please continue to the workroom. Lady Victoria is waiting on you."

"Will we get to pick fabric today?" asked one hopeful voice from the second row.

"I'm not privy to the schedule that Lady Victoria keeps," Sera said with a twinkling smile. "But I will say that I saw a rather laden cart in the back alley this afternoon."

The girls split around her in ranks as they scrambled for the door—though no one ran. They wouldn't dare under Sera's proper, chastising gaze. Many waved and bobbed small curtsies. Lottie smiled back at them. Her heart reveled in their safety.

A soft knock on the door behind them heralded a towheaded maid. "Miss Vale, there is a Sir Ian here to see you. He's waiting in your study."

"Thank you, Melissa." She didn't like the way her entire body sparked. Tingling tension nestled at the base of her spine. Her skin woke, and her bones threatened to melt with anticipation.

He sat in her chair, behind *her* desk. Such arrogance. But he was so handsome that she wanted to forgive him for such effrontery. Almost. "Get up."

He grinned at her, all cheeky insolence. "Did you order me about?"

"Did you seat yourself in *my* chair?"

"I did." He leant an elbow on the chair arm and propped his chin on his loose fist. "I've no reason to obey you, you know."

Was he doing this intentionally? Teasing her and allowing her a moment of ease to get away from the clutching memory of her mother's near drowning? From the weight of the kiss she had enticed him into? If so, she appreciated it more than words could say. She grinned. "No reason, but every want."

"Why do you think so?"

She came closer. Once again she was leaning over him while he sat in a chair. She rather liked the disparity and the possibilities inherent in such positions. "Because if you don't, I'll likely be tempted to kiss you again."

His eyes turned clear and shining blue, like the sky after a summer rain. The noise that swirled out of his throat was a growl. No two ways about it. Lottie's entire body clenched and then bloomed open. Ready.

"For the life of me, I cannot remember at the moment why that would be a bad idea." His voice was all roughness and promise.

"Then by all means." She placed each hand on the tall chair back. With her arms, she framed him in. His dark hair shone against the green velvet upholstery. "Don't move. But..." She drew the last word out into a tease.

"But?"

"I think you should kiss *me* this time."

His smile tweaked up on the left side only. He had stupidly thick lashes that women would envy. She wanted to feel them in the soft spot beneath her ear.

Those long, graceful fingers rose and traced down the front of her throat. A delicate touch that probably said more than he wanted to. "You think so, do you?"

"You want to anyway."

"That much is for damned sure."

His mouth was as hot as she'd remembered. He sipped and took, twining with her in a rhythm that did strange things to her body. Strange and lovely, amazing, fabulous things.

He took his mouth from hers, though he left those delicious hands on her face. Touches tickled over her cheekbones, her jaw, the line of her nose. She kept her eyes closed, and he traced over the seam of her lashes. "Wakie wakie in there," he whispered.

Reluctantly, she opened her eyes. With them closed, she could pretend everything was all right. She first pretended her father wasn't writing daily, ignoring all reports of Mama and only talking about Lord Cameron. Then she pretended the school didn't need another influx of cash. She needed nothing but Ian's mouth back on hers.

With one gentle fingertip, he drew a line from her eyes to her mouth. "You're thinking entirely too much."

She made herself smile. "Maybe that means you're not doing this right. Perhaps you should put more effort in."

Before it happened, she knew Ian would respond with humor. She was certainly right. He folded his mouth into a mock-severe frown and gave a nod. "You're right. Come here."

He kissed her soundly. His tongue took and kept territory in her mouth, and his fingers delved into the masses of her knotted hair. She shivered in his grasp. How strange to think they'd barely touched.

She felt like he knew her.

Though that was incorrect. He knew what parts she wanted to show him. And when she'd shown him too much, she'd kissed him.

She sighed when he ended the kiss. With his mouth on hers, she didn't think about much else. Nothing else, to be honest. Only how her body woke up each time they kissed. Maybe he had been right the other day.

Except it seemed that he wasn't quite so distracted as she was. "Have you heard from Patricia?"

"Finna sent around a note this morning to say she hadn't yet been to the flat." She didn't let her disappointment get the best of her, mostly because he couldn't seem to let go of her.

He ran the pale yellow material of the swag at her hips between his thumb and forefinger. "That will be a difficulty for Finna."

She acted as if she didn't notice the way he caressed her dress. Truthfully, it made her breath catch as she waited for his next move. "I've already asked about to find her a new girl to room with. Maybe two if they need extra help with the payments."

"And Patricia?" he asked, as businesslike as can be. Ridiculous man. "Do you have any idea where she is?"

"No, unfortunately not. I sent around a note to see if she'd been at work recently, but the foreman said she'd not reported in."

His trousers brushed against the bottom hem of her dress. The expensive embroidery made the outfit completely unpractical for nearly any occasion, with its fitted bodice and buttons marching all the way up her neck. It was particularly impractical for the city, with its gray, dirty streets.

"I already went by." His mouth set firmly. "It seems impossible that such a woman is so difficult to find."

Lottie's gaze flicked toward the window. The move was so brief most people would have never noticed, not with the way she managed to keep her smile in place.

Ian did. "What is it?"

She grew her smile into a lie. "I wonder that you call her 'such a woman'. Do you know her, to cast such judgments?"

He scoffed. "I wonder that you so blindly trust her, simply because she's been to your charity."

"The women who come here are determined to improve their lives. That in itself denotes a certain upright character."

"You forget." He pushed out of the chair. "I've known Patricia Wertherby a long time. Longer than you have."

"Not forget, you nodcock." She crossed her arms over her chest in a sullen pose. "You haven't told me. She has something you want. That's all I know. But do *you* know something?"

"I know many things. I doubt I know whatever it is you've got on your mind."

"I've made a decision."

"God save us all."

Her chin lifted. "I've decided I'm not going a moment more without you telling me what it is that you're looking for."

Ian shifted with discomfort. He'd toyed with the idea of sharing the full story on his ride to the school, but that didn't make it any easier. No part of his quiet life left him accustomed to sharing confidences. "A document."

"I know that much."

Even in annoyance, she seemed...different. His mother or Etta would pout, hoping to wheedle what they wanted. Lottie set her terms and held her head high as she waited for him to catch up.

"It's not my story." The words ground out like glass caught between two rocks. Painful. "I would have to ask your discretion."

She grinned wide enough that her nose wrinkled. "You're having me on, yes? After everything you witnessed yesterday? I'm the soul of discretion—or at the very least, not a single soul would believe me. They'd chalk it up to more of my teasing and wildness."

"My sister fell in love."

"I would say congratulations to her, but I think this story may not have a happy ending."

"You'd be right." He leaned against the arm of her chair, propping himself up. "He was a millwright. A step down for our family."

"I bet that wasn't well received."

"No. Plenty of fighting. Father threatened to cut her off. He *did* as a matter of fact. But Archie was never after Etta's money, and they ran away to be married. With them, they took Archie's sister as chaperone for the first half of the journey. The sister was Patricia. Archie died only a year after their marriage. Six months ago, Etta started receiving blackmail notes. We managed to trace them to Patricia, mostly through visiting posting locations, but she disappeared when the noose was drawing tight. The document I seek is the proof she's holding over Etta's head. A marriage certificate."

"I see," she said with a nod. Lottie began to brood over the problem. She did it unlike anyone else he knew. It was almost difficult to spot. She paced a few steps from the desk to the side table and back again, keeping her head up and her features clear. Only her eyes were hazy as she looked into the distance, as if there were something to be seen in the striped wallpaper and wainscoting. Her mouth stayed curved in a hint of smile.

She drew to a halt in the center of the room. "I assume the threat is to ruin Etta's life with the story that she married far beneath her, yes?"

"Yes. We'd hoped to bring her to town after her mourning. Etta is the kind of woman who really *needs* to be married. She deserves a family of her own."

"Then your answer is simple. Incredibly so." She spread her hands wide, a pleased openness on her face. "You're going about this all wrong."

"I suppose you know exactly what I need?"

That smile stopped this side of angelic. "Of course I do, Ian. You're going to learn to trust me whether you like it or not."

"I'm not sure what you're thinking, but I doubt it's advisable."

Her mouth set in a pout that shouldn't have been adorable. He wanted to take that plump lip between his teeth. "You haven't given me a chance."

"By all means. Please have out your idea before I tell you no."

"What would happen if Patricia made known the facts about this marriage in your village?"

He had to think about that for a moment. A few people had known, though they hadn't spoken widely of the truth. The household servants chattered when Archie moved into the manor house for the end of his illness. There'd been whispers.

Baroness Esterby had failed to invite them for her annual dinner.

"Little, actually."

"Good," she said with no small measure of satisfaction.

"What does that matter?"

Her grin was something magical. He wanted it. He wanted to fold it up and tuck it in his pocket, keep that smile for the days of duty stretching out before him. "It means she's well liked. Which means that she's a pleasant girl and our task will be easier."

"What task would that be?"

Initially, she hadn't seemed steady enough for the office he'd found her in. A certain lack of organization perhaps, but it was an office well used, not for show. Lottie spent little time on the frivolous in this place. She picked around a piled-over basket of fabric samples and reached for the doorknob. "Come along. We'll have a lot to get done."

He popped the door shut against her exit. "A lot to get done for *what*?"

"Hmm?" She blinked at him in a slightly protracted manner, as if he'd disappeared and she magically saw him again. "You're going to send for your sister to come to Town. We'll launch her."

"Launch her?" He didn't appreciate feeling like an idiot. "You're mad if you think I'm bringing her to London when there's so much at stake."

Her chin jerked back with the same sharpness as if she'd taken a blow. Her eyes went flat and dark. Her mouth curved in an eerie smile the entire time, and her voice stayed spookily airy. "Don't call me mad. It's in particularly bad taste, all things considered. Wouldn't you agree?"

How did she fool the world so well? Did she even? Or perhaps everyone knew how frightened and damaged she was. Maybe she was the only one who thought she hid the truth. He hadn't meant to hurt her. "My apologies."

The air thickened and turned heavy. If she didn't want to forgive him, he'd understand. She must deal with a thousand petty, poorly chosen words. He'd make sure none came from him.

Finally she nodded. Her smile turned into a shining force he wanted to believe.

"But you see? You prove my point for me."

"How so?"

"My mother really is insane, and yet I'm invited to the Duchess of Marvell's ball several weekends hence."

They stood too close together. What a bad habit this was, this giving into impulses to touch. For now, it got his hands folded around her slender upper arm. "And we country bumpkins know duchesses are all the rage."

"They can't help it. That whole second-only-to-royalty thing."

He laughed. She was so cheekily perfect. "Is that their problem?"

She made a small sound of agreement, and he wanted to curl his fingers around her throat to feel the buzz. "You'll see. You're about to meet a duke's daughter. I assure you Lady Victoria is as high in the instep as any you've ever met."

"I wouldn't be surprised." He stepped back from the door then, giving her room to open it. "I may not be quite the country man of leisure you seem to think me, and when I come to town, it's usually for business."

"Oh?" She led the way upstairs. "Business? The times are certainly changing, aren't they?"

"I'm rather thankful, personally," he said. Taking advantage of the narrow, steep stairs, he set a protective hand at the small of her back. Under his touch would be her shift and corset. Would she be embroidered through there as well? She was the sort. "Otherwise I'd be stuck on a very small piece of land, with hardly any chance of improving my circumstances."

"How very terrible for you. You sound positively feminine. Most of us are stuck where we are, despite the changing times or not."

"Hence the reason for your charity?"

"Hence the reason for my school, yes." They arrived on the second floor, where a small gaggle of women milled about. Lottie clapped her hands sharply, but her smile rang true. "Have you somewhere to be?"

"Not especially, Miss Vale," chirruped one with a minxish wink. She let her gaze wander head to toe over Ian. "If you're to be a new instructor, sir, please allow me to be the first to welcome you."

The small gathering of women giggled and tittered, with a few hiding bright red blushes. One swatted the speaker's shoulder.

"Hush, you," Lottie chided, but she didn't seem particularly fashed. "He's a visitor."

"Will he be at the event this quarter?"

Her nose wrinkled on a cheeky grin. "He will, but not for the reasons you presume. On with you." With a little wave of her hands, she dismissed them.

"What event would that be?" Ian stepped alongside Lottie. Her profile was delicate.

"We hold quarterly soirees where the women get the chance to meet certain subscribers. Men of good background and status who can enable them to move up in the world—through marriage only—should they like."

"And you believe I need to attend this?"

"I do," she said with a decisive nod. "If only because Patricia wouldn't miss it for the world. She's always been quite popular with the men. Finna says Patricia flirted with a certain gentleman at the last event. He might have even slipped her a few bobs. She'll wish to continue, secure his interest and more funds."

The sewing room was the likes of which he hadn't quite seen before. Sewing machines ringed the entire room, and in the center were wide tables with bolts of cloth of every color one could imagine—if all colors were dark.

In the center stood a regal woman. Her pale pink dress stood out among the ocean of dark cloth, her hair piled at the back of her head in a shining blonde twist.

"Lady Victoria, allow me to present Sir Ian. He has a sister."

"Bully for him," said Lady Victoria with dry humor.

Ian tipped a small bow. "I generally do appreciate my good luck in having her for a sister."

"Perhaps you have sense after all." She set down the length of fabric she'd been holding and turned to Lottie. "How can I help you?"

"It depends. How quickly could we launch Sir Ian's sister?"

Lady Victoria didn't suffer any moment of confusion or distraction. She turned back to Ian with an inquiring look. "Is she comely?"

"She's generally considered attractive, yes."

Lottie reached out two fingers and touched the emerald-set cufflink at his wrist. She let her fingertips trace down to the sensitive base of his thumb. "And money? How much have we to work with?"

He ignored the taking, grasping impulse that insisted the nearest bolt of cloth would be plenty cushioning to push Lottie back into. He had bigger concerns and a family relying on him to improve their station. He couldn't afford distractions from wild girls. "If you can promise me effectiveness and my sister's acceptance into society, money is no object."

Lottie's smile turned into the glow of a thousand gaslights. "Exactly the words a girl loves to hear."

Chapter Eight

Not three days later, Lottie stood on the step of a fine townhouse in the oh-so-proper Mayfair district as a carriage rolled up to the curb. Ian hopped out with a sure step. Lottie laced her fingers before her waist. He might be primarily a country gentleman, but that didn't seem to impact the way he carried himself. He surveyed the entire street as if he owned it all. A man who knew who he wanted to be and how he wanted to live.

Half the time, she felt as if she were putting on a mummery show. Doing her best to distract everyone else from seeing the actuality of her life.

Like now. She smiled and pushed open the door behind her. "Sir Ian, welcome to your new home."

He doffed his top hat as he followed her in. That air of inspection clung to him. The money she'd so freely spent over the past couple days had come from tin mines, he'd said. She could believe it. He had ruthless intentions.

She never would have expected it, but her nerves fluttered at the idea that maybe he wouldn't be pleased with his investment. She looked around the entryway with her own inspecting aspect.

It was large, but not ostentatious. She, Victoria and Sera had conferred at length about the houses available to rent. As the city house of a baron who'd fallen on financial difficulties, the establishment struck a balance between available funds and seeming too nouveau riche. The foyer floor was tiled with black-and-white marble and the walls covered with gold-and-cream wallpaper.

To Lottie, the ebony stairs that curled down from the upper level were the loveliest touch. "What do you think? Will you be content here?"

He looked back over his shoulder and lifted a single eyebrow. "I don't think that's the issue, is it?"

"True. But as they say, anything worth doing is worth doing well."

She opened the doors to the front parlor, which was furnished. The decorations were overstuffed for her tastes, with tables and couches occupying most every inch of floor space. The floors themselves were layered with piled carpets worn soft by decades of foot traffic. Dark green wallpaper covered the top half of the walls, but she particularly liked the glowing shine of the wainscoted bottom half.

Ian tossed himself down to a low chaise, one arm hooked over the curled back. His smile was cheeky. Daring. "I suppose it'll do, as long as the other rooms are approximately this standard."

She rolled her eyes. "You are such the arbitrator. And what's your home like in the country?"

"Drafty as can be. A bit small, especially when the snow piles up and we're all in on top of each other. The decorations are from generations upon generations each adding their own bits, so they're a mess. The gardens meander for acres all willy-nilly."

Keen wistfulness wound under her breastbone. "Sounds lovely."

"It rather is."

"You're an ass."

He grinned. His ankles were crossed and his legs extended to their full length, heels on a faded Tudor rose in the carpet. "You really think this plan will work?"

"Did you increase the size of her dowry, as we suggested?"

"Tripled it." His eyes went dark, and lines carved around his mouth. "I don't simply wish her to be married off to the first person who asks."

"You really mean that, don't you?"

Confusion wrinkled his brow. "Why wouldn't I?"

"Many wouldn't." She shook her head and wandered away toward the far door. One finger hooked over her shoulder, she gestured for him to follow.

"Your family obviously would agree."

She let a laugh burble up in an attempt to cover up the sharp spike of pain and regret that overtook her. "This is the formal dining room," she said, throwing open doors. "But why would you assume anyone in my crazy family would agree?"

"I can't imagine that you've had any fewer than a half dozen marriage offers. Yet here you are." He pointed at the mahogany table in the center of the room. It could float a dozen cows across the Dover straights. "That is rather large for our purposes, isn't it?"

"Better too large and impressive than have anyone doubt your place in society. Good rule of thumb in most things." She led him up the stairway to the first floor, her fingertips trailing over the balustrade's cool wood. "Here I am, indeed. Alone and unmarried and exploring an empty house with a strange man."

"I might be a man, but I'm hardly strange. Is there a study or an office? I'll still have work to do that can't be ignored."

She nodded and pointed toward the west. "That way."

"Good."

She liked his satisfied smile entirely too much. Inside her chest was painful hope. Her heart fluttered. "I'm glad you're pleased."

"I am." He opened a door and found a bedroom. A white lace blanket covered a huge expanse of bed. There were likely other objects in the room, but Lottie suddenly couldn't gather impressions of them.

All she could think of was that bed. The wide, large bed with the gold-trimmed and tasseled pillows at the head dominated the room.

She imagined Ian stretched upon the full length.

Her body bloomed and awoke. She knew this. Knew this feeling, and the strange fantasies that were doing their damnedest to strip his clothing in her fevered brain. Unfortunately, never having seen a man in the flesh had her placing his handsome head on the white marble body of a statue. That wouldn't do at all.

Perhaps she ought to do her best to get him out of his clothes and see for herself.

She tucked her smile away behind her hand and tried to turn away.

"Why do you do that?" His voice was a rumble behind her.

"Do what?"

"Hide your real smiles and show off your false ones."

Well, that cured her of the smile problem, didn't it? Her chest clenched on tight, hot fear. She didn't turn around. Some conversations were easier to have with her back turned. "Let me ask you this: why wouldn't you see your sister married off to the first man who happens to ask?"

"Why, because I love her." Confusion colored his tone, and she could imagine the cant of his eyebrows along with his eyes clouding. "I want the best for her."

That was explicitly what she'd both feared and hoped. Some women had people who looked out for them. Many didn't, or her school wouldn't exist. It seemed Etta was luckier than most. Her family, though angry, had hidden her less-than-acceptable marriage and kept her close to their bosom.

Lottie...was forgotten more often than not. "You're right. I've had marriage proposals."

"I'm unsurprised."

She turned around finally, because she couldn't read the tone of his voice, and a scared and frightened part of her trembled whenever she didn't know how to read a situation. The part that looked for the meanness that said Lottie was exactly as bad as they'd expected considering her mother.

She didn't find it. He seemed...curious. Like he was listening to her and no more. She hadn't realized how much she'd wanted that. Needed that.

He leaned against the wall, to the side of the door, with his arms crossed over his chest. Instead of impatience, he had all the time in the world.

"Father never turned any of them down."

Obvious shock pushed him away from the wall and toward her. He walked like a man with a mission, but that wasn't right, since he was headed toward her. "That can't be."

"Perfectly true." She curved her mouth into a smug smile and couldn't help but reach out. Her fingers rested in the center of his chest. Between the plackets of his waistcoat was thin linen heated by his body. "He accepted every one. From penniless Lord Morgan to rich but elderly Viscount Rose. The good viscount has four sons who need a mother. Recently he's developed a penchant for our country neighbor. He has a parcel of land that Father would like."

"If that's true, how can you possibly be here?"

"Here? In an empty bedroom, with you?"

His cheeks hollowed on a moment of annoyance. "The bedroom part is secondary. You know what I'm asking."

"Secondary by your choice, I'd like to make sure you know." When feeling reckless, Lottie certainly went all the way. She'd little left to lose now that her mouth was running away with her mind. "He doesn't actually *care* if I marry any of them. So he accepts, and then I have to go convince them that they don't truly want me for a wife."

"And how can you possibly convince them of that so easily?"

Oh, but she did so love that measure of disbelief in his tone. As if he couldn't imagine what would talk a man out of marrying her. "Usually? I let them meet my mother during one of her...more extreme phases."

Ian heard what she didn't say. She looked up at him through the smoky screen of her thick lashes, begging him to hear her. He shouldn't touch her. He knew that much. But her skin was pure magnetism.

He gave in every time.

They'd had proper teas and visits over the past few days, as they discussed arrangements and she found him this townhouse to rent.

He looked forward to any hours in which he got to speak with Lottie. Her animated conversation lit his days and erased his worries as he got absolutely nowhere in finding Patricia.

But most germane to the conversation was where they commonly had those teas—in her mother's studio.

"Your mother isn't that bad," he lied. A single lock of her hair slipped between his thumb and forefinger like a woman's sweetest slickness.

Her fingertips rested on his chest with gentle weight. "I do believe that's one of the kindest deceptions I've ever encountered." Her gaze flicked back up, this time heavy with heat and sparking green. "You deserve a reward."

Suddenly he was completely aware they stood in a bedroom. His chest clenched. His arms tensed and pulled against the impulse to enfold her and feel her lean, long body against his. Push her down on the bed that loomed to their side. All would be lost then.

He cleared his throat, but he couldn't make himself look away from her pink-tinged lips. "That can't have put everyone off. Someone must be strong enough to withstand your mother. After all, she'd be better than some critical, meddling sort of mother-in-law."

She barked out a short laugh. Her eyes went wide with shock. "I've never thought of it that way."

He shrugged and kept his expression neutral, but really he loved putting that look on her face. Getting taken by surprise was something that likely didn't happen often to Lottie. She seemed so very tired and world-weary beneath the affected happiness. "Your mother might keep life exciting, but she wouldn't be choosing your bedroom's decorations."

"You'd think." She led the way out of the room. "It's possible that I strongly implied Mother's madness is often inherited by the women of our family."

"And is that true?"

She paused in the doorway to another room, one hand at shoulder height on the doorjamb. In profile her smile suggested mystery. Her eyes glittered and smoldered at the same time. One of those strange female gifts. "It's absolutely true. The odds are about one in two that I'll be insane before I'm five and thirty at the latest. Or it could happen after my first child."

His feet jolted to a stop at the threshold. That hadn't been the answer he expected in the least.

The room was another bedroom, though grander. Along the wall was a cherry-wood wardrobe fronted with inlaid decoration. Billowy green curtains draped around the head of the half tester bed. The foot had carved posts to match the armoire.

Lottie stood with an elbow looped loosely around the closest post and her hip leaning against the mattress. "No kind lie to say to that one?"

"You seem perfectly sane to me."

"I do hope that wasn't a lie."

"It wasn't." He shouldn't go closer. Not with the way he couldn't look away from her mouth. "You're reckless. Maybe you're a little wild and entirely too spoiled. But you're perfectly sane."

She rocked back and forth, her hips sliding. Silk caught against the bed's covers. "You know nothing of the sort."

"I absolutely do." He cupped her face, the delicate bones firm under his thumbs. "I know that at this moment you would let me kiss you."

"And more."

"You shouldn't say such things."

She nudged the tip of her tongue across the edge of her top lip. She looked up at him from under lashes weighted with promise, and it went straight to his cock. His entire body clenched.

She slanted away from him, shifting so she leaned her bottom flat against the bed. "Why ever not?"

"Because someone will eventually take you up on that offer."

One by one, she walked her fingertips up the center of his chest. "Don't be intentionally slow."

He lifted an eyebrow. Their conversations took interesting, odd twists at times, but this had to be the top. "There are businessmen who've been ruined for saying similar things to me."

"I don't issue invitations to just anyone." A sharp flash of hurt darkened her eyes. "No matter what some believe."

"I never said you did."

She dug her fingertips under the narrow edge of his cravat and set about unknotting it. His blood stuttered, then rushed hot and hard through his veins. He couldn't breathe. Maybe he *shouldn't* breathe, because then he'd smell her soft scent.

Her touch delved under his collar and across his neck. He sucked in a hissing breath. "Don't do that."

"You still haven't provided me a reason for restraint. I'm beginning to think one doesn't exist."

Ian prided himself on being an average man. He had appetites for womanly attention within the normal realm of a gentleman of his stature, but he had periodically been called upon to restrain himself. His circle of acquaintances was small.

There were his sister's friends, the daughters of his mother's friends and business acquaintances' wives. Not the appropriate circle for rousing romps.

Besides, he'd always selected his partners with care. Not from any level of persnicketiness, but because he couldn't imagine spending a short time with a person if he couldn't also imagine spending the rest of his life with them. If there wasn't a spark of chance, he didn't see wasting the effort.

Damn his parents for raising a romantic.

Because the woman under his hands was every bit of temptation he shouldn't have. He wasn't sure he'd be able to resist.

Maybe he shouldn't have to. Maybe he should take that which she offered.

Her bottom lip plumped out in a soft pout. He traced that tender, damp flesh with a single fingertip. Her tongue darted out and wetted his flesh. His entire body shuddered as he growled. Growled, like some sort of rough animal with no greater sense than to take and rip and shred.

The problem resided in the fact that he didn't feel particularly *normal* around Lottie. No idle hunger that could be sated with an hour of mutual fun.

He wanted to strip her boundaries, pull down her walls. See what she hid inside that gilded heart of hers. See if she was anything like he thought, pure of soul and more troubled than anything else.

"I'm sure no woman has ever had this much trouble getting herself kissed." She knew what she was doing. Teasing humor dripped from every word.

"That's part of the problem." Her neck was delicate as he cupped one hand around her nape. "You're expecting a kiss when that's the least of what you'll get."

If he'd expected wild and reckless Lottie to take that as a warning, he'd been a fool. She crackled with excitement. It zinged off her skin like electricity in a summer storm. She'd been toying with the slender strip of his black cravat, but suddenly that wasn't enough. She pulled it free.

"Maybe you're the one who should stop making offers you have no intention of following through with." Her hands were cool against his neck, and his body awoke. Wanted.

Took.

He stole her mouth, claimed her breath. His lips parted over hers. There was no resistance. She melted and sank against him. Lean curves were completely given over.

He held her pinned against his body with one hand at her neck. The other traveled down, down, to her crinoline-and-wool-covered ass. Firm. Pert. His hands filled with her flesh, and there was nothing more he could think of for a long, long spinning moment.

Until she moaned. With a long, slow dip of his tongue, he gathered the sound.

He shouldn't be doing this. The empty house and the promise of her flesh went to his head. He pulled his mouth away and looked into those glowing eyes. She was hazy again. A tiny, winsome curve adorned her mouth, entirely more real than most of those smiles she flashed like blades.

He kept his hand on her ass, even as he scowled. "Tell me to stop. Tell me, or this will likely go further than you want."

They passed breaths back and forth as slowly as treacle. By pure determination, he held back the wave that threatened to take him down.

Then she did the unthinkable. She crossed her forearms behind his neck and with a sweet, low pressure dragged herself up his length. Her lips hovered below his, close enough that he felt every word whisper over his skin. "Don't you dare stop."

Chapter Nine

Lottie knew this wasn't wise. She'd always flouted the rules, and she'd been the bane of her governesses, but she understood there was a line. A certain level of behavior that couldn't be ignored by society. Rules existed for the neat ordering of humankind within the accustomed boundaries.

She intended to leap right over those boundaries.

Here, now, she had the protection of Ian's arms. A sharp twinge in her chest warned her this closeness would only serve to complicate issues. Eventually she would have to contrast the sure, hard feeling of his arms wrapped around her against the flayed-open effect of losing him.

His kiss swept away the awful fear slithering down her spine. She locked her forearms tighter behind his neck. Held on because that was all she knew how to do.

She wanted more, but she didn't know how to make *more* happen. Or what it entailed. All she knew was that the way his hands spread over her back made her push up closer. Nearer. The fragment of space between them disappeared.

Closing that distance was the least she could do. Rewards came from pressing her chest along his. Heavy pressure in her lungs counteracted the tempting thrust of her breasts against him. The tight pull of her nipples made her breath catch.

A quiet grumble filling the air was another reward. His hands clenched on her back, then one shifted down to her backside. Soft kneading made her rise on her toes. Lean harder into him.

She could believe it possible to let go. Allow herself to put her trust and her body in his hands.

Whatever he took, it wouldn't be enough.

He kissed her jaw, then her neck. Lush and tingling sensation heralded wetness. He was drawing his tongue along her skin, adding nips. His hand along her back spread wider as a single point of steadying calm.

He found supple skin beneath her ear, and she jolted. Her heart and body and insides twisted. Body warming and readying. She'd never been turned inside out like this.

"There's a bed behind me," she gasped. He'd found a place at the center of her throat that made her rock up on her toes. She wasn't helpless, not the way she'd heard the feeling described sometimes, but Lord did it feel lovely.

She couldn't tell if the sensations all came as a result of his skill or the palpable excitement that drove every movement. He was on the verge of eating her up, turning her into some sort of treat for his pleasure.

Which was why she was so surprised when he gave a small shake of his head against the base of her neck. "No."

She shuddered, and it was half from unbearable disappointment and half the implacable control in his voice. "You sound so certain."

He lifted his head away from the delicious things he was doing to her neck. His eyes blazed. Such fire was enough to assure she was on the right track. This was right. *They* were right.

"If I have you on a horizontal surface, I'll fuck you."

Her nails dug into the back of his neck. Firm flesh under soft skin. The ends of his hair trailed over her knuckles. Her body clenched on his brutal words, and she made herself smile. "I was under the impression that men took anything freely given."

His hands were so assured and confident. She loved the feeling of them on her body, holding her still. Holding her in. But she wasn't going to appreciate what sparked in his eyes. That was only confirmed when he chuckled. "What is the world teaching women nowadays? That every man is some slavering beast at the mercy of his body?"

"Maybe at the mercy of my body." Her smile wavered. "If things are going well."

"I like you, Lottie."

He turned them and then backed up until he was seated on a small chaise. She shouldn't have allowed it, but the shocked pleasure that rocked through her at his words left her off-center. He held her by the hand, and those long fingers enfolded hers with more warmth than she'd known could exist. He arranged her beside him so that they were seated together.

"This is a horizontal surface," she pointed out, rather than address his enigmatic comment. What did one say to that? How did one accept it? Particularly when she feared he knew nothing about her after all. Only what she'd shown, no more.

"There's less room for maneuvering." His fingers laced with hers, and his other hand rose to cup her chin. "I'm good, but there're still limits. And trust me, you shouldn't like to see such limits. They're difficult and awkward. Those phrases shouldn't be involved with lovemaking."

There. She was right in giving herself to him. His humor was enough to make her giddy. She kissed him again, this time taking the lead with a fast rush of assurance. She could do this. More than that, it would be lovely and amazing.

He kissed her back, but not long enough. Not for nearly long enough. She started to melt, her spine leaning back and back against the arm of the chaise until she was a crescent that waned and melted.

"I can't do this, Lottie."

She felt her lips bend into something unattractive, a flickering shadow of the frustration that made her want to dig her fingers into his hair and yank. She would put his mouth back at her neck and let him figure it out from there. "You said you liked me."

He didn't exactly take his hands off her, either. He swept up and down her sides in a slow streak that didn't dissuade her. She wanted to curl and preen under the attention, like a puppy in a puddle of sunshine. "I do. That's why I can't continue."

"You make no sense." She loved and hated his eyes. There was too much there. Like he could see right through her, and she absolutely despised the speck of pity. Her neck turned rigid. "No complications. No permanence. You'd be a fool to not take me up on my offer."

He wrapped an arm around her shoulder and pulled her to his chest. Her head shouldn't have been able to bend, not with tension locking her into a brittle collection of straw bits. Somehow she fit against him, despite the lingering conviction she'd fit nowhere. Ever. Her head rested on his surprisingly hefty shoulder.

"You see, that's the problem." He passed a hand over the curve of her head, fingers skimming through her hair.

A tingling burn came and went behind her nose and eyes. "You are a nonsensical idiot."

"You're not sweetmeat to be offered on a silver platter, Lottie. You shouldn't be."

"I want you." She swallowed. "That way."

"No, you don't." She could somehow hear a smile in his voice, though at the moment she stared at a golden pillow tassel. When he'd backed her away from the bed, she should have known this wasn't going the way she wanted. "You have a notion, and you wanted me to stop asking pointed questions about your family."

"My family is an open book. There's nothing that needs asking."

He petted and stroked her head. He dug into the back of her neck, pinching away a flush of stress. Her fingertips tingled. "You talk about the facts. You make jokes and you dance about as if it were nothing unfortunate. But you never talk about the effect upon you."

"Have I mentioned that you're an idiot?"

"Quite recently."

She sat up then. This had gone entirely too far for her preferences. If she gave into it—if she *ever* gave in—she'd be sunk. Drowned under frozen waters and trapped by crisp ice. "You're alone in an empty house with a woman who's generally considered attractive—"

"You're not simply attractive, you're one of the most beautiful women I've ever seen."

She buried her smile against his coat's soft wool. "With a beautiful woman, then. You refuse to do more than kiss her, and you wish to talk about her feelings."

He gave an overly dramatic sigh. "I know. It's a tragic failing of mine, not recognizing amazing opportunities when they're given to me. Maybe I'll shortly change my mind."

"Is there actually any chance of that?" She wasn't sure if she wanted him at this moment, but she was quite curious about his answer. Only when her fingers stilled did she realize she'd been idly twisting a silver button on his waistcoat.

"There shouldn't be." His voice traveled straight to some depraved core of her and woke her again. "There shouldn't be, because I'd always intended to be a good sort of man. But you go to my head."

It ended up taking everything Ian was made of to leave that empty house without tasting Lottie's sweetness. Even so, he cracked and kissed her at the foot of the stairs while her groomsman waited patiently outside. He bent her back against the newel post, and she kissed him so agreeably he almost convinced himself that she truly wanted him. Completely.

But she didn't. Not really. The problem was more that she *didn't* want her other options. She'd didn't have enough happiness in her life to base such choices on.

Coming together like that ought to be a happy thing. Joy to leave both parties fulfilled and feeling better about themselves, before going their separate ways.

Any choices Lottie made would be borne of fear. It then followed that fear would poison that which came after.

None of which was to say that he didn't want Lottie. He wanted her more than he wanted sense in his head.

He put her into her carriage unmolested and then took his own to the railway station. He'd told Lottie the day before of his intentions to go home to collect Etta and his mother. Hence why he'd needed to inspect the house she'd arranged for this afternoon, before the servants arrived.

That didn't mean he'd expected the train ride home to be quite as fraught as it was.

Lulled by the chugging, clambering rails, his mind took the strangest detours, and every inch was a wander down odd roads. What it would be like to make such a trip with Lottie at his side.

He could almost imagine her riding in a private rail coach. To meet her standards, the train would have to be adorned like a tiny jewel box, with her as the prize at the center.

Besides, private accommodations would mean more time for them to indulge. Feel her and know her to take her apart piece by piece and put her back together again stronger and more aware of how amazing she really was.

The station at his village was small, little more than a tidy white-clapped building with a platform long enough for the average train. No one waited for him there, exactly how he'd intended it.

He needed the trip home and the crisp, clean air in direct contrast to the grime and thickness of London. The road he took out of town was one he'd traveled a thousand times. More.

He'd walked this road to church and back again. To the station when his father had died and Ian had been forced to take over the business of the mines. Those weren't counting the trips he'd made in the middle of Etta's disastrous drama—or when he'd realized there was yet more mess to clean up.

Which was part of the obligations of being an elder brother.

Which was also why he could sympathize strongly with Lottie. She had likely gone home to spend time with her mother—or to the charity she ran. Must be convenient to have such a well-respected way to run away.

Not that Ian blamed her in the least. Standing at the end of his drive, looking at the home he'd been raised in, he was shocked how little he wanted to enter. The place had always been a comfort, safe from the rest of the world. Ivy covered the north wall, and he took no small measure of pride in knowing the entire slate roof had been replaced last year. He'd had gas run to the entire lower floors, and he'd recently spoken to a man about having a full plumbing system installed.

All in all, it was a good house. A solid house. The kind of place a man could build a family.

He'd rather be in London, in Lottie's realm. Where he had the hope of seeing her.

Instead his mother's near hysterics needed to be dealt with. She must have seen him from an upstairs window. A scarf dangled from her hand. For middle age, she was small and spry. Her hair was mostly dark, with only the slightest sprinkling of white at her temples and twisting through the braided mass.

"Is it true? Have you rented a house?" She had all the fluttery animation of a young girl.

"A very fine one." He grabbed her up for a fast hug, then put her at arm's length so he could better see her bright eyes. "I went to see it this afternoon."

How very strange. He wanted to tell her all about Lottie. To sit with her in the gathering twilight and have tea delivered to the back garden.

He and his mother had a good relationship, but he'd never felt compelled to tell her about the women in his life. Certain issues were solely for a man's world.

Lottie, it seemed, straddled both worlds.

Maybe the idea had merit. If anything, his mother was excellent at seeing to the heart of matters. Her response might be a hysterical overreaction, but that made the initial analysis no less valid.

"Is it grand?" she asked. She looked half terrified and half enthusiastic. "I've always wanted to stay in one of those grand sorts of places. The grange is nice, but it's nothing compared to some I saw in my one season."

"There's an ebony staircase that spirals down to the foyer. Marble everywhere. And I'm told there's a conservatory."

"In London," she said on a pleased gasp. Looping her arm through his, she led him into the house and up toward the family parlor. "Though what do you mean told? Didn't you choose the place yourself?"

"I relied upon knowledgeable advice."

Though she spoke with an amiable smile, there was no missing the way his mother's gaze narrowed in on him. "From whom? One of your business agents? Please, Ian, I beg you not to leave our living conditions to some man of business. He'll have picked based solely on cost plus how long it takes you to get to whatever offices you're working out of."

"In the first place, I'll be working out of the study as needed. You'll have me as much as you like."

"Oh, how marvelous," she exclaimed with a little clap of her hands. "And?"

"And what?" he prevaricated.

"And first places are always followed by second places. You have more on your mind."

"Ah." His mother made his head spin sometimes. She was so damned...chirrupy. He wasn't entirely sure that was a word, but there it was. After all, he'd contributed to that, conspiring with his father to give her and Etta the best possible life.

They emerged into the family parlor as one. There, Etta waited picturesquely situated by the bay window. Since Archie's death, she'd spent many, many hours curled up there. The part that worried Ian was that she didn't indulge in the novels she'd once enjoyed. Instead she'd begun to read treatises for millwrights. Ian rather thought she could build a paper mill if she liked.

"Ian," she exclaimed, in practically the same tone his mother had used. "You're home. Are you really going to take us to London?"

"I am." He gave her a large hug, then swung them around to face their mother. "And next I've your second place."

Hands clasped before her bosom, she lit up from within. "This is going to be lovely. I can tell. I can always tell, when you get that look."

"Which look?"

"The one that says you're about to be the best son or best brother that could be wished for."

How he loved when she relied on him. They'd grown up in each other's pockets. Etta hadn't had a governess, but they'd shared Nurse Rockaway. Ian's earliest memory was coaxing a butterfly to land on his pudgy young fingers so he could show it to infant Henrietta.

"Surely I'm not so obnoxious as to be self-aware," he said, squeezing her shoulder.

"Surely you are," she said. Her hair was the same dark, dark brown as his, and he realized he had no real concept of how long it was. He hadn't seen it down since she'd married

Archie. It was coiled and pinned and twisted up. "But it's all right with us. Everyone must have a fault."

"Smugness is mine?"

"It seems minor compared to many." Something dark flitted behind her eyes and pinched her features. "Lady Cotrose came to tea. She was very sorry to be the bearer of bad news, but she'd received a letter."

Ian sighed, filling in the blanks. "From Patricia."

"Indeed. Intimating I had an illicit history." Instead of being able to laugh it off, Etta's bottom lip wavered with emotion. "Lady Cotrose already knew, of course, but who will be next?"

He did so hope that she was up to this London venture. "You'll have to forgive me, then. I'm about to be smug when I tell you that I have arranged for a duchess to sponsor your Season, as well as the assistance of a baron's daughter who is quite experienced in navigating treacherous waters. We'll have your reputation safe in no time."

As he'd expected, Mother cooed and clapped and generally made quite the to-do of the announcement. Etta brightened as well. He loved filling her eyes with happiness.

But hers dimmed much more quickly than their mother's had. Her grin faded to a hint of a smile, though she still clasped hands with Mother. "Ian, can I ask... That is, what plans have you for me?"

"You don't have to marry again if you don't find someone you truly wish to."

Palpable relief washed over her. Her shoulders eased. Her arms flew around him for a hug that threatened to snap his ribs.

"Oomph." He pushed her away enough to see her face. "What's that for?"

Her eyes filled with tears. "I miss him. I thought you might be tired of me, and with all the trouble I've caused for the family and for you in particular... I know what Papa would have liked for us." She drew in a deep breath, and her chin lifted. "I'd have done it. I'd have married whom you wish. I still will, if it would help you in any way."

Their mother linked arms with Etta. Her mouth set into a mulish frown. "You'll do no such thing. I haven't raised a martyr. Why, we're not Catholic!"

"I will, if needs be. I've been lucky enough to marry for love once. Who gets that sort of chance twice in life?"

Ian would rather lay money on the chances that she didn't mean such assurances, not really. It didn't matter, anyhow. He wouldn't ask that of her—and it seemed a fairly low man who needed to bargain his family members to improve his lot in life. His parents had married for love, and Etta had as well, though that was a slightly different situation.

Ian had always meant to follow, once he found a compatible woman who'd help bear his burdens. Not add to them with false faces and deceptive smiles.

Even if those smiles were all Ian could think of in the dark of night.

Chapter Ten

Lottie was in the school's kitchens when Isabella, the downstairs maid, came skittering to a stop on the tile floor. A smile wreathed her round face, and she held her skirts in both hands. Her breathing came in pants and gasps. "He's back again."

A giggling, quiet titter rolled like a wave through the kitchen staff, though many choked themselves off when they glanced at Lottie.

She wiped her hands on her apron. The white streaks of flour were almost invisible on the white cotton, except where they intersected smears of coal dust. "Who might that be, Isabella?"

The maid jumped a good four inches. "No one, Miss Vale. That is. Um." Her cheeks turned red.

"Who is here?" She kept her voice calm, as if she were completely unaffected. Really her heart thrummed away, and she thought that she might be sick. In a good way, though.

How very foolish she was. The man had made it more than clear he had no interest in her, at least not that way.

"It's Sir Ian," the girl eventually said when glances toward her compatriots showed no allies. They all kept their noses turned diligently toward the pots they stirred and the dough they kneaded. "He's here to visit you."

"I understand Sir Ian is handsome, but I don't see as how that's such a remarkable thing."

Isabella's cheeks jumped from red to crimson. "We were hoping... That is, Miss Vale, you get so very happy when he comes. We only want the best for you." Her chin lifted, and she breathed pure assurance of purpose into her words that Lottie had never seen on the young girl. She'd once been a hurdy-gurdy girl and on her way to prostitution before coming to the school. Once she was brave enough to leave Lottie's employ, there'd be a reference in it for her.

So as much as Lottie did not want the ladies chiming in on her personal life, she didn't have it in her to roundly chastise Isabella. She stripped the apron over her head and hung it on a peg. "Back to work, ladies. I'll have no idle speculation, or you'll all be scrubbing floors for a week."

He was waiting in her study. Somehow it was becoming too normal to see him lounging in her chair. The dark suit he wore made his coloring that much more dramatic. Near black hair was tousled over his brow, and though he held a book in his hands, he looked up at her with that boyish smile.

As a result, she seated herself in the chair on the other side of the desk. Her feelings were still stung from their last encounter. Stung and yet also strangely soothed. He'd said he *liked* her.

Such simple words were a balm against the hollow compliments of society. Of course, late at night when she tossed and turned alone in bed, they could also seem like a cruel-edged blade. He liked her, he liked her, he didn't *want* her.

"Did your family fancy the house?" she asked once she'd seated herself and smoothed her skirts. Those she wore today were simpler than she would have preferred. He'd been gone a whole week, and she hadn't known when he would return.

Otherwise she might have dressed more finely.

She was a silly girl.

He left her shaken and buzzing. She felt appreciated around him, as if she were some better version of herself.

"Fancy?" he said on a wry chuckle. "You've no idea, do you?"

"No, but I do enjoy the sound of that." She waved a hand in the air between them, as if gathering the potential compliments to herself. Her pulse fluttered. "Do tell."

"My mother was so pleased she had a fit of the vapors." He snapped the book shut and set it down. Though he'd taken her seat with no mind, he placed the book carefully between two stacks of paper, as if he had no wish to disturb them. "Luckily, she managed to hold herself together long enough to swoon on the velveteen settee in the music room."

"Oh, I did think she'd favor that room. All that white velvet is delightful."

He grinned, then let it fade from his agile mouth. Now that she knew what havoc he could wreak on her skin, she could hardly look away from it. But his eyes had darkened to the sea at dawn. "My father played the harpsichord for her."

"Then she should love that piano."

"Except that she has no one to play for her."

Her gaze dropped to his long, graceful fingers. "Not you?"

He shook his head with regret. "No. I was much more preoccupied with learning the business. Henrietta tried, but unfortunately she had a tin ear. I didn't have patience for lessons."

"Such a shame," she breathed. She could imagine his hands playing—on many things. So focused was she on that image, she spoke without thinking. "My mother plays."

"Does she?"

There was no taking it back now, and indeed it seemed fairly innocuous. But there were more words there, lurking at the back of her throat and burning in her mind. "Not only does she play, she's excellent at it."

The room all but spun around her. Or maybe that was her fumbling, flipping mind. She was closer to mad than she'd ever supposed, and all because of him. From him. From the way she dallied with his fire.

"But?" he asked. Gently. So gently. As if he doubted that she'd manage to say anything more.

"But I hate that it was so effortless for her." The words spilled out like champagne from a bottle—gurgling, sparkling, tripping over themselves. She let out a huge sigh. "I wanted to play. She couldn't care less. Couldn't manage to focus long enough to teach me. It...hurt a little."

He leaned his chin on his fist and watched her. "She seems rather...casually cruel."

Her hands locked together in her lap. She forced a smile, one of her biggest and brightest. She needed to change the subject. "It's lucky she's charming. And taught me how to be, as well."

"Reached your limit of speaking of difficult things, have you?" He had a knowing smirk. "No worries. Starting small is fine. Real people occasionally have emotions."

"You're rather a bastard, aren't you?" It was so much easier to be annoyed. That wasn't even the worst of it. She was amused. She found herself hiding away a smile that could turn into a giggle if she allowed.

He gave her a faux put-upon expression. "You come in here and unload your deepest feelings and then call me names and not once have you asked my purpose for being here. If this is high society, maybe I was better off in the country. Or the business world."

She cut her eyes toward the ceiling. "What a load of ballocks."

"Now you curse in my delicate presence." He pushed up from his seat and stalked around the desk. When he pulled her to stand, she went because it would get her closer to him. "There's a penalty for inflicting such language on me, you know."

She couldn't leave well enough alone. Not when she found herself back in the happy circle of his arms and about to be kissed. His mouth hovered over hers, the air between them luscious and scented with mint. Still she couldn't keep her mouth shut. "Thank you," she said on a soft whisper.

"For what?"

Her hands clenched on his firm arms, the fine wool their only barrier. She hardly knew how to put words to it. For taking what she could manage to be and wanting her to be better too.

There were too many confusing, twirling feelings. So she said nothing. Sometimes it was easier to speak with actions. She lifted her mouth and covered the scant distance between them. Kissed him with everything she was feeling—and the feelings rocked straight over her like something alive. She clutched at his shoulders, and his hands curved down, over her back, over the swell of her skirts and ass.

She yanked away on panting breaths. What the hell was that new surge through her body? If it were what happened when one felt for one's partner, she wasn't sure she could handle it. Not in the least. Nothing that overwhelming should be within her realm.

She didn't like feeling that shaken up. She couldn't afford it.

As fast as she could form her lips into the shape, she smiled. Ignored the tremble behind the backs of her knees. "So. Tell me. Why did you come here today after all?"

Ian rather liked having conversations with his hands full of luscious, lithe female. There was something about it that added an extra piquancy to the moment. He nuzzled a tendril of her hair away from her neck. Layer on layer of softness, and most of it covered by the thinnest stratum of gilt he could imagine. Underneath that shine, she was warm and true. Completely at odds with the sides she liked to present.

But she apparently had limits. In talking about her mother's small cruelties, they'd tumbled headfirst into Lottie's capabilities. Well enough. He'd gotten the peek at her tender insides that he needed.

Possibilities were a beautiful thing. He'd founded his entire empire on them, taking his father's happenstance tin mines and parlaying it into a modest fortune. While he was no financial genius, he certainly knew how to work with possibilities.

He cupped both hands around her face. "I'm not giving up on finding Patricia, and I can't promise that there won't be any repercussions for your charity. I'll try, however."

She cut her eyes toward the ceiling. "I suppose that will have to do." She pulled out of his arms and moved around the desk to sit in her chair. The grin she put on was mischievous, and she crossed her legs in such a manner that her skirt rose three inches. Her toes bounced against the front hem. The slippers he spotted were silver with a tiny bow, absolutely frivolous for a day in London. "I can't possibly distract you?"

He hitched a hip on the corner of her desk, though he had to go carefully. A stack of correspondence five inches high threatened to drop like snow across the floor. "You can try. I have about two hours before I'm needed at the townhouse."

She smirked. She tugged her skirt up a fraction above where it had already been lifted.

He swallowed. Hard. His chest jerked and clenched on such a forbidden hint.

"Here," she said on a soft coo. "Lock that door and we'll spend those hours doing...something."

He wet his lips. The turn of her ankle was a mystery he hadn't been privy to. Such a simple thing and only eroticized by the fact of its status as a withheld item. Buried under silks and wool and linen and kept secret from men at large. Her delicate bones tempted his hands. "No."

She dropped her skirts. "You are absolutely no fun."

"You've no wish to be tumbled and taken in a cramped, dirty office."

"My office is certainly not dirty," she said on an offended gasp.

"You get my point."

"I don't, as a matter of fact." Her smirk demonstrated she knew exactly what other sort of meaning could be inferred.

He couldn't help but grin at her. She was astute. Fast. Though she had a terrible sense of humor. "Did you just pun at me? How very unfortunate."

"Don't lie." She leaned back in her armed desk chair, a woman in charge of her world. While true, he wondered how many people realized that was only part of the story. "You want to laugh."

"It's not pointed." He did want to laugh. He was talking about taboo subjects when it came to ladies, and yet rather than feeling risqué, he wanted to revel in humor. "I'd say blunt."

She sat up. Eagerness turned her into something less humorous and more enticing. "Blunt? That has promise. Would you say...thick?"

"You're rotten. I've completely lost track of this conversation."

"I haven't." Her voice was full of good humor. "I've been distracting you."

He had to concede the point, so he tipped his chin. "Indeed you have been. Rather effectively. But I'm easily returned to the topic at hand."

"Or not at hand, as the case may be." She grinned so hard that her nose wrinkled across the bridge. "You *could* put your hands on me. I wouldn't mind."

"Patricia," he said, attempting vainly to get his mind on task. Utter temptation infused her every breath. She was reckless. Exciting. "I came here for a reason, and that reason is named Patricia."

"Oh, pooh." She flicked her fingers. "Fine. She's not here. She hasn't been seen at work or anywhere respectable in quite a few weeks."

"And what about places that are less respectable."

Her head tilted to a cheeky angle. "How clever you are. I ought to make you provide a fee. For every answer I give you, I get a kiss."

"Isn't that blackmail?" He crossed his arms, mostly to avoid displaying how very much he liked that idea.

She shook her head and pressed her mouth together as if she were considering the question with great seriousness.

Really, she didn't seem to have a serious bone in her body, or so she'd have the world believe. Couldn't be possible considering how much she put into her charity, into making sure girls were prepared for the world and to improve their lot in life. He'd seen more of her. A more he quite liked.

"No," she finally said, drawing the word out into a tease. "I'm fairly sure this is extortion, not blackmail."

"All the same. Illegal as can be."

"True." She kicked a foot, popping at the insides of her skirt and turning her into a vision of youth and happiness. "Report me to whomever you like. I shan't mind. And you won't get your kisses or your information."

He hooked one foot in the bottom of her chair and pulled. Tugged. She came near with the same happy excitement he'd come to expect. Locking one hand on each arm of her chair caged her in. Surrounded her. She didn't care. Her chin lifted so that her mouth hovered under his.

"Where is she?"

"Kiss me first."

He'd kiss her first and he'd kiss her after too. So much temptation could only be resisted so long. Her beauty was second to none, but all that ended up falling by the wayside when he'd grown entirely more fascinated with her mind. Though her want for him seemed to grow with every kiss, it didn't explain everything.

It didn't explain her desperate sort of hunger when she sealed her mouth to his. The jolt of their coming together went through his bones every time. Woke his body and made him want to claim and take.

Except he couldn't shake the conviction that something was not quite right. A goal or insistence of hers struck false.

Not that he belabored the issue when his mouth skated over hers and tasted that sweetness. Wet and warm and he couldn't stop thinking about how her creamy skin would taste all over. Whether her nipples would be pale and barely pink-tinged or a secret rose.

Which was definitely his signal to end the kiss before it got out of hand. He rested his forehead on hers in a firm press. "You could tempt priests out of their cassocks."

"I don't want a priest." Her eyes drifted shut. "I want you."

He still doubted that. But he thought the truth of it grew. "Now I want my answers."

"There's a cardroom run by someone I know. I've word she's reputed to be a regular attendee, when she has the blunt."

His mind tossed over and through the possibilities, sorting them out. "If she hasn't been to work for days, she might not have the money to play."

Lottie shrugged. "Those deep in the cards always seem to find ways to gather cash, so long as there's a game available."

"I'll need the address. As well as when they play."

She curled both her hands around the back of his neck. Sweet, heavy pressure dug into the muscles there, which gave up their tension. Until she spoke. "No." Her words were matter-of-fact. "I believe I'll make you take me with you."

"Why in the name of God would you do that?" He sat bolt upright. "A disreputable card game is no place for a lady of stature."

Her smile turned so smug, he wanted to put his fingers across it and make her feel something else. Real desire or want. "I think you'll be surprised how well known I am around there."

"Because you troll the underbelly of the city all the time?" He couldn't help the heavy measure of doubt that laced his voice.

"Not exactly." Her smile was radiant, and he had the strangest feeling whatever she was about to say was going to give him a massive headache. "But I have friends in low places who will be so very happy to see me."

Chapter Eleven

By Friday night, Lottie was more convinced than ever that she'd made the right choice in insisting on going with Ian. She stepped from the carriage with her hand in his. Down the narrow, crooked street, a single streetlamp at the corner threw a sickly glow over a circle's worth of city.

The building before them wasn't much. Only two stories, and the windows were small and dirty. A sign over the door swung in a desultory breeze. The scent of it, thick with salt and rot, implied the air came from the docks a street or two away. If only it had stayed there.

She lifted gloved fingers to her nose as her stomach gave a little twist. "Such a dreadful smell." She dropped her hand and intentionally took a deep breath, the best to acclimatize.

"The city at its finest. And this is supposed to be superior to the country in which manner?"

She bent her mouth inward to hide a smile. "I certainly didn't mean *this* part. The environs I normally cling to are much more amenable. You'll have to take me to Hyde Park tomorrow to alleviate this memory."

"Wet fish rot does have a particular clinginess to it." He presented his arm and tipped his head toward her. His beaver-pelt top hat tilted at a rakish angle. His cheeks pinched on dimples that inspired reckless thoughts. "Tell me your friend's name and I'd be glad to return you to Chelsea so you can avoid the stench."

He'd been right the other day. She hadn't wanted him, not in the body-deep way that grew every time she looked at his mouth. Not really. This was something new. Something that expanded with every smart quip or teasing grin. She liked him. Just like he'd said the other day that he liked her. She appreciated who he was as a person, the way he was determined to shield his sister from the brunt of her choices.

"You'll know the name in a moment. When we go inside. I won't risk you running about without me." She wouldn't pass up such an expedition.

He didn't like it. He'd protested the entire way that she didn't need to be attending any gambling halls, much less one of the lower classes. Then she'd caught him looking when he hadn't realized she could see. The way his gaze lit. The intensity that absorbed him. She liked it. She loved it. Plenty of men had admired her over the years. But never had she felt quite so...fully enfolded. He already knew about her mother and wasn't put off.

"As you wish," he finally said.

The groomsman darted around them and opened the door, releasing a flood of noise and smoke. The air clashed with layers of sounds. Gamblers cheered each other on. Bone-carved dice rattled in cups. The clatter and clink of glasses.

Inside was a madhouse. Tables of all sorts and sizes crammed the room. Across the right wall, narrow stairs led to an upper level. Opposite of that was a long bar which bustled like a beehive with people coming and going at a fast clip.

She let herself lean toward Ian. He was so much larger, he could take the brunt of the crowd's impact. She'd allow him that privilege. Being the big, strong man got rewards such as her clutching his arm more closely.

The way he bent his head toward hers left her feeling sheltered and protected. "It's not too late to back out."

"Do I seem like the sort likely to back out of anything?" Her heart took a strange tumble, and somehow she found herself oddly hopeful.

It mattered, to her, whether he found her good and worthy. Whether she counted in the larger scheme of things, if a girl liable to go crazy as soon as she accomplished her female purpose ever did count.

"You don't." He tucked a carefully pressed ringlet behind her ear. She thought it might be an excuse to touch her because his fingertip strayed over her temple. "You have more fortitude than most men I've met."

Her chest eased and bloomed open. So stupid, yet she couldn't seem to help it. "That's about to be put to the test. Come along."

She led him inexorably toward a plain door at the far back of the room. They had to wade through crowds. Bodies pressed in on all sides, and unlike usual, Lottie hardly noticed. She didn't like strangers touching her—invading her space. But with Ian walking close at her back, she was safe.

She knocked on the unremarkable door and was surprised that it wasn't answered immediately. She had to knock again, her heartbeat trebling with worry that maybe her note had gone astray, before Sera opened the door. Her friend was dressed in a fine evening gown covered all over with silver lace. The cleavage displayed by the plunging neckline was red with a blush, and she was breathing hard.

"I can't believe you actually came again, and at this hour," Sera exclaimed. She hauled Lottie into the room. "You foolish girl, you couldn't at least come through the back entrance like I did?"

"Back entrance," Ian echoed behind her with no small measure of dry wit infusing his voice. "There's a back way?"

"Of course there is. Through the alley, but we keep it well lit and fairly clean back there." Sera led the way to another door.

"So there was no reason for us to arrive at the front of the rooms and make our way through the crowd?"

"Certainly there was," Lottie said. She looked at Ian out of the corner of her eye because there was no way she'd miss his response to this one. "I wanted to."

"Of course." His mouth quirked up on the left, and he glanced at her. "I should have guessed. Isn't that the reason for most of the things that we've done lately?"

She swatted his shoulder, unreasonably pleased with the fact that his firm muscles didn't give. "We shouldn't be here at all if it weren't for your wishes. Don't fault me for taking some small measure of pleasure out of it."

"Pleasure?" he scoffed. "You have no idea of what pleasure is if that qualifies."

Opening the door to another small room revealed a study that was surprisingly cozy for the surrounds. Sera moved to stand beside her husband. Fletcher Thomas sat in an ornately carved chair with red upholstery and gold trim. The thing was as ostentatious as a throne. Any other man would have looked absurd in it. Not Fletcher. He sprawled in the thing like a king of old. A man who'd look more at home grasping a battleaxe than wearing his finely tailored suit.

He scooped up Sera's hand from the chair back and lifted it to his lips for a silent kiss. Sera's blush started in a pink wash at her temples and scored across her cheeks. Her gaze stayed steady on Lottie's as if she didn't feel the kiss. Liar girl.

The glimpses of Sera's marriage that Lottie saw were the few things that made her doubt her resolve to not marry. But then, Sera didn't have the same sort of risks as Lottie did. Childbirth raised the odds of her losing her grip on the world more than anything.

Lottie lived for knowing her friend was happy. She patted Ian's arm. "Sir Ian, allow me to present Fletcher Thomas."

When two men of equal power were introduced, particular magic charged the air. Both Fletcher and Ian were gentlemen of top standing. It was so much energy that a girl couldn't help but feel a thrill of excitement. She held back a shiver, but Ian still saw it.

Her hand looped over his forearm, and he squeezed his fingers over hers. She was firmly held between determination and lean strength. "Mr. Thomas. I'm pleased to make your acquaintance," Ian said.

Fletcher flicked a look up at his wife, who gave a tiny nod. Sera wielded a quiet power over him that had nothing to do with control and everything to do with the reassurances given and taken in turn. "Same here, I'm quite sure." He held out a hand, which Ian took with a brief shake. "I understand you're on the lookout for a paper."

"More, a woman."

Sera gave a teeny, sprite-like smile. "You have a woman at your side."

Ian chuckled. The sound wove through Lottie's body with soft promise. She pushed temptation down, away. Not the time for it.

If she looked too closely, she might have to admit how much she liked being at his side.

Ian had moved on anyway. His gaze focused on Fletcher. "But have I heard of you before? Your name sounds rather familiar."

Fletcher relaxed into his chair. His good humor melted into something more smug. "It's possible. My interests are many."

Lottie laughed. "How droll he is when he wishes to be. Fletcher is one of the largest crime bosses in London at the moment. If Patricia has any intention to indulge in her gambling hobby, she'll come into contact with Fletcher's people."

Ian's eyebrows flew up. His body tensed, and he looked from Lottie to Fletcher and back again. "You're friends with an underworld criminal?"

"Of course I am," she said on a smile. Oh, how she liked discombobulating him. "Doesn't everyone have a favorite criminal?"

"No," he said, feeling rather like the prude and country bumpkin she'd teased him about being. "Most people never come into contact with criminals, not on a regular basis."

Mr. Thomas chuckled roundly, and his petite wife smiled. "Well, now," he said, "I'm not quite as sure about that as you are. I'm of the opinion that you come into contact with criminals nearly daily."

Sera curled a hand over her husband's brawny shoulder. They looked about as mismatched as possible. Fletcher Thomas was a brute, with roughly hewn features and cutting ice-blue eyes. His wife was short and curvy. In her features dwelled calm serenity Ian wouldn't have guessed from a criminal's wife.

Sera smiled at Fletcher before speaking. "It's only the thieves and riffraff you meet simply aren't quite so open about their activities."

"While I see no reason to hide anyone's drinks or gambling. Everyone finds what they're looking for. I candidly afford them the opportunity." Fletcher pushed out of his chair and ambled to a sideboard filled with crystal decanters and squat tumblers. He poured a generous helping of liquor into a glittering glass. "Doesn't seem like horrible criminality to me. Would you like a drink?"

"Thank you." The whiskey burned Ian's throat like fire. "Is there a plan in place for finding the chit?"

Lottie scooped the glass out of his hand, her fingers trailing over his like another touch of that fire. Except this one seared hotter. "Fletcher's men are watching for her, but they don't know her like you and I do. We're going out to the main area to observe."

"Can't hurt."

Fletcher saluted with his glass. "You're welcome to sit with me and my wife at my usual table. Or you can gamble if you wish."

Ian lifted a single eyebrow. "How kind of you."

The other man gave a charming shrug. "It was worth an attempt. And really, I'll spot you the first few quid."

"How generous."

Lottie waved the tumbler of whiskey, which Ian suddenly realized she'd almost fully downed. A whiskey-drinking lady. His mind rather flipped. "We'll sit in the royal booth, thank you very much," Lottie said with cheeky assurance.

"Royal booth?" Ian echoed.

"Lovely," Sera said. Her smile barely curved, but her eyes warmed with true pleasure. "This will be fun."

Thirty minutes later, Ian was rather surprised to find out that was true. Sera had insisted they drink champagne, a very good bottle she admitted came from Fletcher's personal selection rather than what was sold to the regular hoi polloi filling the gambling tables.

Indeed, they hadn't sat among most of the attendees. The seating Lottie called the royal booth was on the second level, abutting the balcony and looking out over the rest of the room. Beneath was a clear view of the gamblers and drinkers and girls working. The table itself was trimmed with gold and inlaid with mahogany stripes across. At the top of the stairs a bodyguard stood silent sentinel, but Ian was convinced by the one good look Ian had gotten of the man's face.

The men Fletcher Thomas employed were not to be messed with.

When a man with a bartender's apron approached, Lottie took the opportunity to lean toward Ian. "This is all rather exciting, is it not?"

If she hadn't such a problem with being called insane, he'd have told her how very cracked she seemed. "You forget I've been to gambling houses before."

She pushed her lips into a pout. "How very masculine of you. I've little opportunity to indulge. Never when feeling so safe as well."

"Oh, goody," he intoned. "You do realize the corridor behind us is lined with women of reduced means who take to their backs to fund their lives, yes?"

"I do. I've been able to convince several to begin classes at my school, but it's rather surprising how many are either honestly pleased to stay where they are or are too frightened to change." She cupped a shallow, wide glass of bubbling wine. "I'll be back in two days to take another run at convincing them to flee Fletcher's evil clutches."

"I do wish you would," Fletcher interjected. "Responsibility for them is drawing me attention in more circumspect company."

Sera patted his arm. "Fletcher is going to be a railroad baron."

Lottie lifted her champagne glass in Ian's direction. "In the meantime, do try to appear as if you're having a good time."

"Are we being watched?" Ian sat too close to Lottie. The hint of her cleavage above her dress's bodice enticed him. "Must I entertain the masses below?"

"No, for me. I tire of seeing such a sourpuss face," she said before laughing. "You'd be surprised how far a little forced enthusiasm goes. In no time, you'll feel it for real."

If anything, he was enjoying himself. But the gambling hall wasn't a novelty. What pleasure he felt came from hers in turn. Seeing her excitement was enough to light him up.

Until a scream echoed through the air behind him.

Lottie jumped. Champagne dribbled over her wrist. Ian was up before he had time to think it through. His chair crashed to the ground. Fletcher scrambled out of his own seat. The man at the top of the stairs started to follow, but Fletcher put up a hand. "Block any crowd."

The scream echoed again, louder this time.

Coming from the second door on the right. The door was locked, the brass handle not moving an inch. "Do you care?" Ian asked Fletcher.

"By all means." Fletcher backed up a step to give him room.

Leaning back, he kicked hard at the knob. Once, then again. The wood cracked, showing pale white unstained by smoke or time. The door gave up completely with a quiet creak.

Ian got only the briefest impression of a small room. In the corner, a tiny blonde cowered and covered her face. Blood dripped from behind her hands.

A ham-fisted man towered above her with his shirt off and suspenders drooped around ample hips. "You've got no right, cunt. None. I'll beat that mouth off you if you say it again."

She peeked out from behind her fingers. One eye was already swollen. Her bottom lip was split. She spat blood across the hardwood floor. "You've the willie of a four-year-old, and it's not my bloody fault if you can't fuck a woman."

The john drew back his foot, roaring with fury. "Whore," he snarled.

Ian launched. Damp, sweaty flesh and the bitter stench of pure cowardice filled his senses. Ian kicked, taking out the man's ankles with the edge of a boot. A flurry of blows and punches flew from Ian's fists. One punch struck the bastard in the throat. No reason to fight fair when the bloke obviously didn't—for it was completely unbalanced to attack a half-dressed woman.

The man clutched at his throat, making a whistling, choking noise as his face turned red and purple. For good measure, Ian punched him powerfully enough that his chin snapped back. The man tottered. First left. Then right. He snatched a knife from his belt, only to try to run. Except he came face-to-face with Fletcher, slashing wildly. Fletcher punched him and sent him spinning back toward Ian. He ducked a wheeling knife swing and connected his fist with the bloke's temples.

He fell.

"Bravo!" cheered a voice Ian should have expected. Lottie stood in the doorway with Sera at her side. Though she still held her glass of champagne, now half-empty, she tapped fingertips against her palm in applause. "Well done, sincerely. Have you spent time boxing?"

"Truly?" His blood pounded in his temples. His fists couldn't unclench. All through him rushed wicked power and awareness of himself as male and Lottie as female. He wanted to take. And she wanted to play games. "You think violence worthy of accolades?"

She shrugged and flicked a glance toward Sera at her side. "When it's for such a worthy cause. Wouldn't you agree?"

"Certainly." Sera nodded. "I appreciate all champions of womanhood, no matter the form."

Behind him, Fletcher had given the woman a robe and was roughly inspecting her face. "I think you've likely got a break along your cheekbone, Melody. It'll be long to heal, at any rate."

"A damn shame." She held still in Fletcher's grasp. "I won't be able to give any of my specials until it's less painful."

"Hurts like a right son of a bitch, doesn't it?" Fletcher asked.

"Language," piped up Sera from the doorway. "You'll slip at the Duchess's ball. Again. We barely got invited back this time."

"You heard my lady wife. Use more respectful language when discussing such woeful matters." His mouth tweaked with a hint of humor. "Now, Melody. What happened to anger the bloke so?"

She shook her head, tucking the robe closer about her midsection. The silken lapels gaped open. Waving a hand through the air drew attention to her ample cleavage. "He called me mummy last time, and spent all his time admiring...*these*. I simply asked if he'd like to again, an innocent-enough question. Surely not worth getting my lip busted over."

Ian's head spun. Rough laughter shook him by the shoulders. He looked at Lottie, who lounged in the doorway sipping champagne as if she hadn't a single care. "This is your world?"

"Part of it. Now do you see?"

He was beginning to understand, at the very least. Why all the truth-laced lies at society parties. Why she put up such fronts and falsities. Part of it had to do with her mother, yes. But in running so hard from her own mother, she'd found an entirely different world full of excitement and life. Her own recklessness didn't seem half so dramatic in such surrounds.

He crossed the room toward her. They were probably entirely too close considering that people encircled them. He touched the back of her neck anyway, that long and lovely length.

"I think I might. I really do think I might."

Chapter Twelve

Lottie hadn't been the one fighting, yet she felt fully absorbed in the moment. Her blood pounded. Shocks zipped down her limbs and turned the back of her neck into a prickling mess. She was caught up in Ian's energy. His gaze locked on hers, and Lottie couldn't look away. Could hardly *breathe*. He was magnetism and power, and he was finally focused on her.

The other times she'd asked him for more touch, more contact, for him to do more to her...they faded. She hadn't known, not really. Not like she did now, when her entire being was absorbed by him. She wanted him, from her toes to her eyes and everything between.

She would do scandalous, delicious things if given half a chance.

When Sera made an inarticulate noise, Lottie thought that she'd read her mind. The smaller woman clapped her hands over her mouth, then darted across to Fletcher. "Fletcher! You've been hurt."

Fletcher looked down. A tiny rivulet of blood escaped his cuff and curled around his thumb. "Well, I'll say. Can't be too bad, I'm guessing."

Sera had gone white. "Don't you be a man about this."

"Can't help it. I am one and all." He shucked off his suit coat. Sure enough, high on his arm was a slice. It didn't look too bad, but Sera swayed.

"Oh, come. Come now." She pulled him toward the doorway and into the hallway. "We'll have to get that fixed immediately. I couldn't stand it if you—"

"I'm not going anywhere, wren." Fletcher smiled down at the top of Sera's head, where she bent over the relatively minor injury. "But I'll get stitched if you like."

"I do like." Worry colored Sera's tone into something higher pitched and strained.

Sera and Fletcher whisked out of the room. Lottie had to step to the side of the doorway as other employees swarmed in. Two women surrounded the whore who'd been attacked, though she seemed well enough to be joking and teasing with them.

"Oh, was nothing," she said on a laugh that Lottie recognized. The cover-up laugh, the one that said maybe it had hurt, but you weren't about to say a word to anyone.

Three burly men pinned the troublemaker. One bound his wrists, another his ankles. They unceremoniously hitched him by the armpits and the legs and set about hauling him away.

"Where will you take him?" Ian asked.

One of them gave a short head shake. "You don't want the answer to that, sir."

"You'll kill him?" He all but vibrated with force, like lightning crackled over him. A storm could explode at any moment.

She wanted the rain to fall on her. She wanted part of that. Subtly, tucking her fingers around his elbow, she pulled him out to the hallway and from the path of busy bees who were cleaning up the mess and assisting the girl. Other prostitutes stood in the doorways of their rooms, lacy wrappers held around their shoulders. Their eyes were wide as they watched the man hustled away to the back stairs.

Ian watched them go as well.

Lottie reached up to touch his jaw and force his face toward her. He was hard, bold, made of heated skin over strength. "Not so far as that. He won't be out of bed for a good six weeks, though."

Ian's head cocked. His eyes were lit up, bright and wicked. "Broken bones take that long to heal?"

"They do." Her mouth was wet. All that attention on her made her feel taller. Stronger. Like she lived fully in her body and ought to take possession of every inch of it.

He encroached on her space. Came closer. His chest brushed over hers until she scooted a half-step backwards. Not from fear or from uncertainty...but because she would wrap her arms around his waist and press herself against him if she didn't soon get a breath free of his scent. "Why did we come here tonight?"

Her tongue rubbed the corner of her mouth. She wanted him there. She wanted him filling all her senses. "Because Patricia was supposed to be here."

"If she comes so often, there's plenty who could identify her."

"Don't you want to see her yourself?"

He put both forearms flat on the wall. She was surrounded by him, which wasn't the same as enfolded. "I'll see her." His voice was a deep growl. "She could have easily been fetched to my new townhouse by the capable men around here."

"I wanted to be there, to ensure you didn't terrify her."

"You're lying again." He touched two fingertips to the base of her throat, where her heartbeat thumped and blood singed her veins. "I can see it. So tell me, Lottie. Why are we both here tonight?"

They were surrounded and yet alone. Inappropriate leaning and talking and nearness would be unacceptable in proper ballrooms and parlors of the aristocratic types. She rubbed the rough plaster wall. She wanted to grab him. Hang on for dear life. "Because I wanted to."

His fingers didn't move from her throat and the tender skin there. He was strong and big. He'd protected a woman who many would have thought beneath him. Decidedly elemental. Her breasts felt abraded against the inside of her corset.

"Nothing's ever so simple with you." His voice rumbled.

"Is that a complaint?"

His mouth tweaked. "The very opposite." When that smile faded, her breath clenched. Something was coming. She couldn't wait. "But it leaves me wondering what's going on."

"Nothing."

His eyes narrowed. His palm spread and folded over the back of her neck. She bent backward against the wall, needing that support. "Is this your attempt to scare me off? I've met your mother—and liked her. Are you trying to prove how wild you are, to drive me away?"

She couldn't help but scoff, even over the heavy excitement that threatened to undo her. Deafening fear washed her hearing white. True and scary, and she didn't like being seen quite so directly. But there was another side to it as well. "There's no need to drive you away. You've not taken what I offer."

He made a rugged and needy noise. "Stop making offers you have no intention of fulfilling."

Her hands curled into his slick, silk lapels. She pushed up on her toes, body sliding up the craggy wall. The rough stucco was trying to hold on to her, tell her what a reckless choice she was making. They were practically in public, of all places.

She couldn't help it. Her need and want had finally flipped over into a life of its own. Her hands traveled up his chest, that expanse that wasn't particularly wide but backed with steady strength she couldn't get enough of. He was hard. Prepared and ready.

Her mouth lifted and met his. He held himself so very rigid, like he'd snap at any moment. But his mouth was hot, wet and mobile. It swept her away to some better place. She'd never been there before, but somehow she knew that it would bring her happiness. Calm. She craved peace that had always been unobtainable.

"I mean it." She breathed the words over his lips.

For a long, strange moment, she wasn't sure what he'd do. It was part of his appeal, never quite knowing which way he'd answer. He surprised her at every turn. Only his single-minded focus on finding his sister's tormenter never wavered. He was so bloody flexible otherwise.

The way his eyes bored into her, the way his lips parted and his chin tipped down...she didn't know what that meant. Which way he'd go, to take or abandon her once again.

Then he broke open, like a wild storm coming to shore. One hand cupped the back of her neck, one grasped her shoulder. His mouth took hers. His kiss was more than enough and not nearly all she wanted. Sandwiched between the wall and his implacable body, she was held still. Held ready.

Not that she was going anywhere.

Her fingers curled around the wrist at her neck. Crisp, manly hair tickled her fingertips. His strength came from the raw accumulation of bone and tendons and ligaments. She wanted to know what he could do to her. Where he could take her.

She needed to know if he could make her forget the lonely stretch of her future.

His kiss was so strong, so hopeful, that she wondered if maybe she had it all wrong. She couldn't marry, and the idea of children turned her into a gibbering mess, but maybe, just maybe, she didn't have to be alone.

At least not forever.

She poured it all into her kiss, the way her body pressed against his. Her arms locked behind his neck. This was everything she hadn't known she'd needed.

A raucous crash and laugh from the level below broke through the haze.

Ian jerked his head up. His eyes were wickedly bright and completely focused on her. Both his hands hooked around her elbows, he walked backwards into the prostitute's room. The very one where only moments ago he'd fought for no reason but what he thought right. He slammed shut the door, leaving them alone. Thoroughly alone.

Lottie gulped. Held down her smile. "Here?"

His eyes flashed wide, and he looked around. The room was small but not unappealing. The space was clean and soft, with lots of white netting and lace. A tiny bloodstain was left in the corner but one had to look close to see it. She had only meant to tease, but concern darkened his features. "I'm sorry. Impatience got the best of me."

Ian knew better. He absolutely did. There were inherent problems with indulging in his wants with regard to Lottie. She wasn't the settling-down sort of girl. At this point, he'd be crushed when she moved on to her next conquest. After all, she had the entire ton on a string.

All that was bad enough. Closing her in a whore's boudoir with him... He was quickly becoming as reckless as Lottie. He wouldn't have the chance to feel her lean curves now.

When she stepped back, then back again, he knew for sure. His hands clenched on air, and disappointment slid down his spine. His brain buzzed at a high pitch that pushed him to the stars, only to let him drop. This was new, and he wasn't sure he liked it.

How did a man ride that kind of energy for a lifetime? He'd be burned to a husk trying to keep up.

Maybe it was for the best that she drew away. Her chin lowered as she looked up at him. Her hands lifted, and he rocked forward on the balls of his feet. Couldn't help it. She reached behind herself, the move pressing her bosom out.

Then her dress gaped, displaying her collarbones and the creamy pale skin that made him want to lick. "I don't mind," she said.

The dress fell away. She gave the tiniest twist of her shoulders, letting the material pool around her waist. Her thumbs hooked in the silk, and she pushed it down over her petticoats.

She was unbelievably pretty and lusciously wanton. Embroidery of rose pink over pale blue covered her corset. It clung to her slim curves, displaying the taut bend of her waist. Her arms were slender but lined with delicate muscles. The straight slashes of her collarbones announced her pride.

She was beauty in her every breath, her every movement. But the way she looked at him over parted lips made him feel like a god. A pagan one who'd rape and pillage if left to his own devices.

Yet his goddamned mouth still wouldn't quiet. "We shouldn't be here."

Her mouth tweaked into a little smile, a real one. "No. We really shouldn't be." She came back closer to him. She stretched toward his ear, and he felt her voice vibrate through him. "But doesn't that make it better?"

"I won't fuck you on a whore's bed." He couldn't keep his hands from clenching over that skinny waist. Under the band of her petticoats, his thumbs brushed the hard points of her pelvic bones. She was lithe. Lean.

She kissed her way down his neck, and Christ her tongue was wicked and bold. "Am I too good for that?" she asked, and the giggle in her voice implied she was teasing him.

"I want you in my bed," he said on a growl. Damn him, but it was true. A shimmering star such as Lottie wasn't meant to be held long, and he didn't want those memories soiled by a prostitute's scent. He wanted Lottie in his world, in his rooms, so that going to bed would mean remembering her.

"Your mother is there."

He turned her, hitching her up so that she sat atop a low dresser that snuggled against the wall. "My mother does not keep city hours." He filled his hands with the pale blue petticoats that had filled out the bottom of her darker blue dress. The legs he revealed were slender and covered with pale stockings. Her delicate ankle bones all but begged for attention. "She'd never notice."

When he sank to his knees before her, her lazy voice turned tight, the last words coming out on a squeak. "My house would be better."

He folded his fingers around the God-crafted piece of art that was her ankle. The length of her leg was beautiful. Something he could hardly believe she was letting him touch. She not only waited patiently, she nudged her knees apart.

The mounded petticoats draped and concealed his prize. Didn't matter. He reached underneath, finding silken skin and the firm resilience of her inner thighs. The gasp that whispered through the room was enough to make him feel frenzied. Rushed. Because the sooner he tasted her, the sooner he'd know her perfection.

"Sera will be looking for me," she whispered. But her hands rested on his shoulders as lightly as hummingbirds. She was flight and excitement and flash. He would taste her even if the place burned around him.

He untied her garter and drew the length of her stocking to her knees, his mouth trailing. Her skin tasted of salt and elemental woman. Behind was a soft, private cove. "We'll leave by the back way." He flashed a grin up at her. "The one you didn't tell me about. She'll never know *when* we left."

Her throat worked on a tight swallow, lines of tendons marking where his teeth wanted to land. To bite and nibble, sucking her taste into his senses. "You're persuasive when you want to be."

Under her skirts, he found the second garter. "You have no idea."

Her touch slid over his shoulders and down his back. She curled over him a little, exploring everything she could reach. "I'd like to find out. Any time you wish to begin."

He smiled against the slender calf muscle he'd exposed, then dragged one slow lick all the way above her thigh. She shivered under his mouth, but the whole time she kept her knees apart.

He wanted her wanton and completely open to him. Her petticoats frothed when he slid both hands underneath. God, her ass was a tight little piece of art. He grabbed it hard, wedging his chest between her knees so that when he drew her forward, she'd stay open. Her grip clenched on his back when her thighs spread.

She breathed his name, and he couldn't help but seize another kiss, no matter what he'd intended. Her mouth was mesmerizing. Fascinating.

He could come back for more, over and over again, and never get enough.

God only knew how he'd feel after he tasted her wettest, most supple places.

"You've pushed and pushed," he said against the small mounds of her breasts above her corset. Every movement of his lips over her delicate curves drew forth a hitching breath from her. "You're about to finally get what you needed. Do you want to know what's coming?"

She nodded. Her hands splayed across the back of his neck with only the lightest sort of pressure. "Tell me."

His hands spanned her waist, then over her hips and up the insides of her thighs. She was tremulous. Whether she had much experience was suddenly called into doubt. Maybe she had, maybe she hadn't. Didn't matter much to him.

The right to touch her was much more important than any concern with who'd gone before. She was no less stunning, no less responsive under his every touch. When he skimmed the slender tendon at the juncture of her thighs, she jumped toward him.

Velveteen, springy curls gave beneath his touch. Her mouth opened on a silent gasp. Those almond-shaped eyes were wider than he'd ever seen. Her hips twitched, and she gave a tiny sound that dove straight into his brain and shook him up.

"Right here," he said. "Your sex. You're already wet for me."

She nodded. Her lips trembled a little. "You did that. Or we did."

He liked that, he really did. His smile spread against her skin. The rake of his teeth over her softness made her surge into his grasp. "Yes, we did. And now I'm going to lick you. This spot. All over." He punctuated his words with a gentle circle of the bud of nerves and mystery that topped her sex.

"Oh, I bet that will feel marvelous," she breathed.

Enthusiasm, thy name was Charlotte. She grasped life with both hands, and if she did so as a lifeline to escape the things she feared, who was he to deny her? Not when it brought him such delicious opportunities.

Despite the thrumming, surging eagerness that tightened his stomach and made his chest burn, he moved slowly. Her skirts were pushed up, out of the way, baring her legs, but he didn't look down. Not yet. He kept his gaze fixed on hers—or maybe it was the other way around because he sure as hell felt held by her.

"After I make you come, I'm going to keep your stockings in my pocket as we leave."

She shook her head as if in automatic reaction. "But why would you do that?"

He smiled against the inside of her thigh. Satin and down. Her skin made him think of absurd things like kittens and clouds. Entirely too childish for a man of his stature and for *this* wicked moment, but they seemed somehow invested with goodness. With a level of happiness impossible to explain.

He drew his tongue over the seam of her lower lips. At the very top, her clitoris peeked through like a tiny pink promise. He set his lips there. Soaking and tasting. The wetness gleaming over her lips was sweet.

Bloody hell, she was intoxicating. He wanted to take her. Fully. His thumbs rubbed up and down her damp, soft lips. Spreading her apart a teeny amount at a time. The first lick burst her flavor over his tongue like sparkling wine. He licked and sucked and took her flesh into his mouth. There was no such thing as too much of Lottie.

And then she moaned. Good. Exactly what he was after. He wanted to make her mindless with desire.

After all, to be on his knees as he indulged in her body, he had to be mindless. Completely so. He wanted her as wrecked as he. One way or the other.

Chapter Thirteen

Lottie was not ignorant about sex. She couldn't afford to be. After all, if babies had made her mother run mad, Lottie needed to avoid them like the plague. In turn she had to know how they were created. Hence several purloined scientific manuals and one rather astounding chapbook that described rather naughty scenarios.

In none of them had there been a hint of this. Searing pleasure that left her adrift and lost in the clouds. Though her hands cupped the back of his head, somewhere along the way she'd gone wandering. Floating outside her body as shocking, tingling pleasure wound through her.

Wet didn't come close to describing his mouth. Nor did heat nor did the fact that he was at turns first gentle, then hard. Firm strokes. Nips that flashed sharp tingles.

He'd found a wicked and reckless spot that made her head jerk back and strange, quiet noises come from her throat because it felt so damn amazingly good. Waves and jolts took her over.

She caught hold of his hair. She tried to pull his head back, away. She didn't know what to do with the bursting sensations rocking through her. But he wouldn't be moved. He licked straight up her center.

His thumbs stroked and circled her. Pleasure at top and bottom. His mouth stayed open and wet and sucking.

Then she switched, pushing him closer to her body. She was not letting him go under any circumstances. She needed whatever he dangled out of reach. Her fingers twisted and tightened in his hair. She hooked her knees over his shoulders.

He was solid. Steady. Though he looked slender and elegant in his proper suits, underneath there was a man who could take her bare heels digging into his back. He shifted in a subtle rocking rhythm that matched the way her blood surged and released.

Her breathing locked down, slipped away. She stopped panting long enough that multicolored stars bloomed behind her eyes. She was sensation and no more, all wrought by his touch.

She cracked open into a million sparks. The joy rocked out from her middle and washed over her. Taking over her.

She felt *good*. Which seemed so unsubstantial, so insufficient, but it was true. Her body, her mind and her soul were bound together in happy joy that took her completely in a tingling surge. She was right with herself for a little while.

She eased back into her limbs, finding herself more comfortable than she'd been in ages. Ian helped by lengthening his licks and softening his assault to gentle kisses. Her muscles and bones fit together perfectly. A draught from the badly fit window frame tickled her soles.

He rubbed his wet mouth against the inside of her thigh, leaving a streak. "There. I don't know about you, but I feel much calmer now."

Her spine melted and melted until she leaned against the wall. She giggled in a way unlike her. "I don't see why. You were the one doing all the work."

"And reaping all the rewards." His eyes were hot, fired with arctic ice.

"I could argue that point, but I'd do myself no favors." Her hands curled in the heaps of her petticoats, her fingers gone slightly numb. She felt less like herself than she ever had before, but also strangely *more*.

"How so?" But he didn't give her a chance to answer. He stood, leaning in toward her. His mouth tasted like something more sweet and slick than before. She realized with a tiny startle that it was her own flavor. She should have been appalled. Instead, she licked the inside of his bottom lip.

He liked that. Or she assumed so, since he gave a throaty growl and nibbled at her top lip.

She was smiling when she pulled back. "Because if I convince you that I've the best of it and you're wrong, you may decide not to repeat the act."

He gripped her knees, thumbs gently rubbing over the tender flesh of her thighs. He cocked an eyebrow at her, that smile tucking up only on the left. "You could try. I'm not likely to be convinced. You taste like a lick of heaven."

Heat flared across her cheeks in a blush. "You've no need to talk so rough."

"This from the wild child?" He drifted close enough to brush his mouth over the column of her throat. "I feel like I've won a prize."

She pushed him and slid down from the dresser she'd perched on. She scooped up her dress and had to twist the sleeves into place from where her impatience had flipped them. As if her dedication would keep away the embarrassment, she kept her gaze pinned on the pale purple fabric. "I'm still allowed to be offended."

"You are. If you actually feel so." He leaned against the dresser, watching her pull the dress on as if she were there for his amusement. His every look stoked her flames higher. "But this time at least it was only an act. And therefore a surprising one."

He was completely wrong, but she couldn't make herself simply *tell* him. In truth, she was disappointed he didn't already know after what they'd just shared. She presented him with her biggest, brightest smile and her wide eyes. Her fingers flew up the line of her buttons. They sealed up as if nothing had happened. As if she didn't still tingle and the inside of her thighs weren't damp under her petticoats. "Our whole world is one big act. It's what makes everyone get along."

His head tilted. "Haven't you anyone to whom you tell the whole truth?"

She wanted to be able to say yes. She wasn't without friends entirely. Sera and Victoria were her heart, her closest. But she'd never told them all of it. She'd mentioned how terrified she was and how much she worried about her mother. Certainly that.

She'd never mentioned the anger. The guilt. The way she got almost a little *relieved* when her mother entered one of her sad periods, because it meant she'd take to her bed and not embarrass anyone for a while.

And how very ugly an emotion that was.

She held her smile up so tightly that her cheeks pinched. The corners of her eyes felt tense. "You must be a nicer person than I, if you can reveal every single thought and emotion."

He came close enough to trace his knuckles over her rounded cheeks. She didn't want him to see through her. Nothing else would leave her as vulnerable. "It's got nothing to do with how nice I am and everything to do with how much I trust my friends. My family."

"Tell me who you talk to." Her voice was raw.

"My mother." His smile was endearing, and she wanted to taste it again, but it didn't seem right where their conversation had wandered. "And my sister. I know, it's unbearably saccharine, but there you have it. I've two close friends from school as well. I don't see them nearly enough. Usually for hunting trips in the fall."

She wanted a part of that life. It spiked through her, washing away the experience he'd given her. This moment wasn't meant to be kept. Not the miraculous things he knew. Not the kindness and gentleness with which he spoke of his family.

She was jealous. She was so very envious she thought she might lose her grip on her senses. How close she trod, everything simmering beneath the surface. Barely in control, layered over with bright smiles.

She'd take him. She'd have him. Full use of his body, however she liked. Because he'd be the closest she ever got to that kind of indulgence and connection. Denying herself that taste seemed ridiculous. Should she walk alone through the difficult world without ever having experienced it once?

She had never been the self-sacrificing type. There was no reason to start now.

But there certainly was business to see to first. She shook her skirts smooth and peeked into a smoky mirror to tuck back her hair. Her tumbled curls hid a wealth of reckless activity, since they never looked neat and orderly. "On with it, shall we?"

He presented his arm. "Tell me," he said as they stepped out onto the landing. "What will we do if Patricia makes an appearance this evening?"

A sea of heads and cawing laughter and round faces with eyes turned red by drink made up the crowd beneath the banister. Cards were shuffled, markers passed. This was the sort of world she knew and yet one she didn't. She surveyed it all with an easy assurance that no matter what happened, she'd have the man whose arm she held at the moment. She'd feel the strength currently under her fingers turn into a force that would leave her mindless. Again.

"At this point? Whatever is fastest, if I have my way. The better to leave quickly."

How strangely surreal this all was. Ian looked down on the crowd with a sense of detachment that lifted him above the rabble. Except his was pure luck. He was no better than the rest of them, but for narrow accident of birth and dint of will. Parlaying his father's beginnings, he'd turned a fairly profitable mine into a hefty income for what remained of his family.

What was the point if not to build more family?

He wasn't any better than the people who gambled and drank below. He was luckier. Throwing that away would be foolish.

If anything, he should be looking to marry.

Not dallying in a whore's rented room. He hadn't stooped so far as to play with those so much less fortunate than him. The woman on his arm was dazzling. She was an amazing example of English womanhood, including her recklessness. That edge of hers conquered nations and made the empire grand.

Now, when she'd been an orgasmic puddle not ten minutes ago, she stood with her chin up and her spine a casual, shallow curve of attitude and arrogance in a feminine package.

He was coming to rather like the combination.

"Fastest," he said, drawing the word into a slow promise. "I'm curious. Have you somewhere better to be?"

She kept her face turned outward, toward the crowd. "Under you."

She'd have felt his response in the full-body jolt that wedged out from his ribs. He'd almost been able to forget his body. He was hard, yes. That became almost secondary since he knew he'd receive relief eventually. Besides, he sometimes liked the slow torture of unrequited excitement. Best to revel.

Not this time. He wanted. Now. He folded his hand flat over hers where it curled around his biceps.

"You think it's so simple as that?" He kept his gaze averted as well. His lurking laughter grew in direct counterpoint to the pull of his lust. "You've tried me before and I turned you down."

"True." She leaned enough that the side of her breasts rubbed against his fingertips. "But that was before you tasted me."

"True," he echoed.

Her mouth curved. Her neck was a white column of tendons and softness mixed together. Locks of red hair curled around her shoulders. "You see?"

At this moment, he couldn't remember one single reason not to indulge and take her. "You're forgetting one thing."

"Am I?"

He liked her. So damn much. "We've nowhere to go."

"Let me take care of that. I already told you my home was best."

He almost laughed. Because really, what in the name of God was going on here? Was he seducer or the one being seduced? Maybe a bit of both. He'd let a little slip of a girl wrap him around her finger.

His body coiled at the memory of her under his mouth. Silken flesh. Tender skin. Her responsive moans and the way she'd clutched at his hair. "Now?" he asked hoarsely.

"In a..." She broke off. Her eyes narrowed. "Near the front of the room. Near the faro table. Do you see?"

A woman stood there, facing the dealer. From his angle, Ian could only see the back of her head, where her hair was twisted into a tight knot. The gaslights shone orange off what appeared to be light brown hair. He snapped from indulgence to awareness. "Is that her?"

Lottie shook her head, nibbling on her bottom lip. "I can't tell."

"Come." He took off, dragging Lottie along behind him. His grip slid down her arm, forearm, wrapping his hand around her. Their fingers laced together as they hit the bottom of the stairs.

The press of bodies was ridiculous. Too close. They could barely breathe, much less track the slip and slide of one person. Ian was tall enough to look above most of the crowd, but the problem was Patricia was short. The woman stepped to the side as a giant bruiser angled across Ian's line of sight, toward the bar.

Frustration boiled out of his throat in a rough noise. "I don't see her."

Lottie muttered something as she craned upwards on the tips of her slippers. "I don't either. I do see..." She shoved two fingers between her lips. The whistle she gave could have burst his eardrums. But it was effective.

Heads swiveled as if spun on pikes. Their mouths were as slack as if they'd been beheaded and stuck on a stick as well. Wide eyes took in the whistling lady like she was a freak at a circus.

She also got the attention of one of the big, burly guards near the front door. He arrowed in on her, but she pointed. "Her! Grab that one. Red shawl and the flower in her hair."

He darted left. With no visible regret, he strong-armed a skinny gambler to the side. As he grabbed the woman by the shoulders, he scowled fiercely, as if the task he'd been assigned were nothing less than protecting the Queen. "Got 'er," he roared.

There were only a dozen feet between Ian, Lottie and the guard with the woman, but it took stupidly long to get through the people who packed the space like cows. The thick smell of sweat and sticky alcohol scented the air. "Come along," Ian said. "Clear out, clear out."

As soon as they were within reaching distance of the woman, Ian knew. Even before the guard turned her around.

It wasn't Patricia. This woman was of similar build and mannerisms, but not at all similar features. Her mouth was full and blowsy and her nose hooked. Her gaze flicked back and forth between Ian and Lottie. She said nothing, cowering in fear.

Disappointment filled his skull with the thudding beat of his pulse. He hadn't realized, not really, how fully wrapped up he'd allowed himself to become in the idea that this would be over quickly. That he would soon be free.

The question remained, free to do what? He hadn't exactly planned on devoting a whole season to displaying Etta to best advantage, but it certainly seemed more pleasant than chasing some low woman all the way across London and back. His hands fisted.

"Damn it," Ian muttered.

"And we made too much fuss." Lottie's face pinched. She turned away, looking out at the crowd, and this time they were all staring at her.

There was little animosity coming from them, beyond the general displeasure that they weren't gaming at the moment. But they'd *noticed*. They knew Lottie and Ian as not part of their type. A tall, skinny bloke with a red kerchief tied around his neck slicked his gaze over Lottie from head to toe. An avaricious gleam dwelled in his eyes.

Ian coiled his arm around Lottie's shoulders. "Come on. It's our turn to get out of here."

"We're under Fletcher's roof. Nothing will happen to us." She came along with him anyway and liked the way she leaned into his shoulder.

They found Sera in the back room. Her hands were filled with linen cloths and a steaming bowl of water. "Gone so soon?"

"We made a spectacle of ourselves," Lottie said with her usual good cheer. Ian wasn't the only one who could see through it because Sera's mouth knotted into a pinch. "We'll have to be off now."

The ladies said their farewells, and Sera took a moment to whisper in Lottie's ear. Probably something about not trusting men one hardly knew or that Lottie ought to be on her guard.

Once they climbed into the carriage and the silence wrapped around them like comfort and temptation, Lottie looked at him with a tiny smile curving her lips. "You're coming home with me, aren't you?"

He shouldn't. Not by any means. There was indulgence and then there was recklessness, and it seemed that Lottie was rubbing off on him. He let his hand delve beneath the curling, soft mass of her hair and felt the delicate dip at the base of her skull where two of his fingertips fit perfectly.

She leaned into the touch. Her eyes drifted half-closed as she looked out at him from under her lashes. They were pale in color but thick. A study in contrasts, like her.

The words came from some deep place that he hadn't known he had. It was also a place that he might come to like. Especially if it came with indulgences like Lottie. "Yes. I'm coming home with you."

Chapter Fourteen

Lottie's groomsmen knew when bringing her home from possibly non-Society-approved locales, they were to take her directly to the back of the house. From the mews, she slipped quietly through the gate and the garden.

Night had always been Lottie's friend.

Even if it weren't a matter of concealing her comings and goings, she'd always liked the way the shadows slithered around the small garden at the back of their house. Flowerbeds closed up at night, hiding away their secrets, but that didn't necessarily mean they were less beautiful for being knotted buds. She'd spent hours there in the dark.

It was safe. She wasn't obligated to sit with her mother or to think about her or to be a good daughter or good friend. When alone, she was no one other than herself.

It was easier that way.

Walking through the garden with Ian trailing behind her like a silent wraith was different. Her steps whispered over the gravel path, but his were absolutely nonexistent. She knew he was behind her by the weight of his attention. She had absolute knowledge that he focused on her.

He'd be hers soon.

She could hold him, so long as she could hold herself together.

The heady rush of power made her float. Like she were both above and in the moment. She let her fingers trail behind, held out. He took her hand. It wasn't only the touch, which sent liquid anticipation trembling up her arms to center in her chest. His hands were finely wrought, his fingers elegant. It was the fact that she'd known he'd reach for her. That she hadn't had to look back or to taunt him.

She'd offered and he'd taken.

How simple and how completely complicated.

The back door, the dark-painted wood slab that opened on the bowels of the kitchens, had been left unlocked for her as it always was. Her liberal control of the household meant that she was obeyed to the letter. The two scullery maids curled up in front of the fireplace to tend the flames through the night had come from Lottie's school and before that a tinwork factory.

The girl on the right rolled over and lifted her head, looking at Lottie, who put a finger to her lips. Eloise had lost her smallest finger in a press and worshipped Lottie as the person who'd gotten her free of that world. She nestled back into her pallet. The blankets twitched over her head in an intentional move. She'd say nothing.

Once Lottie and Ian were in the hallway again, Ian pulled her close. Their hands, still laced together with warmth passing from palm to palm, were tucked behind his back. There was strength in the heavy curve of muscle barely hidden by his proper coat.

The amazing part was that she'd see all of him soon. She meant to touch and take as she liked.

Except it appeared he might be having second thoughts. A single lamp glowed at the other end of the hallway, where it opened on the foyer. Where they stood, dark shadows clung and draped along his features. They turned him into something different than the open, honest man he'd been. "Are you sure this is wise?"

His skin smelled like spice. That would be all hers soon as well. She shrugged, though it felt almost as if her body would buckle if she didn't get her way soon. "Which part?"

"Here. Your family's house?"

He was rather cute when uncertain and at sea. "You'll see."

She led him up the back stairs, the narrow ones that the servants usually kept as their domain. The fingertips of one hand trailed along plaster walls, and Ian kept the other. His grip never slipped from hers. She would know him. That closeness. That warmth. His breath slid across the back of her neck, shifting a lock of hair.

When he hesitated on what should have been the floor for bedrooms, she kept going almost into the attics, where the servants shared rooms. Below was the level that once was a nursery and playroom.

The landing was small, the hallway truncated. The stairs split and turned to keep going upward, and to the right was a single door. She fished a key out of her reticule and unlocked it.

"Here," she said as she stepped in and lit a lamp. Her reticule spun across the petite table she kept inside the doorway. She shrugged off her cloak and draped it over the back of a gold-leaf decorated chair. "This is my...space. For lack of a better word."

"How interesting." He let go of her hand and wandered into the open area of her room. "Where did this come from?"

"Well, when they built the house, there were walls put up. Floors between stories. Windows here and there. The usual." Her mouth stayed bent in a smile, but her fingers twisted in the front of her skirts.

This was...strangely personal. Very few people came to her rooms. Fanny tended to her, but she stayed toward the front quarter, which could generally be called Lottie's dressing area.

That was the problem. The whole area was rather amorphous once compared to most rooms and buildings. This whole stretch...it was open. Wide. There had once been five rooms along here, but the walls had been removed, and now only a series of archways broke up the areas. The one room extended the full length of the building. The front section had dressers and armoires and standing closets in which Lottie stored her clothing. Past that was stacked with books and couches and a chaise lounge perched beneath the window.

Her hands clenched the sides of her skirts, staining them with salt from her damp hands. But she couldn't look at the pale pink blanket spread over her bed or the darker rose curtains hanging from the half tester without thinking of Ian in that space. How very masculine he'd be against those pale colors.

He hadn't spotted the bed. He was wandering about with curiosity writ on his features, much as he had when he'd seen her mother's room downstairs. "Don't be intentionally obtuse," he said.

She moved past him and threw herself down into her favorite chaise. She loved the crushed velvet and well-padded back that stretched halfway down the side. Resting her chin on a fist, she watched him. "But I like teasing you."

He slid a look at her out of the corner of his eyes. A small slice of the London sky gleamed through the window. Half haze, half dark night swirling together. London never slept. He pushed aside the gauzy curtains. "You don't exactly live...normally, do you?"

She was sure he didn't mean that to hurt, but it did, more than she would have liked. Her chest clenched. "You'd be bored if I did."

"Maybe." He sank to the end of the chaise, beside her knees. The way he sat pinned her skirts. She tried to shift and could only move a few inches. "Tell me how this room came about."

"Mama, of course." She shouldn't like that he'd immobilized her. She certainly wouldn't if it had seemed like accidental oafishness.

When he braced his hands on each side of her head against the end of the chaise and leaned in, she knew. He was unaware of nothing. Every inch of her skin, every inch of his body, filled his mind. How they would align. He wanted her still. Wanted her held down.

She shuddered. Her breathing coiled in her throat.

"I doubt your mama held a hammer or a paintbrush."

She could hardly believe they were having this discussion with his mouth only a fraction away from hers. She wanted to be kissed.

She settled for petting back locks of his hair that eased across his forehead. Her lips parted a tiny bit. Wonder made her tentative and appreciative.

"This was supposed to be Mama's studio. She directed all the changes. The windows along the back were put in specially. But once it was done and paid for, she declared it not right. She couldn't create here."

"So you took it over." His eyes were a brilliant blue. He let his arms fold, his elbows tucking down and bringing him closer. His mouth was near enough that his air brushed over her lips. "Creating your own world in what she left behind."

She didn't like the way that sounded. Didn't want to spend her life following in her mama's wake. The very opposite was her intention, after all. She'd left behind any dream of the existence most would expect. Between the school and her friends, she'd created something new that was good enough for her. She didn't like that maybe her whole self was wrapped up in her mother's shadow.

Her fingers slipped around the back of his neck and delved into his hair. She liked the strands, their soft and crisp texture. But it was the intimacy of the gesture. She couldn't remember the last time she'd touched another's hair or felt warm scalp. Never, probably.

She kept her voice contained and quiet. "I always take what I want."

Tonight, that meant him. She tightened her grip in his hair and pulled his mouth down to hers. Then kissed him.

Ian knew what it was like to kiss a woman. He'd done it plenty of times, with results that were more than lovely.

He wasn't simply kissing Lottie. Such words were inadequate and cheapening. He was *kissing* her, she was kissing him, and they came together in a way that was unlike anything he'd experienced.

He wrapped his hands around her jaw, feeling it work under his touch. Her lips were pliable as he drew her essence into his senses. She was sweetness and desperation wound together. She melted under his every touch, then launched. Her body begged as her mouth was taken and given.

With his eyes shut, Ian knew how she looked. So exquisitely beautiful he'd be transported to a level he'd never dared touch before. She was gorgeous. Lovely.

Frightened.

He could feel it in the way she trembled. But when he tried to pull away, she made an impetuous noise. Her fingers wrenched hard enough to cause a flinch of pain. The skin of her cheeks was more satiny than any he'd touched before. She was plush and tender, except when she was mean. Her teeth nestled into his bottom lip.

He hissed. His hand rested in the bend of her jaw to neck, where bones met resilience. "That hurt."

"I know," she whispered in a husky voice. "You loved it, don't lie." Her eyes were so heavy-lidded he wondered if she really saw him. He wanted her to. He wanted to know her and he wanted her to see him inside and out. He cupped her small breast. Her eyes flew open. "So bold."

"You love it, don't lie," he said in an intentional echo.

"So true."

She was wearing entirely too many clothes. He set about unbuttoning and untaping and untying her. She wiggled and shifted, eventually letting him draw the dress down her body. A ridiculous amount had been paid for that tumble of silk for it to end up on the floor, but Ian didn't give a goddamn. He pulled her petticoats off next and they ended up…somewhere.

Her legs were long and slender. Gently muscled. Her knees bent, and graceful toes dug into the cushion next to his hip. She watched him from under those contradictory lashes. "You look at me like I'm something you've never seen before."

He reached out then. Held her thigh in one hand. She had magic in her. Maybe it was that such an accumulation of angles in her sharp shoulders and the jut of her hipbones could turn into something still lushly female. "You're amazing."

She cut her gaze toward the window, her mouth tweaking in good humor. "I'm attractive enough. I've never lacked assurance of that. But you…you look at me like I'm something more than human."

"Are you?"

Her legs were works of art, and he could hardly believe he was petting them. Her knees pressed together, more coy than shy. The corset she wore was both delicate and ornate. Layered with embroidery, it skimmed over her body like another lover. "I'm just a girl."

His thumbs delved behind her knees, testing the fragile hollow. She was slightly damp with anticipation and a thin sheen of sweat. "A woman."

"Yes." Her knees parted a whisper. "Will you be disappointed? If I'm nothing perfect? Nothing worthy of the way you're looking at me?"

"You've little worry on that score." He trailed smooth, slow strokes over her thighs and the brush of curls at the top. She shuddered. "You really are perfect."

Her fingernails dug into his neck. She pulled him closer. "You're an idiot."

"You don't see yourself as I see you." He tasted her mouth again, and all he could think of was the way her quim had tasted, the way she'd been so sweetly enticing. The way she'd shaken apart. How much freer would she be here, in her own room? "You're exquisite."

"Shut up and kiss me."

"Gladly."

He swept his mouth over hers, pushing her into the downy cushions of the lounge. She sank down, her curls spreading over the velvet. She melted and he loved it. Wanted to take and claim. Her skin was pale enough to be marked, his for the owning.

Part of him was tempted to take the corset off her. But it framed her body and her slender waist with such precision. He wrapped both hands around her ribs, holding, caressing. Squeezing tight. Beneath his grip, beneath the corset, she was something new. A wild creature who twisted and stroked her hips upward. Her wantonness waited to be unleashed.

But maybe he'd always been waiting for her.

Her hands found purchase in the front of his shirt, and for a second he thought she might try to rip it off him. Then she wound her fingertip through the material and yanked her mouth away from his. "Off. I want this off. I hate it."

"It's a shirt." He felt his mouth slide up into a half smile and was astonished. The heavy lust that slammed through his veins and turned his cock into a hot pipe ought to have seared away all other emotions. But whenever he was with Lottie, too many emotions whirled together for a single one to stand out.

"It's between us," she muttered. "I want it *gone*."

Chapter Fifteen

How quickly Ian yanked his shirt off over his head. Lottie filled her hands with the stretch of his back, the muscles there that shifted and twitched as he eased down into her arms. She liked being swept up by him. Being absorbed by him.

Her hands coasted up to the back of his head, and her neck fell backwards against the arm of the couch. He overwhelmed her. His mouth opened across her shoulder, the angle of her collarbones. His fingertips sank into her hips, and he ran his thumbs over her flesh. Tingles and jolts dove beneath her skin.

The weight of his body on hers added an extra layer of sensitivity. She wasn't trapped by him. She was surrounded.

Her knees slipped apart with no thought behind it. She had a need to open and take him in. He still wore his trousers, but the warm expanse of his chest pressed against hers. Inside her corset her nipples tightened.

He must have known. Strange magic rolled through the air and turned the breath in her lungs hot and humid. With bold, stroking petting, he eased up her side, then traced across the delicate stitching of her bodice. The embroidered satin there barely covered her nipples, and he wasn't stopped. He touched and claimed.

She clenched the back of his head, but she didn't know what she wanted until his head dipped. Dark, dark hair eased toward her. He delved into her corset, scooping her breast. The rough touch made her whole body curl toward him. When he sucked the tip into the warm, wet haven of his mouth, a wicked kind of cry eased out of her throat.

Her hands framed the sides of his skull. Her lips parted on more of those breathy cries. She sounded wanton. She sounded completely abandoned toward pleasure. Like a spinning-wild version of herself.

She adored every reckless cry, every tingling sensation coming from the pulling draw of his mouth on her flesh. He put teeth to her skin. Bit meanly enough that she jolted. She flushed.

If anything, she wanted to be taken. Filled. Her hips surged toward his but found only the wool of his trousers. She tangled her big toe in the brace that he'd snapped down from his shoulders to dangle about his lean hips. Tugged on it. "This. These." She hardly made sense. How wonderful.

"My trousers?" he muttered against her skin, and the words went through her like a bell that rang her into existence.

"Those."

"Suppose you hate them too?" He flicked a gaze upward and smiled.

She felt positively filthy and marvelously exposed. She scratched over the back of his shoulders, and he must have liked that or maybe he hated it, because he shuddered and pressed closer to her. Suddenly it didn't matter because his hard flesh pressed between her legs.

Even through the barrier of the trousers—that yes, she did hate—his touch did something. Something exciting. Mind exploding.

She gave a soft, "Oh!"

"Maybe you don't hate them after all?" He eased his touch over the mounded top of her breast. She shivered.

"I do," she whispered. How much further could this go? She didn't know which way to push, to grab, to take. "I hate them desperately, because if it's this good now, I can't begin to imagine how much better it could be."

"You're so eager." He ducked his head again, his mouth slicking over her nipple. She clutched his shoulders. "I do like that."

"Good, good," she found herself chanting. "Now more. Now take them off."

He laughed as he reached between them, unfastening his trousers. His knuckles glanced over her flesh, and she knew it was intentional because as soon as he was done, he turned his hand about. He cupped the tenderness between her legs. She gasped. Those long, elegant fingers tucked into her.

She had no idea. All the books she'd read, all the investigations she'd made—none of them had truly left her informed. Not about how it'd feel. Not about how she'd shake with pleasure and anticipation. She almost didn't notice when Ian leaned back into her.

Almost.

Hot, warm skin brushed the insides of her thighs. Ian's legs were dusted with crisp hair that abraded gently. A long, firm weight Lottie assumed must be his member nudged her, beside his hand. Still his fingers delved and ringed the explosive spot at the top of her sex to pull forth cries that left her throat raw.

She opened her eyes and found him watching her. Closely. He was alight with something she hardly knew how to name.

"I should wait," he said in a tone of voice that sounded as rank and rough as she felt. "But I don't think I can."

She folded her forearms behind his neck and hauled herself high enough to assault his mouth. This was no kiss, it was hiding and running and taking. She bit down on his lip. Wrenched a grunt from him that went straight to her body and turned her inside out. "Don't you dare stop."

"I'm not. Fuck, I'm not."

He shoved a finger inside her. Her neck arched back, and she keened, but she never took her eyes off his. Let him see. Let him know how far he took her and how far she intended to take him. His thumb pressed down on the spot that seemed connected right to her white-fire feelings.

She had never felt so good and yet so incomplete. "More, please."

He added a second finger, and it wasn't enough. Her head tossed across the arm of the chaise, and she suddenly let go of him. She reached behind herself enough to hold the carved arm. Her fingernails sank into the wood, but it still didn't make her feel solid and real.

She was both lost and happy.

"Please," she said on a moan. "Please, please." The word turned into a chant, into candied begging. She'd have added more, but she didn't know what she wanted. What she was looking for.

"Here?" He petted those two fingers inside her sheath, tempting and teasing. He did magical things with those elegant fingers. His mouth was a wicked curve until he hid it against the turn of her neck. The drag of his teeth over her throat added layer over layer of feeling. "Here? More here? In this sweet cunt?"

The raw word made her jolt, wicked and hot. Still she agreed. "Yes. There. I want you there."

"As it will be." He took his fingers from her, sucking wet juices off each in slow succession. He surged up from the chaise, and good Christ in heaven, for a long, terrifying moment she thought he was done. Leaving her. Her hands spasmed on the cool wood. "Come on."

He gathered her up in his arms. She was light as air and clouds, the way she'd always wanted to be. With her hands framed along the sides of his neck, she kissed him as he walked. He set her down across the wide expanse of her bed.

She folded up on her elbows. Her abrupt intake of breath was completely involuntary. For the first time, she could see the dense muscles that covered his chest and stretched down to his lean waist. A line of dark hair trailed from his navel, then widened to spread and circle his length. Full and erect, his member strained toward his taut stomach.

She ringed him with trembling fingers. "What do you call it?"

"Pardon? Do you think it separate from me?" He edged one knee up onto the bed, next to her hip. His smile was out to play again. "Should I have named it Richard?"

Her eyes narrowed. "There's a joke in there somewhere, isn't there? No. Tell me the word. I know penis, but that seems very bloodless."

He grunted, and she couldn't tell if it was some sort of regret or from the way she stroked over his satin-smooth skin. She let her thumb play and explore, rubbing a thicker ridge up the underside and across a delicate web beneath the swollen head. "No more."

His hand over hers stilled those motions. He gripped her shoulder, and he tried gently to push her flat, but she wouldn't go. "Not until you tell me. A woman ought to know what she has in her hand."

"You're about to have a lot more in your hand than you expected," he said with a groan. "But it's a cock. Or a prick or staff or dick."

She gave it a small squeeze and liked the way he shoved into her hand. "I like cock. I like your cock, in particular."

"Jesus, woman," he couldn't help but say. He didn't know whether to laugh or to cry or to simply fuck her blind.

The third option. Easy choice.

Her mouth tasted like honey, and they traded her flavor back and forth. He wanted her warmth and her tightness. Their tongues played in abandon. Still she held on to his cock.

He didn't mind because her small forays and delicate advances made him shudder as pleasure made him mindless.

Maybe this wasn't right. Lottie was a woman of stature and out of Ian's reach for any sort of long affair or relationship. But he wasn't about to turn her down.

He'd be the insane one. More insane than her reckless mother ever seemed.

Holy Christ, he couldn't believe they were doing this in Lottie's home. Cold shock trickled down his spine. "Where's your father?"

Her eyebrows flew upward. "Really? Here? Now you mention him?"

He shrugged, but then had to swallow down the clench in his throat when her grip tightened. "It's a valid concern."

"Why is that?"

Folding one arm behind her back, he levered her down. She went slowly, unwillingly, so he flipped them. If she wished to sit up, she could do it from atop him. She gave a small gasp, but then her lips bent into a ridiculously wicked smile.

Her hands flattened on his chest, below his ribs. God, that was good. She was his little vixen. She grinned down at him.

It seemed wrong all of a sudden that her hair was still up. He drew out each pin, one by one. Red locks tumbled around her shoulders. A long skein slipped over her skin and pooled at the edge of her pale blue corset. He framed her breasts through the material, then traced his touch up farther.

"I'm worried about your father's proximity because I'd like to make you scream with pleasure. One could say it's a goal of mine." His gaze flicked back up to hers, and she'd never looked away from him. Her fingernails dug lightly into the center of his chest. Her pinkies scratched near his nipples. His hips jolted upward. His cock notched alongside his wet prize. So near. So bloody *almost*.

She must have liked that, because her eyes eased shut and her lips parted. "Goals are admirable."

His hands coasted up the long length of her thighs. She was everything lean and gorgeous. Between her legs she was delicate and damp. Her lower lips spread over his cock, leaving him breathless. The tiny twist of her shoulders and twitch of her hips worked through his entire body.

They were together. Skin to skin. Any closer and he'd be inside her. His hands involuntarily clenched on her hips.

He couldn't stop touching her. Skimming, long touches that took in the beauty that was her every movement. He didn't want to stop. Why would he, when he had any such indulgence available to his whims? He rather thought he'd die of frustration if he couldn't be inside her soon.

He wrenched her pink and blue corset down far enough for her breasts to rest above. With little tweaks and pets, he brushed over her nipples. Wet his fingers and rolled the berry-tight tips until she gasped.

He loved the way she kept smiling down on him. Between her moans and her gasps, her default mouth position was a smile. She'd more than enough happiness to share. "I've goals aplenty. Is it safe to demonstrate?" he asked.

She laughed enough that the feeling rolled from him to her, between her thighs and her soft quim and the hard length of his cock. So good. He pinched her nipples tighter.

"I promise it is," she said on a breathy laugh. "He's in the country. Still. Mother is drugged for the night. It's safer that way. Being alone on this floor…" She leaned down, down, until her mouth hovered over his. Her lips skimmed a delicate touch at the base of his throat, but then she licked a luscious path along his flesh. Her head tucked under his chin. "I've danced naked in the moonlight and no one has ever known."

He made some sound that was more breath and grunt than word, a full exhalation of air in order to make room for need. He could imagine her loveliness dancing in white-gold moonlight.

Indeed, when she eased back upward, she moved into a shaft of light that poured through the window. With her hands exploring the width of his chest, her eyes unfocused and her hair around her shoulders, she looked like a depraved goddess. Otherworldly.

"I'd have liked to see that."

Her mouth curved into a wicked tease. "I shouldn't have done it."

Her hips slipped and stroked. His cock tucked naturally between her lower lips, seeking her moisture and heat. He held her hips too tight. In the morning, she'd have bruises on her pale skin. "We all do lots of things we shouldn't."

"And you? Am I something you shouldn't do?" She always asked the immeasurably important questions in an intentionally casual tone. This one was tossed out into the space between them as lightly as a flower petal. But there was a hold to her spine that let him know she needed to know. That it mattered to her.

He pushed upward until he was sitting with her on his lap. He kept his grip on her hips, and his fingertips pushed under the material of her corset. Beneath, her skin was silk. She kept her gaze away from his, though he rather liked the way she was looking at his chest and shoulders.

They were chest to chest, but not quite. He finally regretted the corset between them. Nuzzling his mouth across the space behind her jaw, he let his words slide into the skeins of her hair. "Do you feel my hands on your back?"

She nodded. Her arms wrapped around his shoulders, and she combed through his hair. The touch was soft. "Yes."

"Do you feel how they shake?"

"I do."

Even shaking, they were able to untie her corset. He moved slowly, so slowly that their breathing melded together. His hard cock rubbed between them, throbbing. Waiting. But silencing her fears was incredibly more important.

"That's because of you. Because I'm afraid of ballocksing this up. And because I want you so bad that I almost feel as if I'm forgetting steps."

Lorelie Brown

"Forgetting steps? What does that mean?"

He pulled the corset away, and she was so very pretty that he thought he might lose track of where he was. There were long red lines on her stomach and her ribs where the seams had pressed into her. He traced two fingers up and down the lines. Lottie and Ian curved together and apart, a wave of movement.

He kissed the edge of her shoulder, the bone there covered with tissue-thin skin. So many contradictions caused her to become a lie in her own skin.

He wanted to find her truths. With every shiver and shudder and the muffled noises she made, he thought he might be getting closer. Or maybe he was getting closer to some fundamental truth about himself. He hardly knew.

"There's a certain order to these kinds of proceedings. Steps that are usually followed." Putting together a sentence was incredibly difficult with an armful of gorgeous womanhood.

"And we're going about it all wrong?"

He skimmed down her sides, following bone by bone until he reached the taut line of her muscles. His thumbs met down her center and dipped into her navel to ring that shallow bowl. Then lower. He rubbed over her lips first, which added an extra layer of pleasure to the pressure across his cock. She gave a tiny mewl.

When he delved between to catch her clitoris, he took her mouth with his. He wanted to taste the noises pouring from her mouth to his. A promise he was doing well.

He kissed her jaw, her neck. Licked her earlobe into his mouth and caught that tender flesh between his teeth. The whole time he stroked and pulsed over her clitoris, that bit of sensation that made her writhe in his arms. She sank sharp nails into his back, and he grunted. He wanted that mean bite, that assurance.

"You tell me," he finally said once he pulled his mouth from her skin. How hard it was to pull away that small amount. "Does it feel like we're going about this wrong?"

She shook her head, resting her forehead against his shoulder as she gasped. "No. Not at all."

"Some might think I'm being indulgent." He punctuated his words with steady rhythm through her wetness. His fingers slipped and slid around his cock, and it was nowhere near what he wanted. "Some might think I should take you. Shove my cock in you. Here." He ringed her entrance with two fingers.

Her mouth opened on his skin. Wet heat but nothing compared to what he dabbled in. "Not yet. Make me... Make me do what you did earlier."

"You want to come? You want to wet my fingers and my cock with your body?"

"Please, Ian." Her eyes were so wide. Tinged with a hint of vulnerability. But then her mouth quirked upward once again. "And then..." She paused to give a moan when he circled her with a particular stroke. "Then you'll come inside me. Take me. Fuck me."

He growled. Fondled her harder because by the sweet saints did he want that. He rubbed those same circles around her luscious flesh until her eyes went wider and she put her head back. He bit the column of her throat. Her white skin glowed in the moonlight and she came. Came so hard that she shivered and shook over him. Her voice scaled into a drawn-out moan that wasn't near what he was willing to settle for. But it would do for now, until she came on his cock. As he'd promised, juice spilled out over his fingers and over his body where they pressed together.

He notched the head of his cock to her pussy. He wound his fingers through the silken, heavy mass of her hair and pushed her head up so that he could look her in the eyes. "Tell me you want me."

She swallowed first. Her tongue slid across the corner of her mouth. "Ian, I want you more than I think I've ever wanted anything or anyone in my life."

He took her. Or maybe she was taking him, because his cock slid into the soaking, tight clasp of her body. More than her body engulfed him. She felt right in a devious way. He had to drop his forehead to hers and hold his hips still. She was fire and ice.

Everything he hadn't known how to hope for.

Chapter Sixteen

Lottie had expected giving up her virginity to be a faintly violent process. She'd heard all that business with *losing* and *tearing* and those other unpleasant attributes. But with Ian, there was only the slightest burn as the very tip of his cock entered her.

Then pleasure.

A fullness that she'd never dreamt of. Abrading friction that made no sense when contrasted with the liquid rush through her body. She'd nothing to stack this experience against. Nothing that measured up to the way she was transported. His grip on her back stroked and eased, then lowered down her spine, until his fingertips delved between the soft and vulnerable place at the top of her buttocks.

She shuddered, which only meant her body drew closer to his. They pressed together, his hardness to her soft, and between them sparked a power that rocked up her body to coil around her lungs and draw tight until she could hardly breathe.

"Good?" he said on a near whisper. His voice passed from his chest to hers in a rumble. A light thatch of hair across his chest rubbed softly over her nipples.

Her hands tightened on his shoulders. She shook her head and pulled away her hips, but he held her close with his grip tight on her flesh. "I don't know."

His smile tilted up in that left-side-only way. "That won't do. Not at all."

"It's not that it's *bad*." And it wasn't. It had good moments, when he pushed back into her body and all her air escaped her. "It's just...confusing."

"Is that right?"

She had the feeling he might have been laughing at her, and she particularly didn't like that. But there wasn't much she could do, not when he locked one arm low about her hips and flipped them. The room spun. Her head landed almost at the edge of the bed, and when she let her hands fly out for grip, she found only the bedclothes. She twisted her fingers in the blankets. "What are you doing?"

He wedged one arm up under her shoulder and across her back so that his fingertips curled over her other shoulder from behind. She was enveloped. Surrounded. His other hand went to her hip, angling her just so.

And oh, *just so* it was.

She gasped on his first thrust. Sparks lit her from within. Her head tilted back, and she looked up past the draped bed hangings to the window and the barely twinkling stars among the glowing haze that usually clung to London's nights. This was...

Marvelous. She belonged among the stars. She ought to be a star, considering the severe and tingling pleasure that wracked out from her center and through her chest. Her toes curled. She moaned quiet and low, but so very long. Until she'd replaced her breath with more pleasure. More joy.

"There," he said, and this time it was no question. She could practically hear a smug smile in his voice. "There, it's exactly what you like. It's better than good."

"It is," she agreed in a whisper. Her hands were still spread wide, and she wanted to touch him, but she was afraid to move. This was all perfect and good. He filled her and took away and gave again. So much heavy shoving became something more. Something wonderful.

"I like pleasing you, of course."

She gave a little sound that was half laugh and half pleasured moan. "How can you talk at a time like this? Just...do."

"I am." He thrust hard with his hips, into her and out again, making a point of his words. "You know I am. You can feel it in that pretty, wet pussy of yours. The way I fuck you."

Her fingers flew to his mouth, as if to silence him. He grinned at her from behind those fingertips and good God, how that made her clench on his length. On his cock. The newly learned word echoed over and over again in her mind. "You shouldn't say such things."

"Really? Have I found wicked Lottie Vale's limit?" His lips moved under her touch. Soft and wet, and that stupid, small thing of his mouth moving made her eyes drift shut on the feel of him. He slid his grip from the pinch on her hip up her side to hold her breast firm. He rubbed his thumb over the pink, tender tip. Another waterfall of joy rocked her from top to bottom. "You'll say and do almost anything. You'll beg me to take you. But if I talk about your pussy being filled with my cock? That's too much?"

"You can't," she said, but she was breathy and it was good. More than good. The way he stroked into her, the way she thought she'd fly away on the waves.

He lowered his head to her ear. She was surrounded. Absorbed. Her knees hitched higher on his hips. "And you can't lie to me, Lottie. I feel your cunt clench on my prick every time I talk so."

Apparently she really was that depraved. The words set up a chain reaction inside her that led her to abandon. He stroked, and she pulled tight with every fiber of her until she thought she'd never breathe again. Within her was an absence. A feeling that she was waiting and hesitating, but then he'd come into her with a little more force. Plus he kept *talking*. Filthy, depraved things that blended into a grunted chain of *there, sweets, fuck me, yes, harder.*

And she was lost over the edge. Pleasure tingled down her hips. Echoed up through her chest. She pulled tight on his length, and it only amped the pleasure up higher. She was everything beautiful from the inside out. The way he slid over her, the soft blankets beneath and the gorgeous shine of his eyes as he watched her with rabid attention. She was seen. She was his.

For now.

He grunted when her body closed on him. "Fuck, Lottie," he said, all breath and snarl. "You're amazing. Your body. The way you hold me. The way you feel." His words fell away on a mean growl. He stroked into her harder, grinding. His ruthless grip pinched.

The small bite of pain only added to her pleasure. She loved the way he let himself go and only held on tighter to her. She opened fully, absorbing his brute force with wickedness. He withdrew abruptly. Air swirled through the space between them when a moment ago they'd been one.

He wrapped those long fingers around his cock. "Where?"

Her eyes went wide. She knew what he was doing, preventing children. He could have deposited into the blankets, but she was struck with the sudden, instant need to *see*. She spread her fingers wide across her stomach. "Here."

He gulped hard. Still his hand stroked his prick, to the crisp dark hair at the base and then up to the top, where he was swollen and red. Twice was all that was needed, then his release spilled across her skin. She touched it though she knew she shouldn't. Sticky and so very hot. The moment managed to be both depraved and right.

On a contented sigh, she let her head fall toward the bed. Ian collapsed beside her so they were shoulder to shoulder, looking up. Their chests rose and fell on fast pants in tandem.

She felt...strange. Deserted, though she'd shared this brilliant thing with a man she was coming to care about. Maybe it was having to be alone in her body when a moment ago she had held him inside herself. She'd lost something and gained a new part of her soul. New knowledge about what she was capable of that was quite frankly majestic enough to be frightening.

One of her hands was now sticky with his release, so she reached into the small and narrow space between them with her other hand. It felt like a tiny miracle that his hand slid toward hers as well. Their fingers laced together.

She had to lick her lips in order to be able to talk. Her voice had gone raw. "I understand now."

"What's that?" The barest curiosity sounded in his voice. He turned his head toward her. He looked as blasted as she felt. She took a measure of pride in that.

"What?" She'd lost her train of thought, already thinking about his body again. About exploring him at her leisure. While she'd needed to be rid of her virginity, she couldn't see indulging in a life of sin and vice. If nothing else, the risk was too high. Experimenting along these lines too many times would eventually net her a child—the very thing she'd set out to avoid.

That didn't mean she couldn't have at least one more turn.

His mouth curved into a bit of a smirk. He rolled onto the shoulder nearer her. He loomed so well, she wanted to nestle into the shelter of his body. "What do you understand?"

She gave in and entwined their legs. It took her a second to find her thoughts again. "Why they put such proscriptions on such intimacy. Try to convince women that it's horrible."

He coiled a lock of her hair around his finger, then let it trail and drape over her breast. It tickled. She shivered. He admired his handiwork with a pleased grin. "And why is that?"

"Because my only regret now is that I didn't do that years ago. Women would run rampant." She failed at holding back her teasing giggle.

"You didn't know me years ago." He flicked a glance at her from under his dark lashes. His eyes glowed with mischief. "I believe this is where I'm supposed to be offended."

"How delicate men can be at times."

"It's true." He dropped soft kisses along her shoulder. "Completely fragile. It's the real reason no one talks about how good sex is. Because I'd break if you were to kick me out now."

She let her fingernails scrape under his hair. The strands were rough silk. The best part was when his eyes drifted shut. "Might you cry?"

"Maybe. A manly sniffle, perhaps." He flashed her his most cheeky smile. "I could create a tear or two if you thought you might kiss it away."

She pushed up on her elbows enough that her mouth nearly touched his. "Gather up your ballocks and kiss me yourself."

How could he not obey? Before Lottie, he hadn't kissed while smiling, but now he seemed to do it often. She tasted like sweetness and salt, everything good. Manhandling the back of her neck wasn't intended to hold her still. It was so that he could touch as much of her as he could manage. Any space between them was space wasted.

The kiss turned so slow, it was like being drugged in the best sort of way. Deliberate touches. Already Ian's prick was waking again, as if he were a randy boy who'd recently figured out what women were.

He was coming to adore Lottie, her humor and her shine. The very qualities he'd once thought were only gilding, he now realized were fully her. She might lie, but only to protect those most tender parts of her soul. She needed an ally. In this whole wide world, she seemed to show no one her real self.

He wanted to be that person who knew her and protected her and who kept her safe from the rest of the world.

His hand wound deep through her soft hair, his mouth on the heaven of her lips, Ian suddenly realized he had exactly what he'd been looking for. A woman who could keep him twisted up in their life together for the rest of eternity. If he'd found himself a regular country girl, he'd have been bored inside of six weeks. That would never happen with Lottie. She'd always keep him alert.

In the meantime, he would be able to kiss her whenever he wanted. Feel the delicate curve of her waist and ribs. He liked the dip between her breasts. The way her flesh was resilient and elegant.

As he traced his mouth down her neck, heavy on the lips and teeth and tongue, headed with intent toward those berry-tipped breasts, there was a shift in the air. Not sound so much, not at first. A breeze whispered over his bare back.

"Lottie, are you awake, my dove? I had an epiphany about the depth of two dimensionality in my paintings, and I wanted to talk to you about it."

Lottie flinched, jerking upright. "Mama, get out."

Jesus Christ. Ian flipped them and scrambled for the tangled sheet. He yanked it over their bodies, but he rather thought Lady Vale was far enough down the long, narrow room she wouldn't see anything.

It helped she intently studied a book in her hands. "What? Is there a problem?" she asked, without ever looking up.

Lottie slipped out the other side of the sheets, shrugging into a diaphanous robe. She tossed a frantic look back over her shoulder, but besides sinking farther into the bedclothes, Ian couldn't see a damn place he could go. Her bed was set alone, with no furniture directly about it. He'd look for a dressing room sort of door, but all that stuff was piled near the front of the room, where her mother was. Exactly where he *didn't* want to be.

Out the window, maybe? Except he was starkers and they were three floors up. He shrugged, pulling the blankets past his waist.

She rolled her eyes and held a finger to her lips. Sure. He was going to chatter away any minute.

She scurried toward her mother with her hands fluttering as if trying to provide a distraction. "It's past two in the morning. Can't we discuss this tomorrow?"

The older woman pointed at something in the open pages. "It'll leave me if I can't get a grasp on it. See this? It's Caravaggio's. He had it, three hundred years ago. I've been a fool."

Lottie took her mother by the shoulders, gently steering her back toward the door. "Where is Nicolette? Didn't she administer your medicine this evening?"

"I rid myself of it when she wasn't looking." She looked up, blinking. "Is there someone with you?"

Lottie shook her head, frantic. "I'll meet you downstairs if you like, Mama. If we discuss it in your studio, you'll be able to show me examples."

"There is." Lady Vale craned her neck to the side, trying to see around Lottie, who was equally insistently trying to block her view. "A man. Have you a man in your bed?"

Lottie's hand went to her head, and Ian could sympathize. Pressure and tension pinched hard over his skull. He fisted one hand in the blankets. He hadn't ever enjoyed being helpless, and at that moment he completely was. He nodded, though he wasn't sure if she'd be able to see it through the shadows and the length of the room.

He rather wished his trousers weren't on the floor next to the chaise. "Good evening, Lady Vale."

"Sir Ian," she cooed. She waved, twiddling her fingers. "How marvelous to see you again. I should like you to come to dinner some evening. I haven't yet properly thanked you for saving me that day."

He inclined his head, as near as he could get to a bow from his position in Lottie's bed. "Name the evening and I'll be there."

"Wonderful. And do you have family?"

Ian hesitated over the truth, but it wasn't as if she couldn't discover the information if she set out to find it. "My mother and sister are in town."

"Bring them as well."

"Mother," Lottie said with no small measure of exasperation. "You simply cannot."

She flipped her hand in a dismissive gesture. "What? Am I supposed to yell at you? I should never dare be so boring and provincial. Though I suppose you should be thankful your father isn't here. He'd be rather displeased. In fact, I believe you and I should agree to keep this our little secret. And you, as well," she directed toward Ian.

"As you say," he agreed, thankful that she couldn't see his expression and the grin he held back. The whole scene had an air of absurdity he'd have expected to see in one of Shakespeare's more ridiculous plays.

"Mama, you have to go," Lottie said with stressed emphasis. She kept looking back over her shoulder as if wishing Ian would drop through the floor.

So much the worse that he couldn't oblige her.

Lady Vale went out on a push and a rather gentle shove. She continued chattering the whole time, going on about the menu for the dinner they'd have, with a random segue for Lottie to remind Lady Vale to talk about two-dimensional skies the next morning. Lottie agreed.

Then she shut the door. She turned back toward the room, but that took the last bit of her energy. She sank against the wood. Her fingertips rose to her forehead. "Oh sweet saints," she muttered.

Ian shoved out of the bed and stalked toward her. "Did that really, truly happen?"

"She's right. Be thankful it was her and not my father." She spoke with her eyes closed and her head back against the door.

"Didn't you lock the door?" He passed his trousers and grabbed them, pausing only briefly to pull them on. Raw wool rubbed over his ass. At this point he didn't care.

"She must have stolen the key. Again." She opened her eyes and looked at him imploringly. "I am so sorry, Ian. I'm sure that was humiliating."

He shrugged. Finally close enough to touch, he wrapped his hands around her upper shoulders and pulled her face into his bare chest. She went surprisingly easily. "It's all right. I suppose someone else's engagement must have started on a more embarrassing note, though I can hardly imagine how."

She stiffened body part by body part. Her shoulders were first, then her spine straightened. Her neck was last, drawing her cheek away from its press against his chest. "Engagement?"

"That's what I said." He hadn't planned anything of the sort, but once the opportunity arose, the idea felt right. Maybe part of him had only been waiting for the excuse. This moment. "It's the appropriate response to such a discovery."

"Don't say such things." She pushed away, shaking her head. Though the sash of her robe was already tied, she knotted it. "An engagement would be foolish. People would only talk behind our backs when it ended."

"Who says it has to end?"

She smiled as big and bright as she ever had. "Why, I do, of course." She cupped his jaw. Her touch was gentle and silken. "You don't want to marry me."

His hands framed her narrow waist. "It's not the worst sort of option either. Marriage is one of those inevitable sorts of things. Why not with someone I enjoy?"

She stretched up on her toes and brushed a gracious kiss over his mouth. Her arms draped over his shoulders, and after that first gentle kiss she pushed deeper. Swept her tongue over his in what could have been either promise or farewell.

"It's certainly not inevitable. I'm not marrying anyone. If I were tempted by your sweepingly romantic declaration," she said with a dry measure of humor.

"Why not marry?" And why was there an inexplicable twinge in the lower regions of his chest?

Her smile wavered enough that he wanted to touch her supple cheek and make the shadows lurking behind her eyes go away. "Because with marriage comes children. And for the women of my family, children bring the madness. I can't do that to anyone. I'm the last of our line. It'll end with me."

Chapter Seventeen

Lottie had desperately attempted to talk both her mama and Ian out of the dinner. She spent hours in her mama's salon, holding an apple so that her mother could sketch it in the right light, all the while talking. Trying to convince her that this was pointless and a ridiculous idea that was begging for trouble. Mama would be bored with such provincial company.

She'd had Ian meet her at the school, where she'd done exactly the same thing, though she'd left out the argument about less-than-sufficient polish. He'd sat in the chair across from her desk with his hands folded over his stomach and an intent look on his handsome face. Then his mouth had drawn down into a frown that emphasized his strong nose. For a moment, she thought he'd agree. Until he snatched her by the waist, dragged her onto his lap and kissed her senseless.

Once she'd been breathless and clinging to the open plackets of his jacket, he'd said no. That her mother had issued the invitation and he'd accepted. It wasn't her place to withdraw. Not to mention, Etta would be well served by meeting the people who would see her launched to society the next week.

Then he'd left, claiming business to attend to. His sister and mother had to be taken to the shops to ensure they had sufficient wardrobes.

She hated being ignored.

Which was why she crossed her arms over her chest and tapped her toes, standing in the open doorway of her family's seldom-used formal dining room. "Mama! Do you at least promise to behave?"

Lady Vale came to a halt at the head of the table. Her armful of dyed-purple ostrich feathers fluttered like fingers. "Of course I will. How can you ask me such with bald rudeness?"

Lottie sighed all the way from the bottom of her stomach. "Of course, Mother. I'm sorry."

As far as Lottie was concerned, it was a legitimate concern. Her mother always meant well. Always intended to behave. Then she'd end up halfway into a bottle of brandy and halfway out the upper-story windows with her skirts hiked to her waist.

Mama looked perfectly put together. The slim-cut gown skimmed over leanness that spoke well of a woman her age. The dark purple skirt was close over her hips and pulled up in the back to a graceful bustle with swags of rich material.

Lottie's dress was quite similar in shape, narrow-cut at the hips and with a bustle. But where her mother had purple cording along the hem and bodice, Lottie had knotted silk flowers of pale white in contrast to the dark green silk dress. They outlined her bosom and swept down to curve around her waist. Every single one had been set intentionally.

They'd been chosen to torment Ian, to make him want to touch her. Because she'd liked so very much being touched by him. Yet in the past two weeks, he'd kept it almost...superficial. She felt absurd calling it such when she lived for the feel of his mouth on hers. They snuck kisses whenever they had a chance, but there it was. She wanted more. Strange distance dwelled in the space between them, and she wasn't sure where it was from.

Nor was she sure whether she really wanted it to go away. She couldn't afford to become any more involved with Ian. The friendly, affectionate level they maintained had to be enough.

Her mama went back to arranging the slender feathers in an artistic grouping of vases that ranged down the table. "There." She stepped back with a measure of satisfaction. "It's the small details that bring a picture together."

"Small?" Lottie eyed the feathers dubiously. They towered three feet over the table, and the gold-tinted glass of the vases would be difficult to see through. Lucky the dinner guests would have the companions next to them to speak with.

"I wish your father could have been here," Lady Vale said as she brushed off her fingertips and headed toward the front parlor. She made a beeline for the sideboard filled with crystal decanters.

Lottie's stomach flipped as she watched her mother pour a tiny glass of sherry. Hopefully that would be it. She nibbled on the inside of her bottom lip. "Father had business."

Mama shot Lottie a very amused look over the edge of her glass. "As you say."

So what if she wanted to believe Father had business at their estate in Derbyshire? It didn't seem like an evil fiction. He probably was doing *some* sort of business while there. It would be difficult to avoid the estate manager all together, after all.

Besides, sometimes she barely blamed her father. She could do with a holiday in the country now and then. If it weren't for the school to run, she'd have fled for their family's estate as well. Or farther. Run away to the south of France to go mad in peace.

Except when the butler ushered in Ian and his family, she knew that wasn't true. Her heart gave a tiny leap into her throat before delving to her toes. It lingered there, sickly and a little pained.

Why in the name of God did she have to be so happy to see Ian? He looked handsome in the usual white-and-black combo of evening wear. Precisely starched collars framed his sharp jaw. His bright eyes sought her out across the room. "Lady Vale, Miss Vale. Please allow me to introduce my mother, Mrs. Heald, and my sister, Henrietta."

The requisite bows and curtsies and greetings went around before Lottie's mother gave a wide grin. "How lovely it is to meet you, Mrs. Heald. I am ever so grateful for your gracious raising of Sir Ian. If it weren't for him, I'd be buried in the family crypt four weeks past."

"Mother," Lottie said, her cheeks hot. "Don't be crass."

"The truth is never crass." She took a healthy swallow of her wine.

Mrs. Heald smiled graciously. "I'm rather fond of Sir Ian as well. I do love to hear of his various misdeeds."

"Don't be silly, Mother. You know we've never heard a whisper of Ian doing wrong." Henrietta smiled at her brother. "Every story that comes to us proves he's of the highest caliber."

It was more than obvious that she adored him. As well she should. He was moving heaven and earth to ensure her life stayed as smooth as it ought to be. It wasn't only the expense that Ian was going to in order to line up a presentable Season at the last minute. His involvement and nearness itself was remarkable.

Lottie had no idea what that must be like, to have someone support her in every possible way. She found herself rather envious of the black-haired, blue-eyed woman. With her unthreatening prettiness, Ian's money and the support of Victoria's mother, she'd want for little when it came to Society's approval. Henrietta wouldn't be forced into fancy verbal tricks to hide her family's dirty secret in plain sight.

Lottie drifted toward the window, leaving her mother chattering with Mrs. Heald and Henrietta. She twisted her fingers in the curtains. On the street outside a few carriages clattered by in the darkening twilight, but the hand-painted wallpaper distracted Lottie. Lady Vale had spent hours locked in this room only the month before last, turning the striped walls into subtle magic with hand-painted birds.

She knew Ian was behind her before he spoke. The hairs along the back of her neck tingled. "Your sister will do well."

"I'd hoped as much."

He didn't stand too close. He couldn't. There were too many rules between them, as well as his odd silences. She'd caught him looking at her in the past two weeks whenever he thought she wouldn't notice.

She thought he'd want to talk about the things that had happened in the intimate spaces between them. Her heart stuttered as she anticipated.

"I had a note from Patricia. At least I assume it was her."

Part of her wanted to accept the reprieve. "Demanding money?"

"Indeed." He didn't touch her. The absence hurt more than she'd expected. "I sent her a fraction of what she'd asked for. Enough to keep her dangling on in hope of more."

"Yet not enough that she'd be satiated," she said, filling in the blanks. "No hope of tracking where it went?"

"Unfortunately, no. I paid a couple of Fletcher's men to watch the inn where she instructed it be left. An urchin picked up the packet, then the men lost him in Seven Dials."

She nodded. "Not Fletcher's territory. His men would be more easily lost."

Behind her, fabric shifted with Ian's impatience. "Anything from Finna?"

"Patricia hasn't been back, of course. But she remembered that Patricia had been ill lately. It might be what's prompted her to such actions." She didn't want to ask. The question curled and coiled in her throat before slithering out like a snake. "Are you upset with me?"

He jerked to look at her, the change of subject obviously startling him. "Why would I be upset?"

She shrugged, feeling like something small and mean. Jealous, maybe. Of Henrietta and every other girl who had it so easy. She hadn't made half the mistake Henrietta had, but because Lottie's mother was notorious, she bore twice the weight. "What I said about never intending to have children. It's unnatural."

"It's your choice. Therefore it can't possibly be unnatural." His voice looped around her like the touch she craved. "I won't hear you say such things again."

"Do you believe me, though? That I can't ever risk having children?" Her sweaty palm clenched on the curtain, but the brocade would be fine. "Do you understand?"

"Have you been to doctors? Investigated the science behind it?"

"They're as lost as I am." She shrugged and thought she might shatter for the tiny gesture. "But there's Mother, and her mother before her. She filled her skirts with rocks and walked into a pond two miles from the manor house. Mama had a sister, as well. She married well but ran away with a traveling busker."

For a long moment, the silence around them was punctuated only by her mother's beautiful laughter. Then he touched her, lightly and still properly. His fingers smoothed around the curve of her upper arm, above her elbow. She felt it anyway—the meaning with which he imbued every centimeter of quiet touch. "I understand."

Ian understood. He did. Such a history was difficult to overcome, and he was no doctor. He was no god with perfect comprehension to be able to gainsay men of learning.

That also meant as a mortal man he had no words for the uncomfortable, niggling feeling that slipped and slid through his emotions as Lady Vale called them into dinner. Lottie proceeded on his arm. He felt her there, beyond the fingers that rested in the crook of his elbow. The goodness that lay under her flash and sparkle as she turned her head back to chat with Henrietta.

How could he be the only one who saw her underneath the gilt? How was it that no one else seemed to appreciate her loving core and shining happiness?

That she wouldn't raise children seemed all the more a shame. Lottie understood what it meant to keep small souls safe. After all, she did it for her mother. She would also know how to help any children grow into their best selves and have fun while they did it.

It made Ian sad—actually, truly sad in a way no other word would do, to realize that this meant there would be no Lottie in his future either.

His whole world and his whole life had been about hauling his family out of the lower ranks of the landed gentry and pulling them upward. He had never thought he harbored delusions about rising toward the upper ranks, but somehow that wasn't the same thing as ending the family line. There were no convenient cousins, no younger brothers. Ian was it. If he didn't have children, wouldn't his father's work be for naught? All his own work?

He'd never been a man who worked for the joy of it. Look at the past few weeks. When given the opportunity to throw it over for focus on family and his sister's problems, he'd done so immediately. His managers were competent, and they would keep the tin mines going forward, but that wasn't the same thing as all the energy he'd poured into them over the last ten years.

He'd always known he'd have a small but close family in the home where he'd grown up, and his sister's would probably be in the same shire.

If he *didn't* have that life, what was he left?

The table they were seated at was small in order to match their intimate party. Yet the center had inexplicably been set with large vases filled with feathers and twisted greenery so that Ian couldn't see across to his mother or Lady Vale. He and Lottie had been seated together and Henrietta at her far side as well.

As the first course was served, Lottie kept her gaze forward. White tendons traced down her neck, she was holding herself so tight.

She flinched when Henrietta leaned toward them. "Thank you for having me, Miss Vale."

Lottie's prettiest smile made an instant appearance. "Think nothing of it, Miss Heald. My mother is always pleased to have such congenial company. She hasn't much opportunity for indulging."

Etta poked at her fish. Ian knew she had never been particularly fond of the course, but she wouldn't ever be so rude as to say it. "I've heard that Lady Vale once used to be quite the entertainer."

"Indeed." Lottie put down her fork and leaned back in her chair, a glass of white wine cradled in one hand. "She was. I cannot count how many parties and events I watched from the second floor landing as a young girl. My nurse was forever despairing of keeping me contained."

"I can picture that." Ian looked at Lottie, imagining a much smaller version of her face pressed between the railing slats. She'd have had such a pout. "I bet you'd have made it all the way downstairs."

"I did. On many occasions." Though she was looking through the table decorations and likely unable to see through them, she seemed to be smiling at her mother. "Mama always let me have a few minutes. When I was particularly small, she'd carry me about on her hip for a while before giving me a plate of biscuits and trifles and sending me off."

"How wonderfully indulgent of her," Etta agreed.

As if on time, a peal of laughter echoed from around the decorations, followed immediately by the slightly breathier chuckle of Ian and Etta's mother. Lottie leaned toward Ian, close enough that he could smell roses and sugar, the layered sweetness that was Lottie. Concern was written between her brows in a decided wrinkle.

"They're fine," he said in as quiet a voice as he could manage.

Etta must have heard him anyway. "Indeed they are. I haven't heard Mother laugh quite that way in years."

"Mama has a way about her," Lottie said dryly. She took a long sip of the white wine, but then set it down firmly. "She always has. In the coming weeks, it will come in quite handy for you, Miss Heald."

"Will your mother be attending events with us?"

"We only let her out for the most special occasions. And you most certainly count." She looked at Ian. He was missing something she wished him to know or hear or say.

He didn't understand. She was too complicated. Maybe too complicated and delicately wrought for him to ever understand.

Didn't matter. He wanted her, wanted to know her. Like having a lightning bug caught in his hands, he wanted to peek in and see that spark. Then he'd have to let her go again, or risk extinguishing that shine.

If he were really honest with himself, he'd know that he should stay away from her. It would be kinder, both to her and to himself. Otherwise he risked falling entirely in love with her.

His fork clattered to his plate somewhere in the middle of the beef course, sending a delicate spray of sauce across the wide porcelain edge.

Lottie lifted an eyebrow. "Are you all right?"

He wasn't. He was stunned. Poleaxed. A great doddering idiot who wanted to simply stare down at his meal in stupefaction. He wouldn't have thought he was quite the man to indulge in introspection in the first place, much less while stabbing beef with a fork.

Yet here he was.

"I'm well." He nodded slowly.

She was so lovely. The mischievous twinkle of her green eyes and the graceful arch of her cheekbones. Her mouth was wide, with a common curve that seemed always pleasant. But it was more than the accumulation of her features. Her devotion to her mother and her school shone over her. She had constant intention to see the best in the world. She might force herself into smiling so often that it hurt, but that came from the desire to be a better person in a better place. She was crass and reckless, and underneath all that she was *good*.

Even her intention to never have children came from soul-deep sweetness. From not wanting to inflict what she'd been through on anyone else. How could anyone fault her for that?

Yet how could anyone fault him for running away before it was too late? If he were only halfway in love with her, he could still escape and save himself difficulty. It wasn't much to want both love and his dreams of a family.

"Are you sure?" Her head tilted toward him. Her lush mouth drew into something tighter. He wanted to touch her lips and feel the keen edge of her teeth, the sharpness inside her vulnerability.

He picked up the heavy silver fork again, and the cool metal gave him something solid to hold. "I am well, I promise." He made himself smile. "If I weren't, would you soothe my brow with a lavender cloth?"

She snorted, a tiny and indelicate laugh that she smothered behind her fingertips. Her gaze darted over to Etta, who'd bent far to her side to speak to their mother. Across the table, Lottie's own mother might as well have been in the wilds of South America.

Lottie leaned back toward him, close enough that her shoulder brushed his. She looked at the table between them, but he knew it was from no sense of modesty. Teasing, playing. Turning him inside out. Because she knew that if she added the strength of her eyes to the words she was about to say, he'd be completely undone.

"No," she said in a soft coo laced with humor and sexuality. "But if you're unwell, I wouldn't tell you about how I plan to leave the back door unlocked. Or how any certain person who knew how to get to my bedroom would find that door unlocked as well. Then that certain person might find me in bed after the midnight hour. Unclothed."

His body responded before his mind did. He clinched tight. His hand fisted around the fork handle. Not cool anymore, the metal blazed hot with his own temperature.

Then his mind caught up, hearing the implication in her words and, more than that, becoming aware of how desperately he hungered for her.

He was damned. Gleefully so.

Chapter Eighteen

Lottie knew this had to be one of the most foolish things she'd ever done. Not only to issue such a scandalous invitation, but to do so at the dinner table with her mother? With his mother as well?

The final moments of dinner could not come quickly enough. Lottie rolled and reveled in the excitement that shortened her breathing and made her palms tingle. Gooseflesh chased up her forearms. Her toes curled inside her slippers every time Ian looked at her. She knew the weight and touch and promise of his gaze on her skin. She anticipated every one. Breathed deeper and let her pulse surge. How wonderful this all felt.

No wonder people tried to keep young women under wraps. Having once learned how good Ian could make her feel, Lottie didn't want to give it up. She wanted more of him. Everything she could grab with grasping, greedy hands.

Maybe then she wouldn't think about the tinge of pity she'd seen in his eyes earlier.

Mama stood, popping up over the decorations like a jack-in-the-box. She clapped her hands together. Animation and color washed over her cheeks. "We'll do without separation, don't you think, Sir Ian? All of us to continue to the parlor? I'll permit you to have an entire bottle of port if you like, so long as you promise not to abandon us."

Ian inclined his head. From the side, his profile was boldly hawkish, with a great and fierce nose. She wanted his shelter. "I shouldn't like to sit by myself anyhow, Lady Vale."

"Of course not." Then she gave Lottie one of those little wink and nods she was particularly good at before shifting to include Henrietta as well. "Come along, everyone. We've revelry to indulge in."

Mrs. Heald giggled and tittered as she and Mama left the room. Henrietta followed along directly behind them.

Lottie...lingered. There was no two ways about it. She lingered far enough behind that she could feel like she was alone with Ian. Because she rather *liked* being alone with him, though she carefully laced her fingers together before her waist and didn't risk touching him.

"You shouldn't be so bold."

A sharp spike of fear made her lungs clench. His chin up, his expression was kept grave...but for the tiny quirk of a smile that pulled in the corner of his mouth.

"You don't mean that."

"I might. I should, rather." A sudden wash of bafflement clouded his features. "I really should. There're rules to the world, and they're there for a reason."

"Sometimes it seems as if those reasons are arbitrary." Her steps were muffled on the soft carpet runner that ran down the middle of the wide hallway, so there was no auditory proof when she slowed. "And then sometimes as if they're meant only as a means of controlling women at large."

His hand came to rest at the small of her back. She didn't feel like she was being herded. More like he hadn't been able to resist touching her a moment longer. She held down her smile by pure force of will.

His fingers traced a simple pattern over her dress. "There's only one method of control that should be attempted on a woman like you. I'm not even claiming that it would work. Only that it should be great fun in the process."

They were rapidly coming up to the open door of the parlor. From inside she heard pealing giggles. The ladies were having quite the good time.

Lottie held Ian's strong wrist. He was all cruel bones and firm tendons. Her thumb slipped under the cuff of his shirt and found crisp hair. She rubbed. "You can't say such things and not tell me."

"I shouldn't. You'll only take it as a challenge." He backed her against the wall. They were getting too reckless, a little too wild.

She curled her hands in the lapels of his evening coat. No way was she letting him get away. If this time was what they got, she wanted all of it, every possible experience. "I do love a good challenge."

He kissed her then, though so lightly she could almost think she'd imagined it. He tasted like dry wine. Tempting enough that she traced her tongue over his top lip, trying to entice him back. How quickly their air mixed and their breathing turned into something raucous and animalistic.

Ian's voice was rough. "Pleasure. A woman as complicated and amazing and wonderful as you should only be constrained with pleasure. And not the threat of its removal, but as enticement. As promise. Fulfillment, as it were."

She grinned against his mouth. "You think you're as good as that?"

He had her caged in, one of his hands flat on the wooden wall next to her head, the other resting at the small of her back. As if he'd sweep her away and they'd begin to dance. Maybe they already were.

"You tell me," he said, so quiet and low she could have filled in the words herself. Made him the puppet for whatever she wanted to hear. "How did you feel after our night?"

She'd felt sated. Happy inside her own body, as if she'd finally put all her pieces into the right order by taking what she wanted. "You're that good."

"There." He straightened, though he left that one magical hand at the small of her back. "Now, let's go in before we're missed." His next words he must have timed for when they stepped over the threshold of the room, because he waited five steps to say them. At least he had the circumspection to whisper quietly enough that only Lottie heard. "Try not to look like you're thinking of the ways I made you come."

Scandalous, awful, horrible man. She was left standing facing each of their mothers and his wide-eyed sister. Henrietta's eyes were a similar color to Ian's, and Lottie was fairly sure the girl was her same age. But there was a general air of innocence about Henrietta that said, marriage to a commoner or not, she'd been untainted by the world.

Lottie was the one who not only indulged in reckless fantasies, she initiated them. Telling Ian that her door would be unlocked this evening had been outrageous. But they wouldn't have long in the grand scheme of things. There were only so many times Lottie could gamble and risk pregnancy before she'd buckle under the weight of her mind's worry.

That meant she needed him again, and soon. Before it was all too late.

Once Henrietta was properly received into society at the Duchess of Marvell's ball, and once Patricia had been corralled, most likely at the school's quarterly social, Lottie would only have one choice—to push Ian out of her life. Otherwise she'd have to face more choices that would break her heart.

As she watched, her mother was taking on that frantic inclination that did not bode well for the rest of the night. The glass of wine in her hand wasn't helping the situation. The color that had been so attractive on her cheeks only moments ago now stretched all the way up to the dip of her temples. "Lottie, my love. Whatever took you so long to walk down the hallway?"

Mrs. Heald watched Lottie with an air of suspicion. "I'm sure they got distracted by innocent things."

"Yes, Mother." Ian gave a tiny nod of agreement. His collar was sharp and precise. "We stopped to inspect a painting I found interesting."

Henrietta gasped. "Was it the ballerina? I saw that one too. So pretty. I wish I had done better in my dancing lessons, but I never had that grace."

"It was," Lottie said on a smile. She slid a look up toward Ian. "I was telling him about Monsieur Degas's realist style."

Mama took another deep drink of her wine, then looked up through her lashes with noticeably coquettish affectation. "I doubt it was the dancer's grace that Sir Ian was admiring. More like the half-bare legs. I reconsider hanging that painting in such a public place as the hallway every day. Propriety and all."

A hard knot appeared in the center of Lottie's chest between one beat of her heart and the next. She knew that tone. It was waspish, irritated and rather self-satisfied. Her mother never had half a speck of interest in propriety of any sort, either for herself or for others. For some reason she seemed to have decided she was jealous. More likely she felt generally irritable and inexplicably inclined to rage at any moment.

"Mama," she said with the most negligible hint of warning she could manage.

Thank God for Ian. He scooped her mama up by the arm, draping slightly against his side. He was so bloody, thankfully charming as he smiled down at Lady Vale. "With such beauty surrounding me, what need have I of a dancer's legs? As a matter of fact, it was the off-center composition of the painting that I remarked upon. Perhaps you could explain more about that to me?"

Lottie's mother visibly perked up. Ian led her to the far end of the room and deposited her on a sofa, then she patted the cushions beside her skirts. "Why, of course I can. Come sit next to me."

Lottie let herself be drawn into conversation with Ian's sister and Mrs. Heald, but she continually took swift peeks out of the corner of her eye. Her mother and Ian were deep in conversation. She occasionally heard art phrases and her mother's patented barbs about her fellow painters, but Lottie wasn't reassured. She knew that look in her mother's eyes. The hold of her head and the way her hands flew and danced with every single word, which streamed from her in rapid patter. Every now and then, her skirts twitched and shifted while she bounced her toes.

She was on the verge of a breakdown, and there was nothing Lottie could do to stop it.

While Ian had no idea what sort of byplay it was that passed between Lady Vale and Lottie, he certainly knew how to spot fear. It looked like Lottie's wide eyes and the drawn whiteness of her cheeks. The emotion didn't fit her right. She was bolder than that. Better than that. But no matter where she went around the room, her gaze kept returning to Ian and her mother.

"My daughter is all concern and solicitousness, isn't she?" Lady Vale managed to sound rather displeased with the sentiment. Her nose crinkled.

"Many would be happy to have such an amiable daughter. She's a credit to you."

"Not to me." Lady Vale smiled, and in the expression was a hint of her daughter's joy, though tinged with something more sharply bitter. She took a drink of her wine. The gold-dipped rim flashed under gaslight. "Lottie has always gone her own way. If anything, that father of hers has more influence than I."

"I have yet to meet Baron Vale." Across the room, his mother and Henrietta leaned over a sheaf of music that Lottie was showing them.

"He's out of town." Her voice cracked, but then she coughed twice into a loose fist. She blinked fast flutters. "He's often out of town. He rather likes the country."

Ian was wading into murky waters that he didn't quite understand. His own family was close enough that they were often content with only each other's company for amusement.

They were a solid knot. They trusted each other implicitly. After all, their family never would have survived Henrietta's difficulties if it hadn't been for their closeness.

Ian didn't understand why Lottie watched her mother throughout the night like she was wary Lady Vale would turn into a wounded bear and begin roaring. As far as Ian could tell, Lady Vane was eccentric but bearable. There was nothing served by being so on guard.

Except at the end of the night, Ian suddenly realized that both Lottie and her mother had disappeared. Ian pivoted slowly to survey the room, but it wasn't as if there was anywhere they could hide.

Discomfort prickled Ian's skin and made the small hairs at the nape of his neck stand on end. He made his way toward the door.

At first, the foyer seemed silent. A single footman maintained his post at the base of the stairs. "May I help you, sir?"

Ian shook his head—and immediately heard a sharp crash. Most curiously, the footman didn't flinch. His gaze remained on Ian, who looked back and forth between the door from whence the sound had come and the bland-faced footman. "Did you hear that?"

His gaze flickered. Color attacked his cheeks. "Hear what, sir?"

"That noise."

"I'm sure that Lady Vale would appreciate it if you were to return to the party." His cheeks weren't washed with color, they had bright red circles across the apples. "And Miss Vale, particularly."

"I'm sure they both would, indeed." His shoes clicked across the black-and-white tiles. From behind him, a wave of laughter poured out of the open door.

Another crash echoed from the room as he pushed back the pocket door in front of him.

The tableau was exactly what he'd expected and yet entirely more. Lottie held her mother from behind, her arms wrapped around the older woman. Tears streamed down Lady Vale's face. In the corner was a small pile of glittering glass and broken porcelain.

Both women froze, turning toward the door. Lady Vale scrubbed the back of one hand across her eyes and sniffled, but nothing could stem her tears. "Sir Ian. I'm terribly sorry you had to see me like this." She gave another sniffle and her voice broke. Her shoulders bowed on a silent sob.

"I'm very sorry to have intruded," he said by rote habit. Really, he was lost. These were murky waters he'd found himself in. Somehow he was in the middle of the Atlantic, as if he'd fallen off a steamer with no lifeboat.

"Ian..." Lottie's eyes were wide. If he'd thought her cheeks pale earlier, that was nothing on the ghost-white pallor that had taken her over. She shook her head as slowly as an old lady. "You shouldn't be here."

Lady Vale wrenched away from her daughter's arms. She threw herself to the other end of the sofa they sat on, burying her face against her folded arms. "Because you're ashamed of me. I knew it. I've been saying it for years and you've denied. Yet when it comes time to prove yourself, you only wish me hidden away."

"I said no such thing." A touch of exasperation tinged Lottie's expression, but mostly there was weariness. She approached exhaustion. Her movements were as creaky as if her bones had frozen.

Yet she still reached toward Lady Vale. Her hands curled around her mother's shoulders, which shook with fresh sobs. From a drawer she withdrew a handkerchief and wiped what she could off her mother's cheeks.

Lady Vale took the cloth and dabbed at her tears. "I'm so sorry, Lottie. I've ruined the evening. Again." She gave a small, delicate laugh that sounded so forced, Ian filled with grief for her. "I seem to make a terrible habit of this from time to time."

Lottie tugged Lady Vale into her arms. "It's no harm. The dinner itself went well. In a moment, I'll have to leave you to make excuses and say you've a megrim. I'm sure Sir Ian won't breathe a word."

He inclined in a shallow bow, as it seemed the least he could give them, especially considering Lady Vale's discretion at finding him in Lottie's bed. "I wouldn't dream of it."

"Ian, will you pull the bell for me? Twice." She rubbed up and down her mother's back. "See, Mama? I'll send for your maid, and she'll see you to your room as soon as possible. We'll have you tucked in before you know it."

Ian obeyed, finding the silk cord and calling the aforementioned maid. When she bustled into the room, she looked more like a nurse Ian once had than any lady's maid he'd seen. She was soft and round, with salt-colored hair drawn back in a loose bun. Compassion poured out of her every pore. "Oh, Lady Vale. You've pushed yourself too far for the evening, haven't you?"

Lady Vale smiled through a fresh sheen of tears. "I think this bout has been a long time coming, Nicolette."

Lottie whispered in her mother's ear before the kind-seeming Nicolette hustled her out of the room. Sitting on the chaise, her palms facing upward and loose in her lap, Lottie watched them go. Her own eyes pinkened with a wash of unshed tears until she blinked them away.

She pushed up from her seat and brushed at her skirts, though no sheen of dust or dirt clung to them. Maybe she was brushing away her own sadness. "Well, then. I'll be rather busy for the next few weeks."

"Is that how long her spells last? A few weeks?" He crossed his arms over his chest for lack of anything better to do with them. He'd never been quite so aware of his useless, empty hands.

Lottie nodded, moving toward the door as if she wasn't going to stop. He held her by the elbow and turned her toward him. She didn't even try for one of her smiles. "Hopefully. Hopefully they last two to three weeks." Something dark and pained ran across her features. "Once it lasted six months. I was ten and four."

He framed her face in his hands and knew he was a bastard because she was prettier in despondency. That didn't mean he wished such misery on her. But the shimmer in her eyes turned them into jewels, and the contrast between her pale skin and pink-flushed lips was remarkable.

Despite her beauty, he would take that pain from her if he could. "I'm so sorry."

Her mouth twisted into a smile. Her hands looped around his wrists, fingers tucking under the cuffs of his evening coat. "I know. There's nothing anyone can do. She'll have medicine and sleep a lot. In the meantime, I could use some assistance in politely asking everyone to go home."

"Of course," he agreed with a nod. "But first…"

He swept a kiss over her mouth. Partly because she seemed to need bracing and he didn't know how else to give it.

Partly because he was suddenly aware of exactly how useless he was. He'd been patronizing. Thinking that she made too much of her butterfly-like mother and the difficulties that went with her. He'd failed her without ever giving her a chance.

He had no idea how he could fix it all. Maybe he wouldn't be able to.

Maybe she was right and he'd be forced to walk away.

Chapter Nineteen

In the wee hours of the night, Lottie escaped her bed and headed for her desk. Though darkness encroached from all sides, she only turned on one lamp. When she couldn't see the rest of her large, empty room, she felt less alone.

Somehow she managed to march through a phalanx of paperwork. She paid numerous accounts and resolved to inquire as to a less expensive source for grosgrain ribbon. They apparently went through an appalling amount. Likely trimming the girls' assembly ensembles.

She sighed and pushed the accounting book to the side. Her fingertips rubbed at her temples, but it did nothing to alleviate the unceasing pressure that swirled there or the dry-as-dirt feeling behind her eyelids.

A breeze lifted the corner of a report on the behavior of a gentleman who wished to attend the school's events. He'd likely be approved, since he was an up-and-coming clerk in a large firm with sufficient savings in accounts that Lottie was only able to check into because of particular, unsavory connections. The paperwork fluttered as the breeze got stronger.

She set her hands flat on the edge of the desk. Her heart took a tumble. "I didn't think you were coming."

His voice emerged from the darkness like a wraith to twine around her. "I wasn't sure if I was either."

"Too much to deal with, yes?" She kept her back straight by will and the loving support of her corset. Her chest clenched on pure feeling that she didn't know the name of. Her palms were damp, and her heart rushed in her ears. "I have to say after this

evening's display I hadn't really expected to see you. I would have understood if you'd stayed away."

His hands landed on her shoulders when he stepped into the circle of inconsistent light thrown by her lamp. The weight across her back was warm and steady, and she suddenly felt that she could crumple. Fall apart.

She laughed a little. Her hands busily set about cleaning the top of her desk, lining up her pens in an orderly fashion, but she faltered when she realized no matter what she did, there would still be more mess before her. More things she could never quite get control of. She swallowed the knot in her throat and stood.

Wandering away into the dark was easy. She knew this room as well as she knew her own mind. Beneath the largest window, she stopped. Placed one hand flat on the glass and waited for him to come near. She knew he would. He'd come this far, after all.

He caged her in. His hands rested on the wood of the window frame, his head above hers. "I settled into my study with a bottle of brandy," he said in a voice that seemed almost conversational. Casual.

On the other side of the glass was their neighbor's small side garden. Gray shadows draped the bushes and a bench that glowed white under a sliver of moon. She turned to see Ian's face. Wanted to know the shape of his mouth. "But you came anyway."

He traced bold fingertips over her jaw and down her neck. She'd let her maid undress her and put her in a thin white night rail, but she'd drawn on a robe much too thick for the warm weather. She'd nestled into its heavy fabric for comfort. Now she regretted the choice.

When he drew a single fingertip down the folded lapel, she couldn't feel it. Her head lowered to watch. It wasn't the same thing. She wanted his touch on her, not on the fabric around her.

"I came," he agreed. That active, mobile mouth of his that she keenly appreciated was still. She thought he might give his reason, but maybe the way his hand slipped around the back of her neck was purpose enough. "Where is your mother now?"

She sighed. "There's a tonic she takes that helps her sleep through the worst of it. With her nurse overseeing, sometimes she sleeps for weeks at a time."

"Straight through?"

"More or less." She made herself smile. The front of her hair was pinned back enough to stay out of her face while she worked on the school's needs. A few locks fell forward over her shoulder. She pushed them away. "It's the best for her."

He framed her face between both of his warm, strong hands. "Don't do that."

Her eyes stung with tears that she held back through pure will alone. "Don't do what?"

"Prevaricate. Lie. Don't be false, not with me." He stared at her so intently, as if willing her to see beneath the surface.

Not with him, indeed. As if he were special. As if he hadn't withdrawn in the face of her mother's unrelenting and frankly terrifying emotion. She didn't want to look at that. She didn't want to *think* about any of that.

The only time lately she'd been fully without thought had been when she was wrapped in his arms. Reveling in him and the magic they made together.

She laid her hands carefully on his shoulders, enjoying their firmness. She lifted up on her toes until her mouth was within a fraction of his. She knew his scent and his truth. "Make me forget, please. Make it all go away."

"You think I can?" His forearms lowered to the glass, so that the cage he'd made of his body came closer. She breathed him in.

"Maybe. Maybe not," she teased. "But at the very least, you ought to try."

Lorelie Brown

"Gladly."

The way he kissed her was magical, and he scooped her up. His hands went straight to her derriere as if drawn by magnets. Her toes dangled in the air for a moment, but she wasn't exactly the dangling sort. When she lifted her knee, it gravitated toward his hip. They fit together.

Her hands kneaded across the back of his neck. With her eyes closed and her mouth fused to his, her body draped along his, they were one. Maybe that would be enough. Maybe they could hold off the other, sticky sort of darkness. She'd never felt so alone before, but he made it go away. Made her stop thinking about her drugged mother, two floors below, or the fact that her father hadn't been home for weeks.

He shouldn't have known where he was going, but somehow he backed them up until he landed at her chaise. The same one she'd first felt him on, the same one where she'd held his cock in her hand.

She could come to appreciate a piece of furniture in a whole new way.

He leaned back and draped her over his front. Though his hands smoothed and shaped her body, he seemed content to kiss her that way.

Lottie let herself melt. Her knees found a home between his, and the very top of her thigh came to rest against his particular hardness. Her hands delved into his hair. She loved the silken mass, the way he kept it so tidy and combed most of the time. Leaning up on an elbow, she looked down at him. "You're a mess."

His collar had come half-undone, and his skinny ascot was draped around his shoulders. She must have done that. She adored that thought. Her nipples tingled, and her stomach gave a happy lurch.

He chuckled. "While you're not a mess, you're a tousled beauty."

"How well you flatter." She gave a faux-dramatic sigh. "You have a woman lying on top of you. Seems excessive to continue with gross flattery."

"It might be, should I be false." He grabbed her firmly, pulling her leg up over his hips. His cock was hard, insistent and hot beneath her. "But you're so beautiful that it seems to hurt you."

Her heart hopped about in her chest like an insistent and injured bird. "What does that mean?"

"If you'd been less beautiful, people might be more willing to believe you're miserable."

She froze. All the way down to her toes and back up to her head. She couldn't move. Couldn't call up a false smile. "I'm not always miserable."

"You don't have to lie to me." His hands were warm across the back of her shoulders.

The only defense she had wasn't much in the scheme of things. So she lifted up, her knees splitting to nestle around his hips. She pushed her robe down around her shoulders and let it pool at her legs. The night rail was pure white and edged with lace. She unbuttoned it. Part of her knew she ought to have been more frightened. More nervous about being so displayed.

All she could hear was his insistence that she was miserable. She didn't *want* to be sad. No one did, of course, but she had a special terror of it.

She'd push that evil away any way she needed to. Even by using Ian.

Wonder overtook Ian at seeing the mysteries of her body revealed. Her breasts were small but high. Pale skin glowed in the barest tinge of lamplight. The tips of her nipples were tight.

He needed to taste them. One hand flat at her low back, he bent upward. His mouth found her warm flesh. She melted further, as if her bones had disappeared. How right, since he was as hard as he'd ever been. There was nothing between them but cloth, and it was still entirely too much. Heat flared and burned. He needed her clasped in his arms.

Sitting up brought them closer. Pressed mouth to chest to pelvis. He wanted inside her. Wanted to know what secrets she kept.

Mostly, he wanted to make her sadness go away. He needed to know that he could help her. Save her.

Except maybe no one could.

Their hands scrambled and tugged away cloth. She opened his trousers, but then he shoved them down around his hips. She had to lift up for him to push them all the way off the end of the chaise. Her flimsy gown was hiked around her hips, but it was out of the way enough for their purposes.

Once she'd yanked his shirt up over his head, he didn't see where it went. Couldn't bother when it was in the way of getting his mouth on her skin again. From the freckles across the tops of her shoulders to the pale and curved length of her collarbone to the tips of her breasts, he kissed it all. Licked and nibbled. His teeth raked down her flesh, and she only gasped.

Her hands came to rest at the back of his head. She held his mouth to her with delicious desperation that echoed through their every movement. They were frenzied.

Surely that couldn't last. Surely that would eventually burn away. Beyond that crackling fire, the remaining coals would have to be sufficient to support a lifetime of warmth. How could that be without a family to focus on? What else would be left?

Maybe he only wanted to keep the lithe and dazzling woman in his arms. The sweet taste of her skin was beauty and excitement all in one.

"You treat me like I'll break." Her fingers tightened in his hair and held him closer. "I won't. I can't."

"Everyone can break." He molded his hand to the curve of her breast and the sweep of her ribs. He licked down her stomach toward her navel. "Everyone has a line."

"Maybe." Her fingers were cool and delicate as they wrapped around his prick. She moved with such assuredness. Taking exactly what she wanted. Bloody brilliant. "But I can guarantee one thing."

He grabbed her by the hips and angled her up and back enough that his cock notched against her pussy. She was soaking wet and open for him. He ringed his grip around the base of his cock, both bracing as he liked and holding back the hot surge of pleasure.

Some wicked devil took him over. He slid the head of his prick up between her lips, aiming for that twist of special flesh at the top of her quim. Her lips clung and swept over his flesh. Good for both of them. Her little breathy gasps turned into a throaty moan.

"What is that?" she asked. She wiggled backwards. Her grip dug into his thighs. "Oh, right there. What is that you're doing?"

He grinned. He couldn't help it. Having a sensual woman atop his lap was awe-inspiring. "I'm playing."

"Oh my God, why?" The words came out of her mouth, but her wide eyes said she probably didn't care. She thrust up in tandem with the rhythm as he rubbed the head of his cock over her and through her. The soft wet kiss of her pussy along his length was completely worth it. She shook her head suddenly. "It's not the same. Not *enough*."

He knew. Oh Christ, did he know, but he loved being able to twine her into knots. Send her flying on the breeze. "Enough for what?"

"I don't know," she said, and she sounded so very mournful that it took everything he had to not laugh. She wouldn't like that much. "That *thing*. That happened last time. I want that again. You called it coming."

Her nails dug into his thighs. He hissed against the sting. "You want my cock filling you and then you want that explosion, right?"

She nodded. Her hips twisted, seeking further connection. He shifted away. Let her writhe a minute longer. "It felt good. You made me feel good."

A heavy pulse of satisfaction turned him into a more amplified version of himself. Where he'd been man, now he was beast. His grip could bruise, his teeth could mark. He ought to care. But he didn't. He only wanted.

With a growl that increased his link to the animal part of himself, he folded one implacable arm around her ass and back. All of her was for him.

He surged up while she found purchase and shoved downward. Her pussy's tight clasp was enough to drive him mad. Her whimper when her body ground against his hardness rocked through the room.

Immediately they strained together in the give and take of stroke and pull. Her head bent backwards, her body turning into one remarkable arch. He shouldn't be here. If anything, it seemed cruel to them both. He couldn't keep her and stay true to his dreams. If Ian understood anything from her mother's turn for the worse, it was that he couldn't ask her to change her mind. If she wanted to avoid children, that was her right. But he shouldn't be here. Every bit of his cock in her risked her decisions.

And yet he'd been unable to stay away.

Their bodies fit together like parts of a whole. She clung to him with every stroke. Bliss sucked at his bones. The only way to keep from going under too fast was to feast on her flesh and subsume his pleasure in her. Every inch of skin he could reach became a canvas for his mouth.

Eventually he returned to her breasts, lifting her small mounds to his mouth. He sucked and licked, much heartened when an extra flood of her moisture dripped over his prick. He liked knowing how far he'd pushed her. How much she enjoyed it. The soft and pleased gasps she gave were excellent rewards.

He wanted her mad with feeling. Wanted her turned inside out for want of him, though he knew that was an unpleasant thought and something he wasn't proud of. They had want and need. He had to know there was nothing beyond that.

He hitched her higher in his arms, so that her wet sheath came off his cock. The sudden cold was enough to jar but couldn't turn his mind away from getting back inside her. She grabbed tight to his shoulders. Her hair tumbled around them in a private, secret cave. They'd have few secrets between them. None, if he had anything to say for it.

Ian flipped them, then wedged her down into the cushions of the couch. She let go of his shoulder, her hands pushing upward toward the arm of the couch.

Then she laughed. Not meanly, not from any cruelty.

She laughed because she was enjoying the moment. Her eyes crinkled at the corners. Her wide, bright smile rocked Ian all the way down to his soul.

He slid inside her again, taking her harder this time, with harsh jolting movement that thrust her hips up off the velvet cushions. She kept smiling, kept laughing, even when he pinched her clitoris between both thumbs.

She came on a gasping cry, turning her face to bury it against the side of her arm. Her pussy tightened over his prick to suck his brains and his soul right out of his body. The tingles started at the base of his spine, gathered in his ballocks. There wasn't anything he could do, and the fact that he had to remove himself and spill across her thigh seemed like a sin.

A sin he would gladly commit again and again if it got him Lottie.

Chapter Twenty

Lottie usually liked parties, so long as they weren't held in her own home. What wasn't to like about balls? She got to wear gorgeous dresses, speak to elegant people and have an evening off from her worries, when she could pretend they didn't exist. A lovely fictive need. Only the recent evenings spent hidden away with Ian in her room had been more effective.

But standing at the head of the stairs in the Duchess of Marvell's ballroom this time filled her with a sense of dread.

Her father had arrived earlier in the afternoon. Now, he was being announced behind her. Thankfully her mother had begged out of attending—or rather her nurse had affected the same with a large dose of tonic.

How very backwards the world seemed occasionally.

She smiled. She smiled the best she could as long as she could as she made her way through the packed morass of bodies. From the stairs, she'd spotted Sera and Victoria standing toward the head of the room. They were waiting, and they would be her salvation.

Indeed, when she finally made it to them, Lottie felt her smile waver. Sera took her by the hand and squeezed. "You look unwell." Her big brown eyes were steady and comforting.

Lottie returned the squeeze. "Father is home."

Victoria passed over a flute of champagne. They stood shoulder to shoulder and turned to look out toward the majority of the ball's attendees. Unfortunately their average height meant they saw only those near and encircling them in a wall of silk and lace and beading. Lottie swallowed half the glass of bubbling champagne.

"Isn't that better sometimes?" Victoria kept her voice relatively soft.

"Sometimes." There went the rest of the pale liquid, fizzling down her throat. "He hasn't been home long enough for me to talk with him. I was already getting dressed for the evening."

She might be the worst, most shallow daughter in the world, but her one thought when the maid had announced Lord Vale's homecoming had been selfish regret. Her father's return meant having Ian into her bedroom would be nearly impossible. She smiled at a gentleman who passed by. Obviously he had no idea that she was such a terrible daughter.

She should have been happy for her mother. When she was overly excited, sometimes Mama couldn't be bothered with Papa, but she always liked having him when she felt saddened.

Instead, all Lottie could think was that she wouldn't be able to hold Ian tonight. She wouldn't be able to feel him inside her. Or talk in soft whispers between the burning fires they lit together.

"Is there any more of this?" she asked, waving her empty glass.

Sera passed hers over. "Here."

"Thank you, lovey."

"You're not worried about Henrietta Heald, are you?" Victoria's brows rose.

"Certainly not." She was worried about Etta's brother, the great, gangly lummox. Who entirely did not deserve such condemnation.

When she wanted him so desperately, it seemed rather all or nothing. He had said nothing about the future. She couldn't blame him. His entire purpose in hunting down Patricia was about creating a future for his family, which his father had fought hard for. Lottie's whole world was about compensating for her lack of a future. She'd not have children, so she'd create a whole school of daughters. She wasn't blind. She knew that was part of her reality.

But that didn't mean she could give them up either.

"She was certainly pleasant the other day." The trio had joined Henrietta and her mother for tea at their rented townhouse, in order to acquaint them with Sera and Victoria. Sera was always so graceful and kind. It was one of those things that Lottie loved about her.

But she also heard what wasn't said. That Lady Vale was often less than pleasant. Lottie was saved by the announcement of Sir Ian and his small family. "Smile, ladies. They're here."

They met Henrietta in the middle of the ballroom, making a happy and unavoidable knot of womanhood. Lottie held out both hands to Henrietta as if greeting a long-lost friend, dramatically enough that all would take note. Indeed, she did like the girl. She particularly liked the honesty in her face and the way she lit up. "Miss Heald. It's so very good to see you."

"And I the same." She took both of Lottie's hands and gave a small curtsy toward Victoria, then nodded toward Sera. "Lady Victoria, Mrs. Fletcher. It's a relief to have friendly faces in such a crowd."

Ian stood behind her. "Ladies. I'm much relieved that my sister is privileged to enjoy such lofty friends."

Lottie smiled. Really she wanted to throw her arms around Ian and beg him to take her away from the crowd, from the eyes that watched her without watching. So very public, and she was so very tired of it. They were working society's strictures to their advantage.

They'd arranged this greeting in an open manner, designed to garner the most attention. In a moment they'd take Henrietta over to meet their host. Lady Marvell would be instantly smitten with Henrietta's charm and openness. Combined with her friendly good looks, she'd instantly be an accepted member of society. She'd go about making friends as she seemed to do without thinking.

All of it the truth and all of it manipulated in a most base manner to go marvelously according to plan. Lady Marvell loved

Henrietta, of course. Positively beamed at her when Henrietta complimented the particular arrangement of flowers at the lady's elbow. Naturally it turned out that Lady Marvell had arranged them herself and gone against her friend's advice to do so.

"See there?" she crowed, turning to the Marchioness of Ashbury. "She's a girl with lovely and remarkable taste."

Marchioness Starr cut her eyes toward the ceiling. She fluttered her fan made of white fluffy feathers. "As you like. But you're still wrong."

Lottie smiled as she snuck away toward the refreshment table. Everything was working as she'd hoped.

"Should you have abandoned her so quickly?"

She gathered up a glass of champagne and kept walking as if Ian at her side hadn't made her heart leap. "It's best I leave her to Victoria's clutches. She's impeccable."

He looked handsome in evening clothes and fairly pleased with himself. He kept his hands loosely folded behind his back. "You've done a good thing tonight."

"I know." She had a bit of self-satisfaction going on as well. Her chin lifted. "It's a good night altogether, I believe. Finna remembered a clerk Patricia was interested in. He'd even slipped her funds last time. I sent him a note, and he intends to come to our next event. We'll have a good chance at catching her."

Ian smiled with a hefty measure of satisfaction. "That's the makings of a good night indeed."

Except the next time they shifted around a knot of people, it became entirely less so. Her father stood there, which was well enough. She'd missed him. He was relatively handsome, though tired-looking. Deep bags sagged under his eyes and pushed his cheeks into hanging jowls adorned with wiry muttonchops.

"Papa," she said, and she could hear the uncomfortable edge in her voice. After all, she knew the man at his side as well. "And Lord Cameron."

Lord Cameron, her father's most harped-upon choice for marrying her off. He owned the estate next to theirs in Derbyshire, but it was actually the smallest of Lord Cameron's properties. He also owned estates in Kent, a townhouse in London and a villa in Italy. If it didn't come with the man, Lottie rather thought she might enjoy an Italian villa.

Her papa preferred men who invested in land. He said it demonstrated a belief in the future of England.

"Miss Vale," said Lord Cameron. He had dark brown hair with fat curls. "It's lovely to see you again."

Lottie wanted to melt through the floor. Her throat clenched in a sickly fist. But she managed to smile as always, and it certainly seemed as if her father accepted it as true. He beamed back at her. "Lottie." He pressed one flat hand to her shoulders. "You look lovely."

She felt like hell. "I sent for you five days ago," she said quietly. She was shaking, all the way through. If it got any worse, her knees might give way. "Five days ago."

Lord Cameron had the grace to look away across the room toward the dancing couples. Ian stepped nearer to her. Quiet support, she supposed. She hardly knew what to do about that.

Her papa only nodded. "I had a bit of business to attend to. Then Lord Cameron couldn't come to town until today."

"Mama needed you." *She* had needed him through all these years, all these times. Her hands knotted into fists. Pure fury turned her guts into flame.

"It was an inevitable delay. But look!" He put out a hand toward Lord Cameron. "Surely it's worth it when we've such illustrious company."

Lord Cameron nodded. "I can speak for no one else, but I count myself lucky to be in your company."

"As we all are," Ian supplied.

Her father gave Ian a dubious look. How dare he? It wasn't as if he'd been around to pass judgment on her acquaintances. "Besides, I'm sure you've had plenty to keep yourself occupied." He nodded at Lord Cameron, his head bobbing along like an apple on a string. "She has many productive hobbies. Would you guess, Lottie here runs a lovely little charity devoted to the betterment of factory girls and other less fortunate souls."

"How righteous of her," he agreed. His curls fluttered in an errant breeze, which made no sense because Lottie felt smothered. Like all the air in the room was being sucked away.

Maybe she looked as ill as she felt, because Ian put his hand low on her back in a move that was both reassuring and nearly inappropriate. "Miss Vale, I believe I see your friends waving from across the room. Perhaps you'd like me to accompany you there?"

How kind of him to lie. Really, it was likely unfortunate, because all he'd done was give her a terrible idea. A horrible, awful, incredibly brilliant idea grew and grew in her mind.

She smiled. Her bones were brittle and her cries held back by pure will. Her smile grew into a grin. She ignored Ian's attempt at escape and looked at her father. "You're right, of course. Mama didn't need you and I certainly didn't. After all, I was fully occupied. Making torrid, steamy love with Sir Ian every night has kept me...fulfilled."

For a long, heart-stopping moment, Ian thought he'd heard her wrong. She couldn't possibly have said that. Lottie was wild and she was somewhat reckless, but he'd believed that a matter of self-protection. She was showy in order to deflect.

Not in order to set silence rippling away from their tiny knot of people, like the circles that waved outward from a pebble dropped in a pond. Lord Vale's mouth dropped open before he gave a tiny shake of his head as if trying to rid himself of what he'd heard.

Lord Cameron was amused. His eyebrows lifted, and his entire body canted slightly toward Lottie. "Pardon?"

Then she apparently decided to throw a boulder in the pond.

"Intercourse. Sexual congress." She smiled, looking around at the silent crowd doing their utmost to pretend they weren't actually listening while straining their ears toward every word. Not that Lottie was making it particularly challenging. She spoke in a voice as clear as a bell and as bright as when she'd been addressing a dozen of her girls. "A handful of times. I should have liked to experience more, but such matters are surprisingly difficult to schedule."

Ian's first instinct was to roar and fight. His blood raged in his ears. Extra emotion zinged down his limbs and fisted his hands. There was nowhere for that force to go. Certainly not toward Lottie, though she was the orchestrator of this sudden and unfortunate turn of events. "Lottie..."

She smiled at him. "I'm sorry, I did know you wished these things to be quiet. You understand, Father has a recent desire that I marry. And you do know my views on the subject."

"Pardon?" Lottie's father said in a rather befuddled tone. "You can't possibly mean... You and this man..."

She shrugged, then lifted her champagne glass toward the chandelier and peered at it. Maybe she wished for more. Maybe, if she had a scrap of the sense that the Lord had given her, she was wishing she hadn't had quite so many glasses. "I'm sorry. It's a bit gauche of me, isn't it? Probably on par with refusing to come home when your wife is in a time of *need*. When she's *ill*."

Lord Vale heard those words, that much was clear. His face flushed red enough that his cheeks were scarlet apples. "Your mother is perfectly well cared for."

"And me?" Lottie slashed out with her husky voice. A new rigidity took over her normally relaxed posture. She looked like she could break if given the slightest nudge. "Am I well cared for?"

"Obviously not, if you've let yourself turn into a whore."

"Maybe you should have been here. Then it would be *you* letting me turn into a whore. Raising myself has certain drawbacks, after all."

That was it. The freeze that had held Ian still cracked away into a thousand splinters. "Go. Now."

He didn't give Lottie a choice. He hauled her away by the wrist. She went along, but he couldn't tell if it was willingly. It didn't matter. He didn't care. Not like he was giving her much of an option—exactly as she'd stripped away most of his options.

They waded through the partygoers. A wade it was, as well, because everyone looked. Watched. Their eyes judgmental, their mouths set in displeased frowns and open gasps—except for those taking perverse pleasure in the scene evinced before them. Heads tilted together behind fans.

The whispering was beginning.

On their exodus, Ian spotted Etta. Lottie's friends Sera and Victoria flanked her. Though her features were drawn and ghost pale, she waved him on. *Go*, she mouthed. Victoria put a hand on her shoulder and nodded toward Ian.

At least Lottie's friends were sensible, though she'd lost every scrap of rational thought she'd ever possessed.

The heavens smiled down on him in small ways. His carriage waited outside. He shoved her in, not looking at her face. He couldn't. If she appeared the littlest bit amused by her ridiculous stunt, he'd lose his temper unbearably. He snapped directions at the footman and slammed the door shut. It rattled in the frame with less-than-satisfactory solidity.

Lottie squeezed herself into the far corner. "I won't apologize. I won't. I said nothing that wasn't true."

"You jeopardized everything. Everything."

Her face was drawn. In the darkness that swept past the carriage window, she was a ghost who didn't look like herself. Her wide mouth disappeared into the shadows. Her eyes gleamed though, lush and dark. She kept her chin forward as she crossed her arms over her chest. "There's no reason to be so dramatic. Not nearly."

He wanted to shake her. Grab her by the upper arms and shake back and forth until her head lolled and her neck bent. "You're mad."

She jerked her gaze toward him. Her hands dropped to her lap. "I *told* you never to call me that."

"Don't act like it."

Her gloved hand knotted into a fist. "How dare you? I never knew you had such a cruel streak."

"No." He settled back into the padded leather squabs of the seat. His bones suddenly felt weary and yet charged with nearly supernatural energy. He'd never expected this. Of all the outcomes he could have dreamt, some of which would be unpleasant, he'd never even considered this. Not finding Patricia and always having the threat of his sister's marriage over his head, that had been up there at the top of the list. Having Lottie lose her goddamned mind in the middle of a ball was *not* one of them. "It's not cruelty. It's the truth. You've done no one any favors. Not yourself or me, or your mother. Or Henrietta. Quite the remarkable coming out you've given her."

"Henrietta will be fine." Her jaw set to a mulish angle. "If anything, you'd haul down the stars from the sky for her. You'd chew her damned food if you could. Not everyone is so well adored."

"You could have been," he muttered.

"What's that?"

He could have repeated himself. He could have said it louder, or told her that he'd been wondering if he really needed children or if it would be enough to have his days filled with the bright excitement she brought. None of that had taken into account her apparent self-destructive streak. This need to destroy was new. He couldn't help but think it was an unpleasant part of her personality that he hadn't known before. That he hadn't wanted to know about.

"You'll never be able to heal your reputation." He sighed. "I probably didn't make it any better by hauling you away."

"Don't you dare say we should marry. Don't say it. I won't be held responsible for my response."

"I wouldn't fucking dream of it."

They were poisonous together. Anger lived in the space between them. He didn't know exactly where this would end, but no matter what it couldn't be pleasant. Wouldn't be pleasant. No such thing when he was so consumed by fury that his hands tingled and his palms were vortexes of sensation. He wanted to grab and break something. Maybe someone.

"Good." She lifted her chin and looked out the window. "Marriage is expressly what I was trying to avoid."

"I'm not offering," he said with special emphasis. "I doubt it would fix the situation anyhow. My sister's reputation would forever be suspect. I've been trying to bring up my family. Not seal it forever to a notorious woman."

"Don't talk about my mother like that!"

"This has nothing to do with your mother," he roared. "You. You're the notorious one. You did this. You told five hundred people about our relationship."

"What relationship? You're fucking me." Her eyes were wide, her features twisted over a snarl. "And don't lie. I know in part that has only to do with my mother and her madness. It colors everything. It shades over my whole life."

"If it does so, it's only because you let it. Because your fears turn you into someone unfortunate." The carriage drew to a stop, and he put a hand to the door, but he didn't open it. "I have no idea how you could possibly fix all this."

"I have no intention of turning myself inside out to please that man. He's never here. Hell, when he is, he drinks in his study and talks to me like I'm a crony of his. Not his daughter. How the hell can he expect to storm in and marry me away?"

"That's no reason to poison the waters of all Society." He shook his head. "How can you not see what you've done?"

"Because I don't think I've done anything wrong. Damn them all. I'd rather burn their entire world to the ground than endure one more moment."

"You don't hate them. You hate yourself."

Chapter Twenty-One

Oh, how that hurt. Lottie's eyes filled immediately with tears, but she had years and years of practice in beating them away. How wrong this was all turning. She had done this. Brought it on herself.

She pressed her fingertips to her brow, trying to order her thoughts. They swirled along with her emotions and her temper. The skin along the back of her neck prickled. Beneath she was one hard rock of fear and clenching anger. She didn't know her own mind.

In a way, he was right. She'd turned into everything she'd feared being.

"Where are we?" she whispered. There had been no such thing as tracking the turns of the carriage or watching the streets go by. She'd hardly been able to follow the bounce of her own thoughts.

The only positive thing she could cling to was that Mama had been home and not privy to that awful scene. Though part of Lottie wondered if she'd have done it had her mother been there. Maybe. Maybe she'd been bound to crack anyway. That was what this felt like. Cracking open like she'd always feared she would. Like she'd *known*.

He pushed open the small carriage door and stepped out. At least he still provided his hand to help her down. Some small gestures were more than courtesies, they were reassurances. So she told herself.

"You know where we are." He stepped to the side. How severe he looked. His mouth thinned and his jaw was as sharp as a blade. He held his shoulders steady and straight.

The school. He'd brought her to her rented townhouse. The windows were dark under the bare light of the moon. No one had been expected, so not a scrap of welcome in any way had been left out.

She still wanted to grab on to Ian, bury her face in the front of his jacket. Emotion zipped back and forth between them. But she had no words for it and no way to grasp what had been. The moments in her room had been safe. Quiet and exciting.

Maybe she needed to touch him and hold him all over again. Then the awful whispers in her head might go away and she could stop feeling like she'd lost track of herself in the wake of all her fears.

He likely had different ideas, however. She licked her lips as she looked up at the building that had once been so safe. She'd always been able to come here and run away from her home troubles, to feel welcome and wanted and useful. In the dark of night, the building's stones looked different. "Why are we here?"

"I couldn't exactly take you to my home, now could I?" He sneered a little. "Unless you wished to face my mother and explain to her why you ruined Henrietta's big night? Or maybe you should go home and let your father beat you?"

She felt truculent. Petty. Her mouth set into a distinct downward curve as she fished her key out of her ribbon-adorned reticule and unlocked the door. "Father wouldn't beat me."

"No?" He prowled along behind her through the dark corridors. "Because I'm considering doing so myself."

"You wouldn't either." She led the way toward her study because she didn't know where else to go. The tiny parlor where she and her friends retired to exclusive company didn't seem right. She was entirely too wound up to be in such comfortable surrounds. The messy comfort of her desk seemed more appropriate. "You wouldn't dare."

He didn't sit. Crossing his arms, he took up position in the middle of the room as if establishing himself as the palace guard. Suddenly he loomed as big and solid as a castle. Intractable. Unshakable. Enraged. "Don't try me."

She pulled her mouth into a smile and tilted her chin up, as high as she could go without having to look away from him. There was something magnetizing about his eyes when he was furious with her. Particularly when he was so very furious with her.

At least he saw her. He knew it was Lottie at the core. "You're wrong. I don't hate myself."

"No?"

He came closer. Either he saw the way she was looking at him or he couldn't stay away from her any more than she could stay away from him. He wrapped a few locks of her hair around his fingers. She didn't know when they had fallen. His touch skimmed down her neck and across her collarbones.

"I hate the rest of them. I wish they'd all wither and die."

His mouth tweaked. "You don't believe that. You don't want that."

She shook her hair back, out of his grasp. She wanted to be chased. She wanted to be wanted and have him follow her to the ends of the world and beyond. "What do you know?"

"I know you're so goddamned frightened you can hardly see what's in front of your nose. I know you've done something that you'll regret. Desperately. I know you haven't realized how far you've gone or what the repercussions will be."

She snorted, but her chest was clenching tight. "What repercussions? Father won't marry me off. End of story." She made a show of brushing off her hands. "I've money in trust through Mama's family. They knew it was likely that whatever man I ended up with would tire of me. It's the way of things."

"I'm not tired of you," he said on a growl. "I'm so angry that I might break you."

"I dare you to try." She spit the words. "I don't want to break. I only want to get under you."

"So bloody crass," he growled. The rumbling gutter tones of his voice made her nipples pebble and her belly flip. Especially when he spun Lottie around, pushing her up against the desk. The sharp edge barely pushed through her layers of skirts and petticoats. "That mouth has gotten you in more trouble than you know."

Smiling was easy, though her blood burned hot and her breathing was ragged and harsh. "So teach me a lesson."

She thought she'd be in for another of his searing kisses. The ones that spun her inside out and left her panting for more. The whole reason she'd journeyed down this path. His mouth on hers, more of those kisses and then more from there in the set pattern men always followed. Mouth to breasts to the main act.

She loved underestimating a man.

He spun her around again so the desktop dug into her belly. Her hips jerked back under his hard grip. Air flowed over her skin when he scooped her skirts up. She gasped. Her hands flinched and spasmed on the felt blotter. Her elbow twitched into a jar of ink, sending it spinning off the edge.

It clattered and crashed across the floor.

He pulled her bloomers down, and she bit her lip against the squeak that wanted to escape her.

Her sex was wet and blooming, begging for his first touch.

She hadn't known what to hope for. He grabbed her ass in firm hands, his grip unrelenting. Tingles echoed from where he held her apart. She rose up on her toes, and she wasn't sure if she was trying to release that pressure or trying to get closer to him.

"Like this?" His voice descended to such a deep buzz it became difficult to make out words. "Is this what you wanted me to do? Lay you out like a whore or a strumpet?"

She tried to swallow down her apprehension. She was still in control of this situation. After all, he was the one driven to such extreme measures, while she simply waited.

Angling her head, she looked at him. His every feature seemed deeper carved, his jaw too sharp to be believed. "Depends," she said. "Will you make me feel good?"

He'd apparently lost his grip on all words, because what came out of his mouth were pure guttural groans. Then he sank to his knees.

She buried her face against the meat of her upper arm. Silk ruffles caressed her chin, but she barely felt it. Not over the wet, liquid bliss he swirled through her.

His mouth. That was his mouth on her sex again. Her eyes rolled back, eyelids shutting, and she wrenched with sobs. Long, languid licks. He bit, and she couldn't help but grind down against the sparking thrill.

He was all over her. Mouth against her sex, fingers ringing her opening. He rubbed evening stubble against her inner thighs in a soft wash of pain, then dragged his chin over her center. When he plunged his tongue into her, she lost her battle and cried out.

He stroked two fingers where his tongue had been. The embracing, pushing pleasure against the front of her channel rolled clear through her.

Her fingertips scrabbled against the wood of the desk, nails catching and digging. She didn't want to get away, but staying still was entirely beyond her.

"This." He spoke against her skin, against her most secret places, as calm as if he'd asked for a cup of tea. "This is only the beginning. I could give you the world. I could flip you up and down in so many ways you don't know. More than that, I'd make you beg for it."

She nodded before realizing he couldn't see her. She tried to dampen her lips. "Promises, promises," she said, ignoring the fact that it sounded rather more like a croak than an enticement.

She never could have guessed the immense rewards. He laughed. There, with his mouth against her flesh and his fingers in her cunny, he laughed. It rocked through her body, turned her into something less and something more at the same time. And he drew her out into a million crackling points of pleasure.

Ian loved making Lottie come. He swelled with power and satisfaction, combined with the sense of providing for his woman. But underneath it burned frustration he couldn't force away. He couldn't make the growling, animal part of himself calm. The taste of her under his mouth wasn't enough to soothe. Even the idea of fucking her senseless wasn't enough.

He needed base and crude things. An acknowledgment that something could be salvaged of their incendiary explosion.

She refused to give it to him. Her fine and formal evening gown hitched up around her waist so she looked half like a princess and half like a misused whore. His hands slid and skipped over her skin. Softness over the bite of her sharp pelvic bones pressed against the desk.

She tossed her head. Red locks had come unpinned, tumbling around her face. The single light in the room cast long fingers of shadow over them both. She refused to give him reality. Her mouth curved into a grin—that false one he was coming to hate.

"You're all talk. I knew it. Nothing so much of punishment in that." Her jaw cracked on a yawn, and he wasn't sure if she meant it or not. If he *bored* her. "You're not right about everything, you know that? You've your own lies that you tell."

"You're the biggest liar of them all."

"Maybe." Her hands were flat on the desk. Her ass elevated when she rose up on her toes. Between her thighs winked the glistening crescent of her sex. "You have this perfect image of the family you've always wanted. You've never questioned it. A sweet wife and a half dozen children, exactly as you've imagined. Like your father wished for you. But I know one thing that you don't seem to."

He ought to let go of her. With her taste across his tongue, she was temptation incarnate. He wasn't sure what he was resisting at this point. Those bridges weren't burned, they'd been hacked to kindling first. "What's that?"

She lifted up on her elbows far enough to twist and look at him. Her smile was cold. He folded over her back and tasted it with his own mouth. The instant he pulled away, she started talking again, much to his regret. His grip curled into her waist cruelly enough that he pinched her ribs.

"You, Ian. You're not the man you think you are." Her fingers were cool and gracious on his jaw. "You've got a guilty, filthy soul."

Maybe she was right, because his hand delved into the tumbled mass of her hair and twisted tight. Her hips pushed up and out. Seeking him. "Unlike you, I've control of myself."

"No, you don't." She laughed. "If you did, you wouldn't have me pinned to a desk. You wouldn't still need to punish me."

"Not true."

"Do it." She licked her lips with her pink tongue. The way she gazed at him was as savage as he felt. "Perhaps I need a little punishment. I wasn't disciplined as a child. I'm everything reckless. Make me feel it."

His hand flew of its own command. Up into the air, then soaring back down again until he slapped the flesh of her small, curvaceous ass. The sound snapped through the room. He jerked his hand back. There on the white skin was a perfect print, all the way down to fingers and thumb.

He did it again.

She cried out. Her hands flattened. She melted down, her chest meeting the desk. But she pushed her bottom into the third blow. Then the fourth. By the fifth, she was sobbing into her shoulder.

He hesitated. Long enough to feel the press of his cock against the inside of his trousers. What had once been fairly comfortable, innocuous fabric now scraped like a thousand granules of sand across his sensitive flesh.

He was so damned. So wrong. Everything about this was wrong. He should stop. Make this end.

"Do it," she taunted. Her spine curved in a sinuous arch toward him. "Don't you stop, don't think it. Make me burn."

He continued. Five more blows. Her sex quivered at the next to last. She moaned long and loud. The tenth slap was still echoing in the room when he loosed his trousers and stripped his jacket down his arms. He yanked his shirt off over his head, and she was still crying when he sank his cock deep in her wet sheath. "Here, yes? This is what you wanted?"

Her fingers twitched on the desk. Her moans turned into a husky mewl. "You don't know. I get lost. I lose myself. Here..."

He thrust his hips against the heat coming off her bruised flesh. He should have been nicer. Should have backed down from the precipice that he'd found.

Instead he sank his grip into her ass. Her flesh felt different. Firmness came from the swollen flesh combined with pure heat pouring off her. He wasn't appeased. Wasn't comforted. Not in any meaningful way.

He was leading with his body, with his cock. Fucking her deep wouldn't fix any of this. Once he spent, she'd still be as troublesome as she'd been an hour ago. He'd still be unable to forget her, unable to see a way clear of the mess she'd created.

Somewhere these terrible truths made reality, but not so long as he was inside her. Not so long as he could seek the front of her dress and tuck his fingers down her bodice. Her nipples were tight already, and he played and pinched the perfect little beads. Her cunt pulled at him with her wetness. Her cries and moans filled the shadowy room.

He wanted to go away on the pleasure. Wanted to let it coast over him like something dark and meaningless.

That was the problem altogether. It wasn't meaningless—yet it didn't mean enough either.

He withdrew, but he couldn't make himself go far. She reached backwards. Her fingers scrabbled over his hip, to his waist. She tried to hold him to her.

"No, don't stop." She panted. Her eyes were glassy and her cheeks flushed with red. "Don't. I need this."

"Why?" He gathered her close, yanking and pawing at her dress until she shrugged and helped. It stripped off her body and crumpled in a pile to the side. He spun her so her ass pushed against the carved desk. She hissed. He didn't relent.

So very ruined.

She shook her head. "I wish I knew. I...I can't."

Her fingers traced over his chest in a soft caress until she reached the hair above his cock. Her nails scratched and tangled. His turn to hiss, but he wouldn't let go of her hips. He hitched one of her knees over his forearm. She was a lewd masterpiece. He sank three fingers deep in her quim, then moved back up to circle the top of her sex.

"You will," he said eventually. He dragged his gaze up her body. Lean. Long. The bare curves of her breast, tipped with pink. "Tell me you want me."

"I do." She answered so quickly. So automatically. "I don't know much. It's all I can do to scramble along and keep up with the rest of my life. But the one thing I do know is how much I want you. My body craves yours."

"That's because your body knows." He edged the head of his cock over her wet slit, delving between her lips. A tease and back out again. "Because this part of us is perfect."

She arched back on one arm and swept the other around his neck to insist he come closer so that she could whisper in his ear. "And the rest of us is so very wrong, isn't it?"

He buried his face against her neck as he thrust. There was so much of her that he knew to be perfection. She was beauty and grace. And fury. It was the fury he didn't know if he could handle. But it didn't seem right to agree while he fucked her. He claimed her in a deep stroke that made her nails sink into his neck and pleasure rock up through his chest and down to his toes. He was as lost as she was.

"It's all right," she whispered. Her voice was hoarse with gasps and a soft, keening moan when he slid up the front of her sheath. He pressed two fingers to her cunt, pinched her lips against the slide and thrust of his cock. She dug her nails into his ass. "I understand. I wanted you and I took you. All this other stuff is unfair."

"Not unfair. Unexpected."

Their chests rubbed together with every surge. Sweat sheened. Their breathing was jerky, abandoned.

"You were both wrong and right." She bit his earlobe, then licked away the sting. "I don't hate myself, but I don't hate the rest of them either."

His grip above her thigh squeezed. He wrenched her up so the angle of her hips shifted. Stroke and fuck and take. All wrapped together. "Me? Do you hate me?"

She didn't answer. Part of him wanted to take it for affirmation. Except she burst apart into orgasm. Her agreement was there in the husky keening of her cries and the way her body clenched, tried to bind him to her. The clasp was too much. She dug nails into his neck and then pushed him away as fast. Her hand slid across his sweat-dampened chest.

"Bloody fucking hell," he grunted. He slipped out of her sheath at the last second. His release jerked lashing euphoria from his spine and from that guilty, filthy soul she'd mentioned. As spiky pleasure washed him with gooseflesh and loosened his knees, he knew what was coming.

She panted, her arm still looped around his neck, her other hand resting on his chest. Her head stayed lowered. She couldn't—or wouldn't—look at him.

"I don't hate you, I swear it. Me. I hate what I *could become*. What I feel like tonight." Her huge and damaged eyes flashed up at him. He wasn't big enough to wipe away that pain. Nothing ever would be, not so long as she was so very frightened of herself.

Her throat tightened on a swallow, and his chest tightened in tandem. Breath rasped his lungs. Whatever she was about to say, he wasn't going to like it.

"I can't inflict this on anyone else. I've told you that." She pushed him away. A nude study in beauty, from her dips and bones to the softness of her curves. "That includes you. Goodbye, Ian."

Chapter Twenty-Two

The intensity with which Sera and Victoria watched Lottie made her feel like she would fall out of her own skin at any moment. Or maybe that was what came from missing Ian. No matter which, it turned out that she'd found a more miserable way to live. Joy and kittens and rainbows to all.

In the reception hall they rented quarterly for the school's social mixers, she directed a small army of girls in assembling flowers in vases and decorating the walls with swags of bunting. Sera and Victoria sat near the front entrance, counting dance cards against expected attendees.

But they watched her the whole time. Though she tried her best to not look back at them, she knew they whispered. The guilt rained down on her like hail.

"That's it, girls. Continue as you are. Remember, we're aiming for beauty. Not conformity. Have fun at your tasks," she said before patting a girl on the shoulder and heading toward her two best friends in the world.

Victoria's expression was warm, her cheeks rounded. Her smile was small but enough of a reassurance she didn't hate Lottie. "Are you finally ready to talk about it?"

"Certainly not," Lottie said with as much of a chuckle as she could muster. "I don't intend to *talk*. That wouldn't be at all like my family. Who bothers with such nonsense?"

Sera leaned across the small table piled with dance cards and tiny pencils and took Lottie's hand. She squeezed tight. "Those who need it."

Lottie shook her head. If she released one tiny fraction, the rest would come spilling behind. A dam crumbling under the weight of everything she didn't know how to assess. She'd drown. "What I *need* is for this evening to continue without a hitch. We must truly be impeccable. After my recent peccadillo, we must be prepared for a level of examination we're unaccustomed to."

"Peccadillo?" Sera echoed.

She and Victoria traded a measured glance. Lottie wanted to send the perfect squares of parchment flying. Yes, she'd ruined everything. She'd risked all she held dear and then gone ahead and thrown away the one person who made her heart feel whole. That didn't mean she needed her supposed friends passing judgment on her choices.

She had reasons.

As a small blessing, her father had retreated back to the country. He'd packed up the very next morning in typical cowardly fashion. Lord Cameron had gone along, but if he hadn't left the city, Lottie wished him well. There was no reason for her inappropriate outburst to ruin his time in London.

It wasn't as if she'd staked out the entire city as her territory. If that were true, Ian would have gone home to the country.

He'd not. Reports and gossip told her he'd remained and escorted his sister to event after play after musicale. How very lucky he was to be male and rich. Such minor issues were gladly overlooked, while Henrietta benefitted from whispers he'd increased her dowry as an intentional distraction. Sera and Victoria had engaged in only the most minor socializing. Enough to make it clear they were unafraid of the talk.

Lucky for Victoria, her parents were out of the country. They had accompanied Victoria's stodgy fiancé, Lord Ashby, on a diplomatic mission and left Victoria under the aspect of her doddering aunt. By the time the trio returned home, a much grander scandal would hopefully absorb Society's attention.

Not that Lottie could imagine what would be grand enough to wash away the ton's memory of her dramatic *Sturm und*

Drang. Perhaps if the queen married her groundskeeper, Lottie would have a chance.

Her temples throbbed with sudden and abrupt pain. She rubbed them, but it didn't alleviate the urge to run. Flee. Abandon all hope, ye who enter here.

Or enter *her*. An absurd giggle almost overwhelmed her. She'd lost her mind. Completely.

"Why don't you two go home to dress. I'll make sure everything gets finished up here. We're almost ready as it is."

Victoria rose and took Lottie's hand. "We want to be here for you."

Her kindly strokes up and down Lottie's arm were both relieving and frightening and even a little bit annoying. Lottie wanted to draw into herself, not be comforted. She'd crumble if given the slightest bit of encouragement. As subtly as she could manage, she pulled away. "You'll help me best by making sure you're ready to take over if I need you to."

Sera stood as well. They flanked her, one on each side. She wanted to sag. After all, they'd hold her up. But then nothing would put her back together again. "We only want you to know that we're here for you. That we love you. With enough time, everything will pass."

Braced between her two best friends in the world, she could admit to herself she desperately missed Ian. That wouldn't pass. Even if she still couldn't say the words to anyone else, she knew it. She missed the way he'd drop by the school unannounced, offering information about Patricia's whereabouts or the likelihood that she'd be found in any particular place. Or the times she'd finagled him into returning for tea. Those had gone better once her mother wasn't throwing herself into ponds.

She missed talking with him. He'd been steadying. Calming. A safe harbor, a place she could return to and count out her treasures. She missed touching him and kissing him and knowing that she had a measure of connection in the world. She missed having someone who relished her attentions.

Mother hadn't been out of her room for the two weeks since the ball. Some days, she never made it out of bed. She claimed to be recuperating and reading, but many days she didn't turn on a lamp, and she kept the curtains closed against the encroaching sun.

Lottie was going to lose control soon. So very soon.

She smiled first at Sera and then at Victoria. "Go, ladies. I'm well. I promise."

And they believed her.

Of course they did. It wasn't as if she had pushed him away for pure caprice. This constant, unrelenting pressure inside her head was proof of that if nothing else. She was riding the sharp edge of madness. There was no reason to inflict that sort of pain on anyone else.

With plenty more low-pitched words and assurances they'd return before the event started that evening, Sera and Victoria gathered their cloaks and departed. Lottie was left with the half dozen servants and school-goers she directed toward making the room acceptable. The event would go on. This was balance. This was what she'd put her energy into over the years.

The school would go on no matter what. They operated below the rungs of her usual societal acquaintances. So long as they kept their accustomed people, everything would be normal. She hoped.

Fifteen minutes later she waved the girls away so they could return to the school and get dressed in their finest clothing, which had been specifically sewn for the occasion. How thrilled they all were. They walked away in a giggling, twisting spill of happy voices.

Lottie envied them. She shut the door and set about gathering up the last few scraps of ribbon and tulle on the floor. The room was large and empty. Low ceilings weren't particularly attractive, but they'd done their best to make the space pleasant. Once it was filled with eager gentlemen and the ladies Lottie had helped create, it would be entirely different and more enjoyable.

She went home reluctantly, but she had nowhere else to go. She stopped by her mother's room on her way upstairs. Darkness pervaded, of course. Mama was little more than a pile of blankets and pillows in the center of the bed.

Lottie stroked reddish strands of hair that streaked across a lace-covered pillow. "Mama? How are you today?"

She smiled, though it seemed forced to Lottie's practiced gaze. When she squeaked open her eyes, they were reddened. Watery. "Pleasant enough. I've plans for tomorrow. I'm going to paint by the river."

Lottie didn't believe that at all. Mama didn't believe it either. She could barely muster the smallest bit of conviction. But Lottie smoothed back her hair and then straightened the ribbon marking her mother's place in a book. "Mary Shelley? Is that really what you should be reading?"

Her mother's expression fell. She pressed her cheek into the pillow, and her eyes drifted near to shut. "It distracts me."

Lottie's chest pinched and her spine fused. She never intended to hurt her mother, but she had, hadn't she? She'd hurt herself too, but worst she had pushed Ian away forever. Maybe he'd be better off without her, but one thing was for certain.

In this darkened room, facing her mother's unbearable sadness, Lottie knew she needed Ian. She needed his strength and the way that he'd believed in her.

She'd lost him. It had been her fault, as most things seemed to be. "I've a social tonight. I'll be out of the house late."

Mama tried weakly to push up to a sitting position against the pillows. Carefully, she rearranged her features into a pleasant scheme of concentration. Her mouth smiled and her eyes were fixed on Lottie, but she wasn't there. Her sadness had taken her wandering, until she was lost with no way home. She nodded anyway. "You must ensure all the girls are seen home safely. Anything less wouldn't be you."

Lottie was crumbling under the weight of her own fears.

If it weren't for Lottie, her mama would be completely alone. Having a man in her life was no help with the way Lottie's father ran at every opportunity.

Was that what she truly feared? Not the fact that she'd slip into madness herself, but that she'd be alone when it finally happened? Fear licked across her palms in a clenching tingle and streaked up her forearms. Her eyes filled with tears at the very idea, which in itself indicated there might be truth.

The irony was terrible. Awful. If that were the very thing she most feared—she'd ensured it would happen all on her own. All but guaranteed it.

Ian tried to convince himself he was looking forward to the school's soiree simply because they had every reason to believe Patricia would be there. Tonight he'd have his hands on the errant woman and soon after he'd have the proof of Etta's indelicate marriage. Everything tied up in a neat and pretty bow.

How unfortunate that bow didn't include Lottie in any way.

It would be bad enough he'd soon be forced to see her. Though he wouldn't care, shouldn't care.

He had no need for such an example of womanhood. Her beauty and charm meant nothing if everything beneath her surface was false. He'd thought her more than that. He'd thought her someone remarkable and beautiful all the way through.

She'd fooled him, of course, but she had also seemed to fool herself.

The devastation on her face had been awful. She'd refused to talk. Kicked him out. Forced him away.

He'd tried to hold her when the tears started. She'd literally held him at arm's length. There'd been nothing more to do after that, and words failed to break through. He'd sent the carriage off and walked the streets the rest of the night. Part of him had nearly hoped for an attacker. A footpad after a good row. Anything to fight against.

After the whole tumultuous night, Ian would have loved to have been able to plant a fist in someone's face. Anyone's. But there were no enemies in a situation like this. Not when he knew exactly how badly Lottie hurt.

How goddamned stupid she'd been as well.

He had very few hopes with regard to the evening. Finding Patricia and seeing her immediately punished was the most he could look forward to.

Two months ago, that was the only thing on his mind. Now it seemed small consolation as he straggled into the foyer of his house, drawing on his gloves and gathering his top hat from a servant.

His mother appeared in the library doorway. "Good luck, Ian."

He gave her a kiss on the cheek. "I need no luck. Every bit of information I have directs me toward Patricia tonight. You know how grasping she is."

His mother nodded, but the lines that drove between her brows didn't ease. "You'll see Miss Vale tonight too, won't you?"

"I will." He missed her despite how much he shouldn't. Being so decidedly unwanted and venturing forth anyway seemed foolhardy. "Our interactions will be kept to a minimum. You have no reason to fear."

"Good. You need to stay away from that woman." She gave a sad shake of her head. "I never would have thought it the first time I met her, but she's obviously a bad sort. Her mother must be unbearably disappointed in her."

Ian's teeth ground together. "No, Mother. I won't tolerate such talk."

"It's truth."

"I don't care to hear it."

And yet that was all he could do in her defense. Lottie had decided she didn't need him in her life. But what would be worth fighting her stubbornness for? Why did part of him keep slamming up against that wall in his mind, over and over again?

He should have given up already.

There was no *reason* for this.

He bade his mother farewell and let the carriage convey him to the address he'd previously obtained from Lottie. The reception room was in a middling sort of area of town. Below stairs was a tailor, a butcher and a confectioner. Upstairs, Ian found three women gathered around the entrance. He nodded. "Ladies."

"Gor," one of them whispered as he passed. "If they're all like that, I'll be coming every time."

Inside was more crowded. Men and women stood about in groups. A general atmosphere of awkwardness was found in forced giggles and the stiffness of men's shoulders, but it was also mixed with a healthy dose of excitement. The air fairly swirled. The decorations, while simple, had transformed the large room into a taste of anticipation.

Ian stood inside the double doors and looked about.

He saw Lottie, and then he knew why his mind had been unable to let her go.

She looked beautiful. The pale lilac of her dress played to her creamy complexion. It seemed she'd tried to mute her beauty, because the dress was absent of any sort of decoration or adornment. There was no helping it. She was the most beautiful woman in the room to Ian.

Because he loved her.

What a bloody fool he was. No halves or almost about it. Nothing should have been able to push him away. Not if he'd had a scrap of awareness. Or if he'd realized how much he needed her. She lit him up from within.

And yet he could see the strain in her. She held herself carefully. The smile she flashed was not real as she slipped through knots of her girls and introduced them to men. Not really. Her skin was whiter than her usual cream, barring two hectic flags of red high on her cheekbones. The pinched way she walked made each step brittle.

It only got worse when she saw him. She tossed away the smile she'd been clinging to as if throwing it into a coal bin. Discarded.

Loving someone who was determined not to be loved seemed an exercise in futility. He'd never been the sort, but he'd found no shortcut to get rid of these feelings. His arms burned with the need to wrap around her.

Except she was all prickles and nerves as she approached him. "You're here."

"Did you expect any different?"

Her gaze darted over his face like she was looking for something. "Fletcher's men are already here." She flicked her fingers in a little circle about her shoulder. "Here and there. Dressed to fit in."

"And Finna?"

"Waiting in the corner." She pointed to where the young woman sat, her hands folded in her lap. "Patricia will come. Either for money from you, or from the sympathetic gentleman."

His fingertips curled against the impulse to touch her throat. That vulnerable length was beauty and strength, with a flutter at the base above her collarbones. She wasn't comfortable.

He ought to feel bad about that. He didn't. He wanted her uncomfortable. He wanted her as miserable as he was. If he were to be alone in love, he'd not be alone in the pain. "Have you been well?"

238

She turned large, liquid eyes up toward him. Her voice was husky. "You're not the sort to be unnecessarily cruel. I know you better than that."

He needed her desperately. This all seemed ridiculous. "Maybe I don't know myself."

"I know you." She looked out toward the crowds as she spoke, and kept her voice so soft he almost thought he'd imagined it. "I know you more than I know myself, I think."

Except he hadn't any chance to follow up. A tiny flurry of activity near the back of the room caught his eye. Finally. Something to *do*. Someone he could direct all this rage at. "I see her."

He found himself grinning with feral intent as he stormed across the room.

Patricia must have felt his focus upon her, because she flinched and turned. It was certainly her. That she was well put together and nicely dressed only aggravated Ian further. For someone who had been on the run for two months, she had a healthy flush in her cheeks. Her eyes flashed wide and her mouth dropped open—but she didn't look surprised. She looked...pleased.

She ran.

Patricia's movements were rushed and flailing. When another woman accidentally stepped into her path, Patricia shoved her to the side. The blonde fell to the floor, but she was quickly surrounded by plenty of friends.

He almost preferred that the bitch ran. Giving chase forced a rush of energy through his body and down his legs. It was an outlet.

They darted around and through the groups and to the back door. It banged behind her as a gentleman in a narrow-collared jacket stepped in front of him. "God damn it, move!" Ian barked.

"Now," added Lottie.

He was startled to realize she was right behind him, but then he shouldn't have been.

The man moved. The back door slammed shut. Ian ran for it, jerked it open.

There was no one there. "Blast it."

"Down the stairs." Lottie pointed at another door across the landing. "It's the only way out."

The stairs let out onto a narrow, stone-lined alley, but there was still no sight of Patricia. "Where the hell did she go?"

Lottie turned in a circle. Her hair fell around her shoulders from the dash down the stairs. The far end of the alley opened on the street. "The alley doesn't end, it bends."

He rather regretted not having Fletcher or one of his dense bullies when he turned the shallow corner.

Patricia wasn't alone.

Chapter Twenty-Three

Of all the things she'd expected, it hadn't been that Patricia would be aligned with such a proper-looking man. Patricia herself was blowsy. Though her dress was nicely made, it fit badly over her stomach and pulled tight. Her hair was well pinned but lank and greasy, as if she'd not washed. Over her whole face was a slight sheen of sweat and oily nerves.

The girls who'd attended Lottie's school regularly knew better than to let their hygiene drop to such unappealing levels.

The man at her side was another matter. He was...normal. He had brown hair, a decently sewn suit of brown wool and was of middling height. His waistcoat was an inoffensive green that brought out flecks of color in otherwise brown eyes.

But those eyes were cold and empty of compassion.

Lottie's stomach did a nifty little flip and landed somewhere around her throat. She tried vainly to swallow it down. "Patricia," she said as calmly as she could. "You've not introduced me to your gentleman."

"Are you mad?" The woman tipped her head. "It's not as if this is some sort of tea party."

The man stepped forward. "Do forgive my wife. She's feeling a bit puckish lately. I'm Bertrand Heeler."

"I couldn't give a shit." Ian tipped forward onto the balls of his feet. His shoulders snapped taut. "I want the certificate."

"And I want a life of comfort." He gave a rather suave shrug. "This means we must have the money you promised."

"I haven't got it."

"That's unacceptable. After the piss-worthy amount you sent last time, you'll forgive me if I came prepared for more of the same." Seemingly out of nowhere, a pistol appeared in the man's hand. Lottie gasped. Ian yanked her to the side and pushed her behind himself for protection. His hand remained wrapped around her forearm. He gripped her too tight. A pinch of pain ran up her flesh.

She stayed where he'd put her. She liked it. Liked that he'd put himself before her. Maybe that was petty or childish. It most certainly wasn't noble of her.

But it was what she'd wanted all along. On the most elemental level she'd craved a man willing to take care of her.

Only to push it away once she'd finally found what she needed.

What a great, bloody fool she was.

She stepped to the side so that she could see the desperate Mr. Heeler, though she didn't try to pull her arm away from Ian. Let him hold on to her. She didn't mind. "I'm sure you are unsurprised that we haven't got it."

"Bugger off, cunt," Patricia screeched. "I need that money."

"Such language," she said in her most airy way. "You obviously should have come for many more classes. We could have found you a more long-term venture that would give you the life you'd like."

"As a shop girl, married to a clerk?"

"Are you with child?" Lottie asked abruptly.

Patricia's hand flew to her belly. The curve wasn't pronounced until she drew the material taut. Then it became as clear as day. "That's none of your business."

Lottie sighed. "Is that why you resorted to blackmail? Your...husband couldn't sustain you sufficiently?"

She shook her head and snapped her chin toward her husband. "I found me the right man."

"You should have run off with him. You made a terrible mistake in coming after my family. Or in coming after Lottie," Ian said. "I protect those who are mine."

"And damn you for it." Patricia sidled nearer to her husband, but he held her off.

"Got the pistol, lovey," he said in a not-unkind voice. "Don't break up my aim."

She fluttered her lashes at him. The girl was pleasant-featured. How sad that she would fall to this level. "See?" she said to Lottie and Ian. "My man takes care of me. In return, I follow his ideas."

"So that's why you tried blackmail after a year of silence." Ian shook his head. "I'd wondered. Put in a bad way by the blighter, were you? Does he gamble?"

"I'm a card player, not a gambler or blighter." Heeler's face turned red. "But I am getting damned irritated with this conversation. If you haven't any money here, I know you've access to plenty." He twitched the gaping barrel of the pistol. "Walk ahead of me. Down the alley. We're going to take a trip."

"To where?" Lottie asked, as kindly as she could manage. For what it was worth.

"You tell us," Patricia snarled. "Where can you get the most funds in the shortest amount of time? I know you, Sir Ian. Arthur said you always had a bit of blunt in your study."

Nudged by the invisible hand of the pistol's aim into walking side by side, Lottie and Ian exchanged a look. It was a short one that lasted only a second, maybe less. In his eyes, Lottie saw more than she'd ever thought possible. Trust. Determination. Even the oddest hint of humor, at a time like this.

Her love.

She shuddered as she jerked her head back around. That was this never-ending pain, the feeling that she'd gone off the rails. Not madness. Not the edge of dropping into nothingness and her mother's damnation.

It was love for Ian.

How insanely terrifying.

Her footsteps faltered. Something cold and hard poked her in the back. Terror skittered down her spine and turned her veins to shards of ice.

If they made it out of this alive, she'd never let fear manage her life again. Somehow. She'd figure it out.

With Ian. If he'd have her back, though maybe he'd be a fool to take that risk. Not like she'd proved herself particularly reliable.

The mouth of the alleyway opened before them. Night draped the street in shadows the streetlamps could barely push back. Lottie's slippers crossed the threshold of the entryway and stopped.

"Move on," Heeler said. He poked her with the barrel of the pistol. "Let's keep on now."

Slowly, so slowly, she shook her head. "No. I think not."

And then she screamed.

Ian launched into immediate response. He spun, knocking a hard blow into Heeler's chin. The other man flew backwards. His elbow landed in Patricia's side, but the woman didn't go down. She screeched.

Lottie kicked her. Really, she was aiming for the gun in Heeler's hand, but that proved too fast of a target and limbs were flying and things happened. Her toe connected with Patricia's ribs. The other woman flipped and scrabbled toward Lottie.

Ian wrestled with Heeler for the pistol. It exploded with a pop in the small alleyway. The rocks pinged with a sharp sound. The bullet, probably bouncing wherever it liked. Lottie flinched, narrowly avoiding Patricia's nails across her cheek.

She kicked again, this time intentionally aiming for ribs. Patricia dropped to the flagstones. Her eyes pinched shut around fat, welling tears.

Ian punched Heeler. Harder. More. His fists flew into a blur and made raw meat of the other man's face. His lip split, and Ian's garnet ring cut his temple. Blood ran down his face like thin ribbons. He tried to fight back, but Ian gave him no quarter.

Eventually, Heeler was a writhing lump of man on the ground. Ian stood above. His chest heaved on heavy pants. His hands were still fists at his hips. He kept his eyes narrowed on the other man, as if watching—or hoping—for another attack. It didn't come.

Heeler was a defeated, lost man.

Out of nowhere, three of Fletcher's men arrived. Her screams had likely drawn them. "Thank God. Can you help us with cleanup?"

"Of course, Miss Vale. Mr. Fletcher told us to help you however you like."

She said nothing in response because otherwise she'd cry. Too much. All of this was too much at once. She pinched the bridge of her nose. "Why did you have to go this route, Patricia? I'd have helped you if I could."

"You don't understand." Patricia was curled onto her side, one arm over her stomach, but she pushed up to a seated position. Her shoulders were a downward slump that rivaled the droop of a sunflower without water. "In honesty, it had naught to do with you."

Lottie blew out an exasperated breath that sent the hair around her face bouncing. "Then what *did* it have to do with?"

"Henrietta."

"You leave my sister out of this," Ian growled. He was still visibly agitated in his harsh breaths and tense muscles. When she set a comforting hand on his arm, she found pure, hard muscle bunched tight. "You're not fit to say her name."

"Of course I'm not. I never have been. You've no idea what it's like to be almost equal with someone and completely not at the same time. We were the same age, the same sort of pretty, had the same sort of friends. But just because she was a bit of the gentry, she got away with everything." Patricia's eyes blazed.

"She got away with marrying my brother! And them's none that should have sanctioned that. But they did."

"I've met Miss Heald." A bit of wry humor turned Lottie's mouth into a smile, though it seemed nearly absurd considering the situation. "Only a handful of times, of course, but do you know what? I could hazard a guess why Miss Heald could get away with everything you couldn't."

"Could you now?" Patricia spat.

"Indeed. And it has nothing to do with her being gentry. In fact...she's nice. That's all. She's nice and you're not. I hope you enjoy thinking about that in the brig."

Lottie waved in Fletcher's assistants. Two of them hitched Heeler by the armpits. His head lolled. Completely out of it. Patricia screeched and tried to fight the third, but the burly man with cauliflower ears threw her over his shoulder.

They were carted away with surprising alacrity.

Then Lottie was alone. With Ian.

Alone with Ian, her love for him, and her fear. What an awful mess she'd made.

When he looked at her, she knew. She knew she'd do absolutely anything in her power to fix it no matter what.

She thought she might cast up her accounts from the excitement of the previous moments combined with her nerves.

This was no time for flagging courage.

Ian found it to be rather handy to have compatriots in less-than-savory circumstances. After only a couple brief words of assurance that they'd have the culprits on a boat to Australia, Fletcher's hired men carted them off.

Leaving Ian alone with Lottie, who looked up at him as if he'd hung the sun, moon and stars in the heavens.

Naturally, he liked the feeling. "Let's get you home."

"I don't want to go home."

"Sometimes we don't always get what we want." He knew that one completely. Invariably.

Her mouth tweaked up at the corners. "Come to think of it, yes. Let's go home."

He got her bundled into the carriage in less time than he might have expected, and then home again. The whole way there, he sat on the bench across from her and watched her watching him. They existed above the moment. Exhaustion sucked at his soul and yet he was refreshed and energized for having her to look upon.

He was an idiot. He pressed his hands flat against his thighs to withstand the urge to gather her close.

When they pulled up to the curb before her house, weariness had him nearly lethargic. "You'll understand if I don't see you up."

In the darkness of the carriage, her eyes were wide, but he sensed a determined cant to her eyebrows that didn't bode well for him. "I do not. Please. Come upstairs."

"No."

Never in a million years could he have guessed her reaction. She sank into the space between them, coming to her knees. With her fingers laced together in a supplicant's position, she put her hands on his thighs. "Please. Come up. I beg of you."

"Lottie..." He wasn't sure why he warned her. Perhaps he warned her against getting his hopes up. She was damaged. Broken. He'd once thought their pieces fit together, but that was before she'd crushed new parts of him. "Don't embarrass yourself."

"I shall." She spoke with a determined resoluteness. "I'll embarrass myself every moment of every day until you listen to me."

He was shaking his head. There was no way...

And yet he then nodded. Almost without thinking it through. "Get off your knees. I'll come."

She marched him right through the front door, which he hadn't expected. But then, that was Lottie. Flaunting the expectations of everyone around her. The footman who'd been nodding off at his post seemed startled as he watched them go up, and yet he raised no alarm. No hue and cry.

When she stopped on the first floor and advanced down a hallway, Ian could pretty much only follow behind. She held him by the hand as she knocked on a door and swiftly opened it. "Mama?"

"What? Yes?" The older woman sat upright in bed, though she was partially hidden by the mound of blankets that fluffed up around her. "Lottie? What's wrong?"

"Nothing. I only wished to tell you something."

Lady Vale wiped delicately at her eyes. "Yes, then?"

"I want to apologize, actually." She pulled Ian closer to the bed. Her fingers were cold and chilled in his. "I've held you responsible for your illness, in a way. Part of me thought that with our family's history, you never should have had me. It's painful sometimes."

"Oh," her mother said on a soft whisper. The shimmer caught by the moonlight coming through the window started in her eyes and rolled down her cheeks as tears. "I'm so sorry."

"No, that's what I mean." She leaned down to hug her mama. "I thank you. If you hadn't risked it, if you hadn't endangered your own health, I wouldn't exist. If I didn't exist, I wouldn't love. I love you. And..." She trailed off, looking up at Ian. "I love Ian."

"I knew that, you silly goose," Lady Vale said. She sniffled tears away, but she smiled as well. "How could you not? I told you the first time you brought him home that he was different."

Lottie nodded. "He is. He's very different."

Ian shook his head, but somehow his hands rose to cup Lottie's delicate, beautifully shaped face. "Lottie. Don't. It's unfair."

Her throat worked on a swallow. "Wait. Don't...don't decide yet." She leaned down to kiss her mama's pliable cheek. "Sleep now, yes? I'm sorry I woke you."

Lady Vale shook her head. "It was worth it."

Lottie pulled him back out of the room, then up the stairs. She first lit the lamp by the door of her room. The one on the desk went next. She circled the room like a silent ghost, lighting every lamp and candle she had around, until they all blazed like sunlight and firelight and the stars all mixed together.

She stood in the center of the room, near the chaise and bookshelves. Her fingers shook before she folded them together and faced Ian with a new resoluteness to her mouth.

He shouldn't be there. He should have left. There wasn't anything new that could be said because her *I love you* wouldn't count if it were only backed by fear. He couldn't love her so strongly while still being alone.

If she were still afraid, it would do no good.

Of course, he was all talk, wasn't he? It wasn't like he was going anywhere. He waited.

He had the feeling he might always be willing to wait for her. "Enough lights?"

"I wanted them all for a reason."

"Do tell."

The color in her cheeks was hectic and pink. Her wide eyes glimmered with an ocean of emotion. "So I can burn away the dark from between us."

"Pretty words." He folded his arms over his chest. Mostly trying to hold himself back from already reaching for her. "Pretty words don't make a future."

A tear glimmered on her bottom lashes. "Even now, you're too good for me. I wanted to be right for you. I still do. I always will."

"I don't understand what you mean."

The tear broke away and skated over her cheek. "I want a future. That comes first." Tendons pulled tight in her throat. "I'm not sure I always believed that. But I do now. Because of you. I want a future. Something good. To run my school and have happiness."

"Isn't that what you've always wanted?"

She shook her head and stepped closer to him. Near enough that the scent of lilacs rose from her skin. She looked up at him through her lashes. Tears ran down her pretty face completely unchecked. "No. I was marking time. I didn't think I deserved anything. Not when Mama had been robbed."

"You deserve everything good and right in the world." Christ, he couldn't stand seeing those tears fall. He brushed them away with his thumbs first, then his lips, tasting salt and love together. "You're a small miracle in your every breath."

"Jesus," she said on a harsh sob. "You're so good, even at a moment like this. God, let me apologize. Let me tell you how ridiculously sorry I am. I came so close to ruining everything beautiful between us. You've shown me that I can be centered. *You* center me."

He curled over her with his arms around her shoulders and his chin on the top of her head. She felt right in his arms. "This is our center. Us together. But I have to warn you, Lottie."

"What?" Her words came out muffled against his shirtfront. "Anything. I'd give you anything. I'd be anything for you."

"I only want you to be yourself." His hands closed across her narrow back. "I'll warn you this once, and then that's all you get. If you accept this between us...there will be no going back. I'll never let you free. I'll chase you to the ends of the earth."

She shuddered, then craned up on her tiptoes. She covered his jaw with kisses, then his mouth. She was sweetness and strength in one. "I need that. Chase me. Don't let me go." Her voice cracked. "Love me."

Every word loosened the clenched knot inside his soul. This could work. Christ, would it take work of the highest order, and Ian wasn't stupid. He knew there would be plenty of problems over the years. They'd probably be the sort to have epic fights. But so long as they came back to each other, everything would be worth it in the end.

He framed her face between his hands. Probably he wrenched too tight, but he couldn't help it. "Say that again," he said.

"Love me." Her every thought flickered in her eyes. "Love me like I love you. Love me to the end of the earth. Love me and be with me. A marriage and a life and most of all being together."

He growled and kissed her deep. There was no softness there. All fire and promises. "I'll love you until the world ends, Lottie. Most of all..." He kissed her again. "I'm keeping you, goddamn it."

Epilogue

Five years later

Playing with a baby made Lottie feel calm and composed in a way that nothing else quite resembled. Sitting on a large blanket beneath an apple tree, she held two tiny fists between her own fingers.

"Pussy cat, pussy cat, what did you there? I frightened a little mouse under her chair," Lottie sang in a cooing voice.

Her reward was a toothless baby grin and a drool-filled giggle. Lottie laughed. "Oh, aren't you a marvel. You're going to be a gorgeous and beautiful little heartbreaker. Your daddy is going to have to shoot half the city to keep you safe."

Sera scooped the infant out of Lottie's lap. "Don't say such things. Fletcher is a railroad baron now. Strictly righteous."

Lottie leaned back on her elbows and turned her face up to the sunshine. "I know. But once your little one there is grown, I plan to tell her all sorts of awful stories." She waved a finger in warning at Sera. "Not only about Fletcher, either. I have plenty of stories about you."

Sera shoved her nose up in the air, but quickly smiled down at her small daughter. They'd all gathered at Fletcher's country estate. He'd bought the biggest and the best, naturally, which made it logical to congregate there for summer happiness.

Further afield in the meadow, Fletcher, Ian and two little boys tumbled about. Lottie shaded her eyes against the bright sun. "Is Fletcher teaching them to wrestle?"

Sera sighed. "It's not new. In fact, I should probably go break it up before someone cries. It's liable to be Fletcher. Silly man."

"Silly man who you worship."

"That's so." Sera headed toward the pile of males with her baby girl on her hip. She was every bit the picture of womanhood.

Ian tossed himself down to the blanket by her side. "Those young heathens are likely to steal the French crown before they're twenty."

"You think small," Lottie scoffed. Across the dark green grass, Fletcher scooped his infant daughter from Sera's arms. "They'll own all of Europe, I believe."

"Do you regret our choices?"

She looked down at the husband she adored. The tree above them dappled shadows across his beautiful eyes. His eyebrows lifted with curiosity. She traced a line over his brow before continuing. "To avoid children? No. I don't. Do you?"

He snapped off a stem of grass and ran it between his fingers. "There was a period when I might have."

"When Etta married."

"We discussed it, remember?" He shrugged, but when he turned his face back up toward her, that mouth she loved so well tweaked up on the left. He bit his bottom lip. "But then I was over it. I've you. Not some fantasy dream of a life that I was always told I wanted. Instead I get what makes me happiest with the world."

"You're a lucky man." She leaned down close enough to kiss him in the pretty little glen, beneath a gnarled oak tree.

He kissed her in return, his fingers slipping under the collar at the back of her neck. His touch was cool and comforting and also tinged with fire. "No more than you are a lucky woman."

She was filled with love for him. It swept over her like easy comfort and soft waves. She combed short dark hair back from his forehead. "That, my love, is entirely true. Fear has no part of me now. Because of you."

About the Author

After a semi-nomadic childhood throughout California, Lorelie Brown spent high school in Orange County before joining the US Army. After traveling the world from South Korea to Italy, she's returned home to California. But not the cool area. She can't afford that yet.

Lorelie has three active sons and a tiny shih-tzu who thinks he's son number three—not four, he's too important to be the baby. Writing romance helps her escape a house full of testosterone.

In her copious free time (hah!) Lorelie co-writes contemporary erotic romance under the name Katie Porter. You can find out more about the "Vegas Top Guns" and "Club Devant" series at www.KatiePorterBooks.com or at @MsKatiePorter. You can also contact Lorelie either at her website www.LorelieBrown.com, or on Twitter @LorelieBrown.

It's all about the story...

Romance

HORROR

www.samhainpublishing.com

CPSIA information can be obtained at www.ICGtesting.com
Printed in the USA
LVOW08s2036240214

374948LV00003B/66/P

9 781619 218994